Printed in the United States of America
First Printing, 2016
Cover art by Dan Strange at thinkstrange.co.uk

Acknowledgments
This novel is dedicated to Mickey Spillane, for all the palaver.
Also to Bob Gouldy, for the first letter of encouragement a reader
ever sent.
To Dave Arlington, for a valuable piece of cover advice.
And finally, to Robert Grey, for deeds of wonder worked so well
he's to be made an Honorary Citizen of Gold Coast City,
entitled to all the rights and benefits this title grants.

Chapter 1

White collar regs love to meet in the grime. I prefer my office, but the snooping business is consumer-centric, so it was at the request of my only client, Toby Teenie, that I was standing in muck under the crosstown bridge at one AM, with the stink of still water up my nose, and a large, brown folder in my hand. Fortunately it wasn't long until all three hundred pounds of him pulled up in a little red sports car. He threw it in park, dislodged himself, and came waddling over to me in his tailored Italian suit like a pregnant yak. "Did you really get them?"

I held out the brown folder. "What's it look like?"

Moving fast for a soft man, Toby snatched his prize and peered inside. "I can't thank you enough. I'm telling everyone I know about the Dane Curse Detective Agency."

I grimaced at the thought. "I'd rather you didn't, if-"

A blast of black lightning streaked down the road beyond the bridge. It sent a fierce gust of wind that smelled like ozone and scattered the trash at our feet.

Toby froze. "Who's that?"

"Doctor Velocity, I think." Keeping a sharp eye out, I took a few seconds to be sure before saying, "But she's long gone, we can rest easy."

"Not her," Toby said, and pointed over my shoulder. "Him."

I turned around. A navy blue sedan was creeping our way. It stopped thirty yards out. The door opened and a guy stepped onto the street. Thanks to the bright headlights I couldn't see his face, but the silver Thompson machine gun he held stood out well enough. "Hey Toby."

I looked at the fat man. "Friend of yours?"

Toby stood frozen, save for the thick beads of sweat running down his cheeks like clotted cream. "That's the guy who's blackmailing me. I told you he couldn't know I was involved, and you led him right here."

"That folder was the only thing in the safe," I said. "He'd have put it together."

The blackmailer laughed. "Your bulldozer's right. Though

maybe if he hadn't ripped my safe open I wouldn't have noticed so fast."

Toby turned to me. "Why didn't you pick the lock?"

"My way's faster," I said.

"Be that as it may, my boss wants those photos back, plus what you still owe." He aimed his weapon at my client. "And I'll take both now."

Toby looked at the envelope and said, "Alright." Then he deflated like a punctured parade float, and shuffled towards the man.

"Toby," I said, "you take one more step and I'll break you in two after I'm done with him."

The guy took his machine gun off my client and put it on me. "Shut up. Or I'll add some red to that gray suit."

I shook my head. "No."

"No? You may tear through steel, but super strength don't make you bulletproof."

I stood firm. "The photos stay here. And if you threaten Toby one more time I'm going to pull out your spine and choke you to death with it."

"Choke me to death…" The unknown man tsked. "Everyone's a white cape in this town. Hey Toby, be sure to mention this to the next hero you hire." He raised the Thompson and pulled its trigger. The fully automatic cannon made a loud rat-a-tat and spit a series of slugs into my gut.

I looked down. There were now a lucky number of holes in my white shirt, each one belching out a line of smoke like an old slot jockey. I leveled my gaze at the shooter. "Is that gun a Tommy, or a Tammy?"

"What the hell?" The guy looked at his weapon. Then he aimed higher, and blasted away.

I snapped my face to the side as another half dozen bullets bounced off my cheek, doing less damage there than they did to my shirt.

"God damn," he said, "you're invulnerable."

"That and angry." I reached into my jacket and plucked my Thumper, Rico. He's a meaty handgun that holds four different bullets: high-velocity, target seeking, explosive, and electro-stun. Each one's connected to a different trigger in the grip, and aiming at the blackmailer I loosed a stunner.

But my lead went high, and hit the wall behind him. "How the hell?"

Even though I couldn't see his face I swear he smirked. "Not the only cape under the bridge tonight, huh?"

"Maybe not. But I'm the only cape with a Kapowitzer."

The guy lowered his heater and took a step back. "A Kapowitzer?"

Slipping Rico back home I pulled the right side of my jacket open to reveal Lois, a futuristic silver pistol. "Yeah, let's see you dodge scatter shot."

"To hell with this." Leaving his bravado behind, the guy jumped into his car and reversed fast.

I sprinted after him. And in three long strides I caught up. Reaching low I grabbed his bumper. He dragged me a few feet like a water skier, but I bore down, and lifted the front of his car off the ground. The rear tires kept spinning, but he was at a full stop.

"Going somewhere?" I said.

"Yeah," the guy yelled. "Away."

Suddenly the car felt a lot heavier, like some invisible force was pulling it to the ground. I fought hard, but the metal tore free from my hands and he shot backwards at an impressive pace. Then he hit the brakes, spun his sled a perfect one-eighty, and tore off into the night.

As his taillights shrank I returned to my client. "You could've mentioned that guy had telekinesis."

Poor Toby was green, and shook like he had some awful palsy. "God damn it. Why didn't you shoot him with the Kapowitzer?"

"You ever seen one go off?" I said. "Her blast would've leveled the block."

"The block? Who cares about the block?" Toby wiped his slick brow dry. "Do you have any idea what I've already given them for these pictures?"

"Don't know. Don't want to know. You asked me to fetch those and fetch those I did. Now give me my lettuce."

Toby steadied his sausage link fingers long enough to reach into his pocket and produce a white envelope, thick with bills. "Here."

I grabbed it, and started counting the dough. "Thanks."

"Oh no, thank you."

The sarcasm got my attention, but when I looked up to give Toby the stink eye he was already waddling back to his car with the folder full of shame tucked under one arm. He opened the door and said, "By the way, I won't be suggesting you to my friends."

I went back to counting. "Got a lot of those, do you?"

Toby slammed his door and drove away.

I wasn't sad to see him go. But I wasn't thrilled either.

Because like I said, he was my only client.

Chapter 2

The alarm clock's short hand was tickling ten when the sun got the nerve to kick open my eyes. Throwing the covers aside I got out of bed, shuffled off to shave the face an ex of mine called "knobbly," and once I had the undergrowth pruned, I slapped on a gray suit and hat with a black overcoat, filled my twin shoulder holsters with Rico and Lois, and headed out the door.

My matte black Jalopy was parked out front. I got into it, and headed towards my office wishing I had sunglasses every mile of the trip. Not because of the daylight. No. It was the town itself. That's the thing about Gold Coast City, whether morning, noon, or night it's got a shine that shames Vegas at Christmastime. Some think it's because of all those big, silver buildings in City Centre that twist as they climb through the clouds. Others believe the glow comes from the aura of our frontier past that's still rife in neighborhoods like Blackwood and Cobbles. And the tourists swear it's because we have more capes per square mile than any other burg around. But the simple truth is Gold Coast City is the greatest jewel in the world's tiara, and it shines accordingly.

Even in Falling Rock, where my office is located.

I pulled up outside the brick Tanziger Building, hopped out, and took the elevator up to the fourth floor where my suite resides at the end of the hall. And while I have no problem locating it, others think it's nearly impossible to find because over my door, hidden in the smoke detector, is a deceit device which produces a hologram of a dead end. From a distance it can fool the sharpest eye, but once you get close enough, like within five feet, the illusion stops working, and clear as day you'll see a glass door with the freshly painted words Dane Curse Detective Agency.

I marched through it, and into the waiting room, to find my secretary at her desk. She had on the tailored peach suit I always mistake for pink, and her silver hair was pulled into a bun you could confuse with a cue ball. Keeping both eyes on her romance novel she said, "Carl never came in this late."

I closed the door. "Good morning, Mrs. West."

"Morning? It's practically noon."

Pointing at her hair I said, "You got a lock out of place."

"What?" She snatched a mirror from the desk and studied her do from every angle. "Where?"

I shrugged. "My mistake."

Scowling, she replaced the looking glass. "It's not surprising you have no respect for precision."

I hung up my coat and hat, then pulled out last night's kale. "Here, this should cheer you up."

"Is it from that awful Mr. Teenie?" She took the money and started counting. "You know, Carl never had to work for regs, either."

"Yeah. You've mentioned. So how long will this give me?"

"Until you need another client?" She finished and did some math in her head. "Six weeks."

"That's all?"

"If you don't run the electricity too much. Whatever happened to all that money you made with Dread Division?"

"I blew every kroner on a dame."

Mrs. West rolled her eyes. "Why does that not surprise me?"

"Probably because you're just so smart. Don't bother me unless it's important." I walked out of the waiting room and into my office, closing the door behind me. On my desk was the day's copy of The Chronicle, and a brand new bottle of whiskey. I sat down, cracked the booze's seal, and poured myself three fingers. It wasn't nearly enough to give an invulnerable like me a buzz, but still, I took a sip.

And spit it back out.

Earl Grey.

Mrs. West switched out my liquor with tea. But the seal was unbroken. So how did she do that?

The urge to scream rose, but I beat it back down. No reason to let that batty dame know my goat was got. Instead, I dropped the bottle into the trashcan, and turned my attention to The Chronicle. Splashed across its front page was a story about Hard Drive, a black cape who was killed the day before in a melee with Al Mighty. Below that was a puff piece on tomorrow night's Save the Finch gala, and at the very bottom was a story covering the progress of I-93's construction.

Finding none of that interesting, I tossed the paper in with the tea and leaned back in my chair, figuring a nap might put me to rights.

But before my eyes were halfway closed the phone rang.

Through the opaque glass wall that separated me from Mrs. West I heard her pick up the receiver and say, "Carl Cutter... I mean Dane Curse Detective Agency. Yes he is. Really? I'll inform him." She hung up, walked over, and popped her head through my door with something on her mouth that almost resembled a smile. "Dane, you got a client on the way up. And it's a black cape."

"That's not funny."

"Because it's no joke. They'll be here soon so straighten your tie. And that mess above it."

I opened my mouth, but before I could use it she closed my door and was back at her desk.

Then someone tall entered. They traded muffled pleasantries with Mrs. West, strode to my door, and knocked twice.

I said, "It's open."

The door swung aside and in walked a woman. She had a long, flowing overcoat atop a tailored black suit that hugged her hips like an old friend it hadn't seen since high school. Her broad brimmed hat cast a shadow over a pair of almond eyes so smoky they could teach a Navajo communications course, and with two full lips as red as the menace that scared my ma she said, "Mr. Curse? I'm Mandy Marcus." She closed the door and crossed the room with one hand extended.

I stood up and shook it. "Nice to meet you. Please, take a seat."

"Thank you." She obliged, and removed her hat releasing a waterfall of thick, brown tresses that splashed off her shoulders. "May I ask where Mr. Cutter is? I thought this was his agency, but the name on the door says otherwise."

"Carl's gone," I said, sitting down. "He retired a few weeks back. Did you know him?"

"Of him. The black capes I've talked to say he..." She took a few seconds to find the right words. "They say he could be trusted."

Trusted. That was cute. "Yeah. He was good like that. So what's this about?"

Ms. Marcus shrugged off her overcoat revealing four arms in total. And that was all I needed. Mandy was The Widow, a member of an all dame spider themed squad of black capes called the Spinnerettes. I'd met her boss Six Eye, along with Trapdoor, and the venomous Redback, but I never shared space with The Widow. "It's about my brother. And his partner."

"What're their names?" I said.

"Leonard and Tony."

"And their other names?"

"Thermite and Firewall. They were killed last night." Her eyes went shiny. "Trying to steal the Coconut."

"The Vandenberg Coconut?" My jaw fell slack near python wide. "Are you kidding?"

"No, I'm very serious. Their bodies were found a few hours ago-"

"Outside the museum."

"No," she said. "Inside. On the floor of Wentorf Hall itself."

"On the floor of Wentorf…" was all I got out before my throat closed up. I took a hard swallow to get it greased. "I'm sorry, how's that even possible?"

"I'm not sure. I saw it on this morning's news. The police are saying that Tony and Leo broke in to steal the diamond, but instead killed each other before the job was done."

I nodded. "That makes sense."

"No." Widow's eyes got dry and narrow. "It does not."

"Uh, you've seen the Coconut, right?"

"Of course."

"Well if there's anything that could convince me to turn on brother, mother, or country, that rock's it."

"But you're not Leo or Tony. A third man killed them. I know it."

"Alright," I said. "So you think someone circumvented the world's most difficult, and secret, security system in order to gain access to a room full of gems worth billions, only to kill their two partners without taking a thing?"

Her smile was so wry she could've used both lips to make a Reuben. "I don't know what happened. I just know they didn't kill each other."

"What makes you say that?"

"Because those two have been inseparable since grade school. They got special together. They put on the black cape together."

"So far that's not enough."

"Well this should be, when they were picked up on a burglary that got them half a decade in Impenetron the state made them a deal: the first person to squeal on the other gets to go free. But neither one did. Even though this offer stood open for every day of those five long years. That's how I know they didn't kill each other."

"They wouldn't talk to walk? Ok." I grabbed a pad and pen. "That is something."

"So you'll take the case?"

"I will. Now, tell me everything you know about the boys."

Widow relaxed and settled into her chair. "My brother Anthony, Firewall, was a converter, and he had talent. I don't think there was a computer system he couldn't mentally interface with by touch alone. We weren't particularly close though. Maybe we'd talk once a year. Exchange birthday cards. I visited him in Impenetron early on, but after a few months he refused to see me or accept my letters. I didn't even know he was out. His partner Leonard Thebes, Thermite, was a flamer. He couldn't fly or anything, just produce regular fire from his skin."

"And their current address?"

"I don't know."

"Place of work?"

She shook her head.

"Ok. You mentioned a possible third man, did the boys have any enemies? Someone who wanted them dead?"

She looked at her lap where all four hands were doing the busy fidget. "I don't know. Maybe."

I put my pad and pen down gentle. "That's ok. I can find out the rest myself."

"Thank you." Widow got to her feet. "I appreciate your assistance. Obviously I won't be going to the police."

"No one who comes in here can. But before you leave," I said, "I'll need a retainer."

"Will this do?" Mandy reached into her pocket and produced a wrapped stack of bills.

I took the dough and read the band. "Ten thousand? Yeah, and you'll get back change."

"I'd prefer answers."

"If they're out there," I said, "I'll find them."

#

On the way out Widow left her details with my secretary, but me in no better a mood than when she arrived. Sure, against all odds I had a client who wore the black cape, and solving her case would shine me up in the eyes of the powered villain community which would definitely help keep my agency running, but I didn't see this whole thing coming together like she hoped. In fact, I had the feeling this was an open shutter.

But Carl, my former partner and mentor, always told me to base my hunches on facts, not the other way around, so I turned on my computer and booted up Sandtrout, a piece of software capable of wheedling all sorts of information from databases across the city. I entered the names Leonard Thebes and Anthony Marcus, and pressed enter. It would take hours to finish, but when it did I'd have a report on everywhere the boys' paths intersected. Ideally where they both worked, lived, and who they knew.

That took care of their private lives.

Now for their very public deaths.

The first thing I'd have to do is visit the crime scene to see how they broke in. Then I wanted to learn what impossible technique they used to bypass the defenses. And finally, I'd have to know the cause of death. Once I had all that done I'd know if Widow's theory was right.

So, pocketing half of her cash I made for the door.

As I passed by, Mrs. West said, "I don't think she trusts you."

I slipped on my coat and hat. "Most dames don't."

"But you'll still help her, right?"

I couldn't stop the sigh. "We don't help people here. We work cases."

Mrs. West glowered like only nuns can. "That's not how Carl ran things."

"Well I'm not him."

"I'll say. For thirty years he was the only person in this city that helped grieving black capes and their families find the answers they needed. The kind of people the law ignores. I don't know where they'll go for help, if you lose this agency."

"I'm keeping this agency afloat partly because Carl was like a father to me, and partly because I'm done with dark deeds." I stepped through the door. "Not because I want to help grieving people."

Mrs. West tut-tutted. "That's a wonderful attitude. Why Carl loved you I'll never know."

I spun around and poked my head back in. "And yet why he didn't love you is abundantly clear."

Mrs. West opened her mouth. But I was gone before she could use it.

Chapter 3

Wentorf Hall resides inside the Gold Coast City Museum, a five-story castle made of massive, gray stones. It sits on a grassy hill overlooking the downtown business district, and while the thirty million tourists that stroll through this burg annually almost exclusively come to spot a white cape, enough of them still stop in for some culture, and maybe a mug. So the cops would want the crime scene spotless as soon as possible, which is why I rushed there with minor regard for traffic laws.

Parking out front, I ran up the white marble stairs, past the gold plated gates, and into the lobby where, towering high, was a statue of Poseidon. He cast his godly gaze over me and the other visitors as they moved back and forth like schools of fish, happily chattering in whatever language Babel saw fit to stick them with. Pulling my hat low I pushed through them, and fed a fiver into the donation box before making my way towards my target: the gem room.

It was in the center of the first floor, and when I crossed its threshold, for a second I forgot why I was there. The highly polished brass ceiling was as shiny as the parquet floor, but the lush purple curtains softened the shine and absorbed the sounds so it felt quiet and intimate, like a giant potentate's jewel box. The dozens of displays that ran around the room were filled with rare treats like tanzanite, black opals, and even a block of quartz Pinnacle pulled from Mars. But despite their rarity, or otherworldly origin, each shiny rock looked like a dull pebble next to the pride of the exhibit.

Its display took up an entire wall.

There were tools from its excavation on the left, while to the right sat pictures of the Danish family who first found it, but dead center, lounging on its pink pillow like an empress on her litter, as big as a bowling ball and sparkling like the promise of prom night, was the largest and most valuable diamond in the world: the famous Vandenberg Coconut.

I dare you to gaze at it and not ooze some ahhs.

Normally the rock's visible from every part of the room, but today it was partially obstructed by a ten-foot blue police partition in the middle of the floor which protected the bodies I'd come to study.

I took a loop around it to get the lay, but only made it halfway before stopping dead.

Standing next to the diamond's display, previously hidden by the partition, was Al Mighty. He was nearly seven feet tall, four feet wide, and while I could lift seven tons tops he could press thirty without a grunt. The costume he had on beneath his blood red beard was half orange, half white, and it shone with the distinct tinge of Wonder Weave. He struck an imposing gaze across the room, I suppose to remind us that the diamond was still as safe as ever.

Obviously his presence wasn't welcome, but it wouldn't deter me. I needed onsite intel. So I got in line with the rest of the tourists and strolled past the Coconut, but while they all stared at the rock with wonder I studied the unbreakable Kessel Glass, searching for a ding or dent. But there wasn't one. I mean not even a scratch.

Once that was done I turned around and walked past the partition, trying to get a look inside. But there were no gaps between the panels, so I'd have to get creative. Keeping one eye on Al I turned to the nearest stone and pulled out my hand scanner, a useful tool that can record all sorts of clues from chemical residue to ambient light waves, and set its lens to X-ray. Dropping it to my side I pointed it backwards, and moved around the room's perimeter, clicking away.

When I'd completed one full circuit I changed the lens to zoom, aimed it at the shiny brass ceiling, and took a few more shots, using the reflection to get some normal pictures from above. Then, with the crime scene on film, I moved to the next room, leaving Al to gaze upon the rubes and rubies, because now that I'd seen how far the boys got, I needed to find out how they entered the museum itself.

#

The room next to Wentorf Hall was the Amphibia Theatre, a large kid-friendly auditorium. All around were scientific displays of oceanic specimens, while scale models of different whales hung from the forty-foot ceiling. To the right was a wall of blue windows that, despite being covered with iron bars, cast an azure hue that made the place feel like it was on the bottom of the sea. And while all that amazed the children, the most impressive thing was the floor. Supported by a marble perimeter, it was a single sheet of bulletproof glass that protected a fully functioning, yet perfectly isolated, ecosystem packed with water and green bioluminescent algae.

And dangling a few inches from the center of that magnificent floor was a rope. The other end was hanging from a vent in the ceiling, which opened above the model orca. I walked to it, aimed my scanner up, and snapped a few pictures. They'd serve fine, but I wanted a closer look, because if Widow was right, then that vent would be able to hold the weight of three men. And yet from where I was standing it didn't seem too sturdy, though I'd have to wait until the cops buzzed off before I could sneak up to the roof for a peek.

So I wandered the room, looking at the displays, wondering how many I'd see before the cops left. But I barely made it to the far wall before noticing that, in every display, I saw the same thing. It was the reflection of a blond man, in a brown suit, with a bulge in his jacket that could only come from a pistol. And the way he was staring at my back reminded me of how a starving man leers at pork chops.

Now I've never been good at math, but I know that if you add all that up you get cop. I always double-check my work though, so I spun his way.

But instead of scoping me Blondie was looking nonchalant at a nearby trilobite.

Yep, I'd been made. *Damn it.* My rooftop visit was now canceled and I had to beat a retreat before the badge alerted Al Mighty and he put me in traction. But I didn't want to lead him to my car, so before I escaped I'd have to shake my new pal like a British nanny.

Leaving the Amphibia Theatre, I walked down the long hall to the Egyptian wing, the busiest part of the museum. It was also the largest room in the place with a lofty pyramid squatting in its center, painted ankhs decorating the ceiling, and lining the walls on all sides were dozens of statues on square pedestals. I walked through it all at a slow pace, dragging my friend with me. And as he followed my scent I searched for an opportunity to leave him behind.

It presented itself quick.

Right in front of me, two large tour groups were coming my way from opposite directions. One was following the flag of Japan, the other Brazil. They were seconds away from converging on one another. I paused for a moment, and spun around.

My blond tail had already turned aside, and was gazing at a nearby mummy.

I used the moment to slide between the passing parties, and as they crossed paths the two groups cut me off from the cop. I ducked low, and keeping mum and humble, charged across the floor and slipped behind the statue of a jackal faced man. Seconds passed.

Then Johnny Law sprinted by.

Peeking around my cover I watched him go.

He ran to the center of the room. Searched right. Then left. And when he didn't spot me he raced to the end of the room and disappeared through the door to Aerospace.

And now with my shadow properly shunted, I slipped both hands into my pockets, abandoned my cover, strolled down the hall, and ambled out the main gate.

There's something about beating a lawman. It makes the sun feel warmer. The air smell sweeter. I took a deep breath of both and bounced down the stairs feeling easy and free, with as much spring in my step as there was on the breeze. But upon reaching the bottom I stopped short.

The cop was already there. Leaning against my Jalopy.

I walked over, shaking my head. "That's some nice work, officer."

He gave me a hard look with his baby blues. "It's detective."

"That explains how you found me."

"A big ogre like you's not too hard to find," he said. "Though I have to admit, that was one sly fake you made around Anubis."

I looked back at the museum. "Anubis? That wasn't Pharaoh?"

"Life's not Pharaoh."

I laughed hard for real. "A funny cop's rare. No wonder they got you in a museum. So what can I do for you?"

"Keep away from the Coconut."

"And if I don't? You going to get your pal Al?"

"I don't need a white cape's help to arrest you," the cop said. "Just like I don't need any more dead thieves on my watch."

"Wait, you think I'm casing the joint, learning from their mistakes so I can do better?"

He didn't say anything. But he didn't have to.

"Listen, you got nothing to worry about, copper. These days I walk a path that's straighter than a beam of light."

He waved a finger in my face. "Light bends, genius. Now stay away, or prepare to spend a lot of nights in the pen."

I stepped around him. "Thanks for the advice."

"Take it." The cop snatched my sleeve. "It's worth a lot more than the fin you paid to play."

"Good to know." I swatted his hand off me. Then I got in my Jalopy, and pulled into traffic with an eye in the rearview.

The cop was mugging my plates, scribbling the number onto his notepad. Fat lot of good it would do. It's registered to an address that doesn't exist, so my identity would remain clandestine. But still, I was shaken.

That cop tagged me so early he not only knew how much I put in the donation box, but also which car I drove.

He was rarer than I thought. Smarter, too.

So I'd wait until the Viking was off shift, and return after sundown for my peek at the roof. In the meantime I'd print up the pictures to see how the boys died. But to put them into context I'd need some information about Wentorf Hall's security system. I also needed a drink.

Fortunately there was a place I could do both.

Chapter 4

Henchmen's was a speakeasy that catered exclusively to the black cape set. There's no better place for a powered thug to go for a finger of Octane, or info on the underbelly of Gold Coast City, but it's always best to be on guard because it can run rough on the smoothest of days.

I entered the empty dive bar that served as its front, and the door hadn't closed behind me before the far wall parted like I was strolling with Moses. I stepped through it, made my way down a darkened hallway, and after slipping between two red curtains I finally arrived inside Henchmen's proper, my second home.

Thanks to its rough-hewn wooden walls the place smelled like a catcher's mitt filled with sawdust and beer. The juke in the corner was pumping out an old swing tune loud enough to rattle the plaque from my teeth, while the bar on the right was stacked three deep with black capes all drinking and fighting and making a fuss. The rumpus looked like a real fun time, but I aimed my loafers to the booths in the back.

And as I went the drinks stopped clinking. The conversations died. Someone even quieted the juke.

I turned to the crowd.

Every eye was on me.

Opening my jacket I pointed to the hanging hardware within. "If anybody's nervy enough to run gums, there's literally no better time to do it than now."

The gang traded dark looks and risky whispers.

"No takers?" I said. "Lois and Rico will be real-"

"That's enough of that," someone behind me barked.

I turned around to see my first real smile of the day spread across the face of Dastard Lee, last surviving member of the Derby Vicious Boys, and the owner of Henchmen's. She had on a black striped shirt with a pair of cammo pants, and running down her thick, white mane was a streak so black it could've been painted on with pitch. "Hey Dane, what're you in for?"

"The usual," I said. "Booze and a chat."

"Well your timing's perfect, we got both on tap. Follow me."

Lee led me to the furthest booth in the back as the music and chatter resumed in our wake. I sat on one side. She took the other, and waved to the barman.

"Pretty chilly reception," I said.

"Considering what's happened you can't expect summertime."

"Guess not." I dropped my hat on the table. "But what's up with this crowd? Kind of busy for a weekday afternoon."

"It's Hard Drive's wake," Lee said. "But skip that noise, where's Cutter? You got him stashed in your pocket or something?"

"Nope. Snooping solo."

"I heard that, but didn't believe it. This burg won't be the same without the man who solved the Night Jack murders."

"No," I said, "it won't."

A barman with skin as dark as onyx, and two giant white eyes, arrived at our table. He dropped off an ice water for his boss, and a pint of whiskey with a beer back for me. I swallowed the liquor in three quick gulps, then started sipping the brew. Together they provided a gentle buzz.

"So you've had your hooch, let's make with the chat."

I leaned in. "You hear about last night's pass at the Coconut?"

Lee's eyes got so bright they could've brought a blind seaman safely through British fog. "You know I did."

"You think there's anything strange about it?"

"Not really." Lee half cocked a smile. "Do you?"

"No. But the cape who hired me does."

Lee turned bubbly. "A cape? Hired you? That's great." But then she lost her fizz. "Why? It's pretty clear those two dunces went for throats once they laid eyes on the diamond."

"You know, I thought the same thing at first, but that pair did a nickel in Impenetron together, and were offered a way out if they ratted. Neither one did. Seems Denmark rotten they'd go all Caining Abel now, especially before filching the diamond."

"There's nothing odd about it. I was so sparkle struck the first time I saw that rock, if I had a baby in one hand and that gem in the other, and you told me I could keep the one I didn't smash, I'd have pulled a Lady Macbeth faster than you can say 'the king grows mad.' And the smart money says those boys felt the same way, I don't care how flummoxed they left the prisoner's dilemma."

I just sort of nodded.

"But," Lee said, "you're Carl's boy so you're still looking into it, and you came here to learn what makes Wentorf Hall so scary from the Coconut's original fan."

"Absolutely. Nobody knows that system better than you."

"Well, except the curator herself. And the people who built it."

"True," I said, "but they're not answering my calls."

"That sounds like them. Ok, I'll give you a quick tutorial, but listen good, I'm running a business here and I don't got time to repeat myself." Lee rolled up her sleeves. "Now, there are three issues facing any team trying to gain access to the Vandenberg Coconut: the entry, the interior, and the display itself.

"First, the entry." She grabbed my empty pint and placed it between us. "Wentorf's walls, doors, ceiling, and floors are all reinforced with sheets of Trumite, so you can't teleport or tunnel in, you got to walk." She tapped the glass. "Right through the door. And its sixteen-digit encrypted code. But if by some miracle you do that..." She pulled the coaster from under her water and put it next to my pint. "You got the floor. It's composed of thousands of weight sensing tiles that'll pick up a pound faster than a Scottish miser, and over top of this floor is a series of motion sensing lasers." Lee took the bottle of mustard from the condiments and squeezed a few yellow lines on the coaster. "The gaps in the grid are tighter than a gnat's ass, and both are controlled by an independent system set into the far wall.

"But, if you can make yourself light enough for the floor, and small enough to sneak between the beams, you still need to contend with the thickest piece of Kessel Glass ever made." She picked up her ice water and knocked it against the table twice. "It can't be blasted open. It can't be drilled through. And if you try..." Lee had hyper reflexes, which allowed her to move at incredible speeds for brief spurts, so her hand blurred as she lifted the water glass up and shattered it against the table. "It's attached to a tremor gauge that, like the rest of the defenses, will alert a private security firm, the police, the FBI, and the God damn National Guard."

I looked at the mess on the table. I couldn't tell the shards of glass from the ice. "That's about as bad as I expected, but then how'd the boys get so far?"

Lee grabbed a napkin and pushed the remains of her drink onto the floor. "What were their power sets?"

"Firewall was a converter and Thermite's a flamer."

"Well, if Firewall was good enough he could've unlocked the door. Maybe."

"And then disarm the inner defenses."

Lee threw her hands up. "Weren't you listening? A converter has to actually touch the system they're manipulating, and the one that controls Wentorf Hall is set inside one of the walls, behind a curtain. He'd have to physically walk across the room before he could fiddle with it. Unless..."

"Unless what?

"I've heard of converters using fiber optic filament to manipulate software from a distance. If he had one thin enough he may've shot it between the beams and into the control panel."

"Leaving Thermite to burn through the Kessel Glass."

"No way," Lee said. "No flamer burns that hot."

I thought about it. And she was right. But, "Can the glass be removed? I mean how did they get the diamond into the display originally?"

"Clever boy. The short answer is I don't know. But the long answer is I don't know."

"Which means it's worth checking on."

"You do that, kid. And tell me how it turns out. But just remember, it won't change the facts. Those two thieves, they killed each other. As sure as I'm sitting here, they killed each other."

"Well that aside, can you ask around for me? See if anyone knows where the boys lived, who they ran with?" I raised my left eyebrow as high as it would go. "If anyone wanted them dead?"

"Sure thing, hon. What was the flamer's name again?"

"Thermite."

"Got it. Thermite and Firewall. I'll see what I can see. Now I got to get back."

As I watched Lee walk away I toyed with the idea of working the room myself. But the looks I was getting convinced me otherwise. So I got up and made for the exit.

On my way there a woman stepped in my path. She was a foot taller than me, had spiky blond hair, beauty queen carob skin, and a purple suit with a crimson K on her chest.

"Kalamity," I said. "You're in my way."

She shook her head. "Bad enough we lose a real black cape, but now a snitch shows up at his wake?"

The whole place went quiet.

And I pushed up into the big dame's space. "Careful K, Dread Division's still family, so say that again and see what happens."

Another girl joined us. She had the same height and build as her friend, but her grill was ugly enough to put a surgeon off dinner, and the skin that covered it was as hard and fair as a Protestant judge. "I got family. That don't mean I wouldn't send them upriver to save my skin."

"Is that so, Slamazon?" I said. "They must not be valuable, considering the worth of that trade."

"Why you…" She took a step forward.

And ran into Kalamity's arm. "Easy, Slam."

"Listen to your girlfriend," I said.

"You huff and puff big for a has-been liar," Kalamity said. "But I'm betting you'll shrink when we get outside."

"Is it just us," I said, "or is your date coming too?"

A smirk slithered from one side of her mouth to the other. "Don't need backup to split you asunder."

"I'd love to see you try, but right now I got business." I took a step around the giantess and continued on my way. Then something small struck my spine like a bullet. But there was no blast. I untucked the back of my shirt, and out fell a dime. I turned around. "Cute."

"Figure you might be running low," Kalamity said, "since you drop so many. Snitch."

The whole place burst into snickering jeers.

And I stepped back into Kalamity's space.

She said, "You want to go outside now?"

"Here's fine." I plowed an uppercut into her ribs, and she dropped to the floor sans the air in her lungs. Quick as I could I spun towards Slamazon to give her a licking.

But instead I ran into her fist. It sent me flying over the dance floor and into the wall.

The bar exploded like we just won the pennant.

"Kill him, Slam."

"Break his jaw!"

I straightened up and shook my head.

Slamazon was already on top of me. She threw a high haymaker.

I slipped beneath it. And kicked her shin. It sent the big broad tumbling face first into the wall.

Grabbing the nearest table I lifted it up high, and brought it down on her back like a roustabout setting a spike. The oak exploded into splinters. And shut the crowd up. I said, "Stay down, beautiful."

But instead of taking my advice Slamazon rose to her feet. And brushed the wooden bits off her shoulder. "You hit like a boy."

Once again the black capes cheered.

"Maybe," I said over the din, "but I fight like a man."

"Like that's ever scared me." Slamazon threw a jab. I weaved clear and put a right hook into her gut. She doubled over and gasped. And I stomped on her foot. Slamazon fell to one knee screaming, and clutched her bruised piggies.

I grabbed a fistful of her hair with one hand. And punched her mouth with the other. It was like hitting granite. Pain shot through my knuckles. I dropped her coif and cradled my hand. "Son of a bitch."

From behind two big arms snatched me tight. They belonged to Kalamity. "Get off her."

I cocked my head forward, ready to thrust it straight back into her face. But she squeezed. Hard. And it stopped me cold. I tried to breathe. My ribcage refused to oblige. Then Kalamity hoisted me up.

"That's enough," a loud voice barked. "Next person to throw a punch gets banished."

Kalamity dropped me and said, "Sorry Lee. We didn't mean nothing by it."

"Yeah," Slamazon said, joining her friend. "Sorry Lee."

I stood up and pointed at the dames. "They started it."

"We did not," Slamazon said.

Lee shook her head. "Like a bunch of children... Ladies, get to the bar and pay your respects. And you, shamus. The next time you mean to put your head into someone's face don't cock forward. Just thrust it straight back."

I reached down and grabbed my hat. "Thanks. I'll remember that."

She pointed towards the exit. "Remember it outside."

As I left the bar I reflected on this less than stellar morning. I'd been rousted by a cop, got thumped on by criminals, and all I had with me was a set of sore knuckles, and no real answers.

Though I also had a better understanding of Wentorf Hall. And the film on my scanner.

I took both back to my office, ready to find out what really happened the night before.

#

Mrs. West was out to lunch, so I printed the photos in peace, and placed them on my desk. By arranging the X-ray shots in a circle around the ones reflected from the ceiling I had a complete picture of the crime scene. And it was interesting to say the least.

The bodies were stacked on top of each other, and the floor around them was scorched black. Next to their feet was a coiled red cord along with a silver canister, about the size of a cigar. That lariat had to be the long-range filament Lee was talking about, but what was the canister?

I grabbed the magnifying glass from my desk and held it over one of the photos, focusing on the container. There were no markings. Nothing to imply a purpose. I wondered how I'd find out what it was. But then I realized that would be the least of my problems.

Because lying right there, just a few feet from the tools, was the impossible.

Chapter 5

I blinked a few times. Then stared at the photo. Yep. I was right. Both boys were badly burnt.

Both boys.

And that made no sense. Sure, Firewall was a converter. He'd light up like a stogie. But Thermite was a flamer. Able to produce fire from his pores. That meant his body could handle a whole lot of Fahrenheit or he'd have cooked himself years ago.

So what could've scorched him?

Whatever it was had to burn hotter than normal fire. And only one thing fit: a chemical accelerant.

The boys must've meant to use it on the Kessel Glass, but instead Firewall sprayed it on his pal. A tough break for Thermite, but good news for me because a chemical that burns hot enough to toast a flamer would be rare. So rare that only a few places in town would even carry it. Thus, if I could ascertain the type, I could find out where it came from, and who bought it.

And if it wasn't the boys then it was the man who killed them.

I had to get a sample.

But how?

The floor of the museum was no doubt scrubbed clean, and the container itself would be in police custody.

Then it hit me. There was one place that had the information I needed. And while it wasn't as secure as cop central, it wouldn't be easy to walk into, either.

But I needed answers. So I grabbed my hat and ran for the door.

#

The morgue that deals with dead black capes resides in the basement of Gold Coast General Hospital, and by now the two boys would be there, waiting on the coroner's scalpel. But before the slicing started I needed to take a reading of Thermite's skin.

I parked outside the hospital and took the steps down one floor. The morgue's entrance was at the end of the hall. Nothing stood between me and it. I crept along the wall quick, but not so quick I made any noise. The last thing I wanted to do was attract attention, especially from the coroner. But I arrived at the entrance without seeing a soul.

So far, so good.

I pushed the doors open a crack and slid in. The cold smell of mentholated antiseptic hung thick in the air, and white tiles, the kind that don't stain, covered the walls and floor. A row of corpses ran down both sides, each lying under a black shroud. The only parts left uncovered were their right feet, and each one was adorned with a toe tag that hung limp like a flag at half-mast.

Except for the two on the end. They were still in the bag.

I walked down the aisle passing familiar names like Slugfest, Dinky Dee, and Landslide before getting to Thermite. Sitting next to him on the gurney was a dish filled with melted spare change, and a business card, which I slipped into my pocket. Then I unzipped his bag.

The hot smell of cooked pork and scorched iron wafted out like I popped open a grill mid-barbeque. I pulled back and gave the thick stench a moment to pass, then pinched my nose and leaned over Leonard's corpse. His face, chest, and arms were all charred so black he looked like a struck match. I ran my finger down his arm. It felt like bark. And there was a misshapen hunk jutting out from his bicep. I looked closer.

It was a hand.

Which had to be Firewall's, because Thermite still had both of his, though each paw was missing a few fingers. That meant the boys had melted together, and had to be pried apart, implying a struggle. Not good for Widow's theory. Speculation comes later though. For now I needed info. So I pulled out my hand scanner and put it up to Thermite's flesh to get a sample of any residue the accelerant left.

But a woman's voice said, "Stop immediately."

I spun around. It was Doctor Lockter. She had on a lab coat as white as her skin, and bright red eyes that matched the close cropped hair atop her head. "What's the meaning of this?"

"Just here to inspect the bodies. We missed some stuff earlier and-"

"Who are you?"

"A detective," I said.

"Let me put it another way." Her red eyes glowed. And with a voice that was both male and female, angry yet seductive, she said, "Freeze."

And I didn't just hear it, I felt it. Every muscle I had went slack like a wet bag of prickly pins. Which was just what I wanted to avoid. Because Lockter was a puppeteer, able to control an individual with just her voice.

"That's better." Lockter walked over, pulled the wallet from my coat, and opened it. "Ah, so you meant private detective. Dane Curse. Have I heard the name before?"

I clenched my mouth tight. But those jaw muscles loosened on their own, and with my two-faced tongue formed the words, "I don't know."

"What did you do before you were a detective?"

No. If I said "black cape" she'd press me on who I was and what I've done. Then I'd march myself to Impenetron for a ten-year stay. So I pushed my memory back. Back past Dread Division. Back past Raymond's gang. Back years and years when, "I was a dockworker."

"Interesting. Now tell me for true, why are you here?"

"I'm investigating this murder."

Lockter looked confused. "But the police say these two killed each other."

"They don't care if that's true or not. I do."

She searched my face like she'd seen it before. Finally, she slipped my wallet back home, and in her regular voice said, "Get out. And stay out. If I catch you in here again I'll call the police."

My body woke up from her numbing effect and I ran out of the morgue, practically knocking the doors off their hinges. Moving quick down the hall I looked back. *God damn Lockter, now I might never-*

And I crashed into a busy custodian.

He fell to ground and said from his back, "Watch it, pal."

I was about to say, "Why don't you?" but then I looked at him. He was middle aged. With the paunch of a former high school sports star. And there was glory in his eyes that died a long ways back. So instead of my original sentence I extended a hand and said, "Sorry about that, pal. I wasn't paying attention. Just got chewed out by Lockter."

He accepted my help and stood up. "Dames, right? Give them some power and they think they own you. What's she done now?"

"Well, I got to inspect a black cape corpse, but she won't let me without the paperwork."

"Can't you come back tomorrow?"

"No," I said. "And even if I could the Fletcher Act makes cape DNA a controlled substance, so they usually burn or bury the unclaimed ones in shockcrete within twenty-four hours, and if I don't get my samples before then I'm toast."

"But she won't let you," he said. "Typical Lockter."

I smiled. "Right. Anyway, you know when she goes home?" I pulled out a hundred, and held it out.

Falcons don't grab field mice as quick as he snatched that bill. "Around midnight every day."

"Thanks," I said, "I'll swing by then."

I resumed my walk to the stairs.

But the guy called out, "Hey. Don't be late. Security seals those outer doors at two, and only Pinnacle can pry them apart."

"Between twelve and two, got it." I walked outside. The sun was nearing the end of its shift. Soon it'd be night, and I'd be busy. First the museum to study the vents, then the morgue to collect some residue.

But in the meantime…

I pulled out the card they found on Thermite. Its edges were toasty, but one word was still legible: Wetlands.

And all of a sudden my night got a whole lot simpler.

Chapter 6

Wetlands was a Brazilian dance club that had a running sideline in less than legal hard-to-find hardware. It was owned by a black cape named Swamp, and while we normally don't speak I'd just found his card in the pocket of a dead man. A dead man who died near two pieces of hard-to-find hardware. And it reasoned that if he supplied the filament, and the canister, then he provided the chemical himself, or knew the person who did. Either way, I could be one big step closer to solving my case.

I drove to the club and parked out front. The sign on the door said closed, but I pushed it open and looked around. Normally Wetlands is exciting and mysterious. Its nighttime darkness provides cover for forbidden fun, and makes the cream colored furniture look like a naked model's firm skin.

But now, under the fluorescent lights, you could see every floor stain from spilled drinks of weekends past, and the sofas seemed more like dead, bloated bodies.

That's the thing about dance clubs, they're just like hookers. You don't want to be inside either one when they're well lit.

Across the room was the VIP section, a raised metal platform that floated ten feet above the floor. I walked up the hovering stairs to find Swamp, sitting on a couch. He had deep dark skin, a shaved head, and wore red leathers. Parked next to him was a slim, pasty white guy dressed in black.

"Hey team," I said. "Don't get up."

The pale boy hopped to. "What're you doing here?"

"Keep it shiver, Vec," Swamp said. "But my boy's got a point, Dane. Why you here?"

I crossed both arms up high on my chest, and tickled my pistol grips. "A better question is why're you so jumpy? Got a guilty conscience?"

"In my club I act how I like," Swamp said.

"While I'm here that's not entirely true, is it?"

"Screw this." Vec stepped towards me. "I'm going to lay you out flat."

I pulled Lois. "Be easy paleface, before I give you a tan."

Vec kept coming. "I'm not scared of that blaster."

I clicked off her safety, and depressed the trigger halfway. Lois' barrel glowed green and doubled in size and width as twin bracers leapt from the grip, and ran up my arm in a crisscross pattern, lashing her to me. "You're about to be."

"Hem that up," Swamp said.

Vec stopped, and looked at his boss.

"Dane, before this gets messy why don't you tell me why you're here."

I kept my piece on Vec, but put my eyes on Swamp. "It's about Thermite and Firewall. They-"

"I got a TV." Swamp's skin turned a light shade of green. "They killed each other trying to steal the Coconut."

"Yeah," I said, "next to hardware you sold them."

Vec snickered. "Who says?"

"Me. I do. Now start talking, or I'll blast you through that back wall and leave a hole so big that when the Feds, cops, and city inspectors arrive to investigate, they'll have no trouble finding whatever illegal gear you got stashed downstairs." I clicked Lois to scatter shot.

All of a sudden Vec's arrogance was gone. He looked at Swamp.

Swamp looked at me. "Ok. They're both dead so who cares, right? About a week ago I sold them one spool of fiber optic filament, and a canister for a grade nine liquid substance."

"Grade nine?" I said. "That's some potent stew. What were they hauling?"

"How should we know?" Vec said. "Those type of chemicals require special storage tanks. You see any around here?"

Swamp said, "We sold the thermos, not the cola. You know I don't deal in chems, they're not something my clientele go in for."

That was true, actually. "So where'd they fill it up?"

Swamp shrugged. "When you spend as much as they did, I don't ask questions."

"Fine. Was there anyone else with them when they picked up the goods? A friend maybe?"

"A friend?" Vec said.

Swamp laughed. "I don't think those two were interested in a third man."

I looked back and forth between the pair. And slipped Lois back into her holster. "Fine."

Both men relaxed.

"But know this," I said, "if you're lying to me I'll find out. And then I'm going to have to come back and do bad things to both of you."

Vec said, "So we got nothing to worry about."

"We'll see." I turned to leave. Because what they said jibed. While Swamp provided that canister the boys must've filled it someplace else, and I'd know where after tonight's trip to the morgue.

But when I got to the top of the stairs I paused. There was a girl on the dance floor coming my way. She had on knee high boots, a black dress that would have to do some growing up before it could pass as a napkin, and every inch of the too much skin she showed was covered in tattoos. As she walked her thick hair flowed behind her like black fire, and I could feel the heat from where I was standing.

She glided up the steps, passed by me without a glance, and threw her arms around Swamp. "Do I really have to go to the meet tonight alone?"

"Not now, kitten." Swamp motioned at me. "We got company."

The girl turned my way. And went statue still. "What's he doing here?"

I had on a smile. The dewy kind. "Hey Doodle, you look great."

"Doodle?" Swamp said. "Who's Doodle?"

She rolled her eyes. "It's Sketch now. Nobody calls me Doodle anymore, Dane."

"Really?" I said. "Dane?"

"Yeah. You don't expect me to call you Dad, do you?"

Chapter 7

The last time I saw Doodle she was about as big as a baby bird. Now she looked a lot more like her mother. And not in the eyes, nose, and chin way. It was her stance. The attitude. That hard soft skin around her pout.

"I'm not expecting it," I said, "but Dad would be nice."

"Wait, hold up," Swamp said. "Dane's your father?"

"Yes," I said.

"No." Doodle crossed her arms. "Mom said-"

"Tera says lots of things. Most of it's not true."

"Don't talk about her that way."

"Why?" I looked around. "Is she here?"

"Somewhere," Doodle said. "Why are you?"

"I'm getting some information, but now that I'm done maybe we can talk?"

"Information?" she said.

"Yeah, I'm a detective."

Doodle laughed. "That's pathetic."

"Hey baby," Swamp said. "Your old man wants to catch up, why don't you take him outside for a chat?"

Doodle looked at him, then me. "Fine. That ok with you, Dane?"

I smiled. Again it was the dewy kind. "That's great."

She led me down the steps and across the floor, but when we neared the exit a woman with a heavy Filipino accent said, "What're you doing here?"

I turned around. It was my ex, Tera. She was five-foot four with skin as brown and warm as a cup of coffee. The light green dress she wore made the curves running around her look like rolling hills, and I couldn't help but notice that all their peaks still pointed up. "Get out of here," she said.

"I was doing just that. Let's go, Doodle."

"No." Tera jumped in front of me and shoved a finger in my face. "She stays here. We have work."

"Pipe down, I just want a word." I grabbed Tera's shoulder, and light touched her aside, but she managed to find the floor just the same.

"My arm," Tera yelled from her back. "You bastard."

Doodle said, "Mom."

I rolled my eyes. "Aw cripes."

Tera made a big deal of getting to her feet. "Did you see that? He shoved me."

"You fell on purpose," I said.

"You were always like this," Tera said.

"Sketch," Swamp called from up high on the platform. "Outside."

She took my arm. "Right. Let's go talk. Unless you don't want to."

"No, I do." I let her pull me away, and once we got outside I said, "So how long you been in town for?"

"A couple of weeks."

"A couple?" *That hurt.* "Why didn't you call?"

"Don't have your number."

I pulled out my card and a pen, jotted down my home line, and handed it to her. "Here. Now you do."

Doodle shoved it in her pocket. "Thanks."

"Sure. How long are you sticking around for?"

"Until the… I don't know. We're on vacation."

"Yeah, right. Tera said work, what's she got you doing?"

"Nothing I don't want to do myself."

"Jeezus, you're seventeen. You should be in school. This is-"

"What I want," Doodle said. She crossed her arms and stared up at me. Her eyes were so full of anger. But I wasn't seeing Tera.

This time it was like looking in a mirror.

So I softened my tone. "Alright. This obviously isn't a good time, but maybe later we can get together, while you're still around?"

"Sure," she said. "Tomorrow."

Each chamber of my normally hard heart inflated. "Really?"

"I don't know. I'll call you."

"You promise?"

"Yeah, I promise. I'll talk to you then. Goodbye." She slid me a casual wave and walked back inside.

I got in my car. And heaved a mighty sigh. I didn't know what was worse, that I missed all those years of Doodle growing up, or that she was obviously running jobs with her mom. Either way I swore right then to get her out of the life and on the right track.

But as I started up the car I realized how hypocritical a thought that was.

After all, I was about to go pull half a heist myself.

Chapter 8

The sun was way below the horizon when I hunkered down behind the thick bank of trees that sat fifty yards from the Gold Coast City Museum's rear entrance. My black overcoat was doing a fine job of keeping me hidden, but I also had on my old mask. It only went around my eyes, but that would be enough to fool the dozen wall mounted cameras that were staring down on the parking lot between me and the building, if I was dumb enough to get seen. Each one was shaking its head at a different pace, which was going to make this tricky. I had to wait for them to find a rhythm, and all look away together. It was tedious. But necessary. If I got pinched inside these walls I'd be locked up in Impenetron for years. Unless it was Al Mighty who did the pinching. Then I'd be buried under Ayers Hill, with nothing but a John Doe carved into my headstone.

So I waited. Twenty minutes. Until finally every security camera turned inward. And then swiveled away in near perfect unison.

Exploding from my cover I sprinted across the lot. I pumped my arms hard. And opened my stride. But by the time I made it halfway a few of the one eyed vultures were already turning back.

So I ran harder. Hitting the wall without slowing down I used the gaps between the massive stones as handholds and climbed. I got to the top in seconds, and slipped over the ledge. There I waited. Five more minutes passed. And I was still alone.

It was time to get moving.

I started my onsite investigation by studying the short wall that ran around the roof, looking for any scratches or holes. But there were none.

Interesting.

I made a note of it, and walked to the ventilation access hatch. It was sealed with an impressive lock. Reaching into my pocket I removed my pick, and slid it into the keyhole. I fished the thin shiv side-to-side, all with Carl's voice in my head saying, "Learn to use this. Muscle isn't an all-purpose tool."

I know Carl. You've mentioned.

After a minute the first tumbler clicked into place. Thirty seconds later and another joined it. Then, after what felt like forever,

I twisted the pick, and it snapped in half.

Which was the same thing that happened the night before when I tried to retrieve Toby Teenie's pictures from the safe. So like then I ignored Carl's advice, and ripped the door off its hinges revealing a dark shaft that ran straight down. Pulling out my hand scanner I clicked on its light, and slid in face first, pushing both elbows against the vent's sides hard enough to slow my going. After descending thirty feet the tunnel forked in two directions. I turned west, and crawled until I reached the Amphibia Theatre access tube.

There the vent dipped down, then turned and ran parallel over the model orca's back before ending at the grate. I slid down. And the vent's metal bottom made a resounding boom as it bent and shook from my weight. Gently, I slid forward. The shaking slowed, but the next section of vent made the same loud noise. I don't know how it sounded on the floor below, but inside the duct it was like cannon shot. And I wondered if it would hold me. Let alone three guys.

Still though, I slid forward to the end of the tunnel. Below the grate was the hanging whale, a forty-foot drop, and that glass floor protected ecosystem full of glowing bioluminescent algae.

Ignoring all that I turned the light, and my attention, to the grate's edges.

And I couldn't believe it. Just like the roof there wasn't a scuff. And that wasn't just interesting, it was impossible. Sure, the boys may've climbed the outer wall like I did, but the rope they used to get down from here required an anchor, like a hook or a magnet, and those leave marks.

I don't know if Widow was right, but something smelled wrong about this job. And I was in a vent that delivered fresh air. But I couldn't learn anything more by hanging around, so it was time to vanish.

I inched backwards. And the Amphibia Theatre's lights clicked on.

Looking through the grate I saw ten men with rifles and black riot armor charge into the room and fan out over the glass floor in formation, like the SWAT team's older, meaner brother.

"Team leader," a radio squawked, "do you have eyes on the intruder?"

"No eyes yet," one of them said. "We know you're here. Come out with your hands up."

"Where is he?"

"The room's empty."

"No." This voice was calm. And certain. "He's here alright."

"Where?"

My breathing turned shallow. But I wasn't concerned. There were no motion sensors in here. No alarms. They could search this room all day and never find me.

Then one said, "Look up, he's in the vents."

All ten turned their rifles upward and fired. Bullets punched a hundred holes through the metal around me. A few hit my chest. More clipped my thighs. All of them bit deep, but my hide stayed intact.

"That's enough," their commander said, "cease fire."

And they stopped the assault.

"Did we get him?"

"Is there blood?"

All around me the vent was filled with holes. Thin beams of light stabbed through them. I looked back. Beyond my feet the duct ran about two meters before it turned up and disappeared into the ceiling. If I was fast enough I could-

"Focus your fire where the vent meets the ceiling."

No.

Again the bullets flew, only this time each slug was concentrated at a spot one yard behind me. They chewed a sloppy line through the shaft's four sides. Even over the gunfire I could hear the vent groan. And buckle. Then it tore free from the ceiling.

I slipped out the open end and fell all forty feet, hitting the glass floor face first. But I scrambled upright, only the storm troopers already had their rifles aimed my way. The closest man's barrel was an inch from my eye. "Don't move," he said, "or I'll put one into your skull."

I froze, and stared down the black hole.

"Yeah. That's right, invulnerable. We know your weakness."

Chapter 9

The guy was right. My skin's harder to get through than Advanced Latin, but neither eye would stop a slug. And the lids that protected them offered less protection than you'd think. So I put my hands up. "Don't shoot. Please."

"Smart." He pushed a finger into his ear. "Central, this is Commander Waters, we've apprehended an invulnerable black cape. Request immediate dragon wagon for one."

The radio barked, "One wagon en route. Good work, commander."

He popped his visor. But kept the rifle aimed at my left orb. "Now we wait. In the meantime you want to tell me your name?"

"Puddin Tame," I said.

Waters smirked. "We'll find out soon enough."

He was right. We would. If I hung out. Instead, I snapped my face to the side.

Waters blasted away. His bullet struck my temple. The rest of the team joined in and their slugs hit my head and neck. With one hand I covered my open eyes. With the other I grabbed Waters' rifle, and pulled it to me. The commander came with.

As he stumbled I slipped my arm beneath his chin, spun him around, and held his back tight against my chest like a human shield.

And the gunfire stopped.

I peered over my new friend's shoulder.

His men were all at the ready, aiming their weapons our way.

"Hold your fire," Waters said.

"Didn't expect this invulnerable to have super strength, did you?" I dragged him back one step.

The nearest gunman barked, "Stay where you are."

"Ok." I moved my head to Waters' other side. And took another step.

"Hey," the trooper said. "Don't do that again."

"Sure thing." I shuffled back some more. And hit the wall.

Waters said over his shoulder, "Run out of road, strongman?"

I looked down. He was right. Both my feet were on the floor's marble perimeter. I said, "All part of the plan." Lifting one knee up I took a sharp breath, and stomped down hard. My heel struck the floor and it completely shattered, sending up the smell of old gym socks as all nine cops were swallowed by the green stew below. As they splashed down the bioluminescent algae exploded, filling the room with bright blue, yellow, and red sparks.

I shoved Waters into the soup, and then with my back tight against the wall, I shimmied towards the window on the right. When I got there I leapt up, grabbed its iron bars, and climbed them like a ladder.

Below me Waters cried, "Bring him down."

And more bullets flew. Some hit the wall. Others cracked the glass.

Despite the heavy fire I reached the top in seconds, putting the model orca's tail ten feet behind me. Then I bent my knees. And sprang backwards. Twisting through the air I reached towards the tip of the great mammal's tail. But bullets ripped big, black chunks from my target. And those tiny harpoons tore every bit of fake skin and blubber off, leaving only the metal support cable behind, which swayed as it dangled.

Stretching out I opened my hand. And grabbed the thin, metal wire. But the bullets kept flying as I swung back and forth like bait on a hook. So I scurried up the cable, jumped onto the portion of orca back that still remained, and scrambled up the wounded beast's spine.

When I got to the vent, now just a hole in the ceiling, I jumped up into it, and punched my fingers through the metal, making a pair of handholds. And just like that, hand-over-hand, I clambered skywards like a mole with its tail on fire.

When I reached the rooftop I spilled out onto the gravel. Getting up I looked around for Al Mighty.

But there were no white capes waiting. It was all clear. I moved towards the ledge.

And a deep voice said, "Nice night, huh?"

"Al?" My guts dropped and I spun around.

"Wrong again." It was the blond cop that rousted me earlier. And his pistol was pointed right at me.

Chapter 10

"What're you doing up here?" I said.

"Don't worry about it. Now put these on." He pulled a set of cuffs off his belt and threw them over.

The bracelets sailed past me, and landed on the roof.

"Very funny," he said. "Pick them up."

I didn't break eye contact. "No."

He clicked the hammer back on his piece. "I can always shoot you instead."

"With a pistol?"

Blondie queer eyed me. "Yeah."

He didn't know. "Ok then." I turned and took two steps towards the cuffs. Then two more past them. And jumped off the roof. I fell through the air towards the blacktop, plunging five stories in seconds. Hitting the concrete hard I rolled forwards, and came up on my feet, already jogging away. As I went I looked over my shoulder and waved to the cop.

Who was running for the stairs.

What the… Was he in pursuit?

I picked up my pace and bolted across the parking lot.

Behind me Waters said, "Stand down detective, that black cape's invulnerable."

I reached the road and looked back. Four of the storm troopers, dripping in green grunge, were outside.

And the cop charged right past them.

He was. He was giving chase.

I turned and darted across the road. Right into the path of a large, red truck. It mashed on its brakes and hit the horn. I jumped left. And just missed it. But now I was staring at an oncoming blue compact. I rolled into the next lane as it sped past.

Just three more lanes to go.

I ran across the first two. But in the third a bus was coming fast. I dove towards the sidewalk. And the people mover plowed into my shins. I spun through the air, and slammed into a brick wall, then flopped to the ground.

A woman in blue looked down at me. "Oh my God, we got to get you to a hospital. I'm calling an ambulance."

Hopping to my feet I said, "No thanks. I'll jog there." Running past her I ducked down the next alley. I sprinted the whole way, and reached the far end in seconds. It emptied into a sidewalk filled with pedestrians.

Which way was my car, left or right? Right, definitely to the-

"Stop, police!"

I turned around.

The Viking was at the other side of the alley. With his gun drawn. But with so many civilians around me he'd never shoot.

So I pulled Rico.

His eyes got big. "Drop your weapon."

Lining him up real nice I said, "No," and pulled the trigger. Rico blasted loud. And his slug hit true. The cop spun around, and smacked the concrete.

Around me the citizens screamed and scattered.

"He's got a pistol."

"Run."

I holstered my rod amid the mayhem. "It's only a stunner. He'll be fine."

Sooner than I thought, because right then the cop rose up slow. He turned to me with the gun still in hand, and a hard expression on his face. "Stop. Right. There."

Unbelievable. That electro-charge should've knocked him out cold.

I bolted right, running as fast as I could. My car was two blocks down, and I reached it quick, jumped in, and laid the gas flat with both feet. One block rolled past. Then two. I turned right, then left, and then right again before traffic got thick and I had to stop.

I checked my rearview. No sirens. No crazy cop. Finally, I was safe. Stuck in traffic, but safe.

I wiped the sweat from my face, then removed my mask and laughed. I'd never met a cop like him. What breed of bull charges down a powered perp on foot after he catches a stunner an inch from his heart? Not one that wants to spend their pension. He must've-

Something rapped my window.

I looked over. And into a determined pair of Swedish blue eyes hovering above a gun. The cop said, "Open... Your door."

Unbelievable. I put it in park and got out. "How'd you find me?"

"Shut…" He gulped some air. "Up. You're under arrest."

The light ahead turned green. And traffic started to flow around us. Behind me a car laid on its horn. The driver leaned out and yelled, "Come on already."

The cop shouted, "Stand down, I'm-"

Moving swift I swatted his gun. It fell to the ground, but the cop didn't shrink. Instead he threw a fist into my jaw. I rolled with his punch, but he still screamed and cradled his hand. "You bastard."

"So," I said, "you are human." Grabbing his lapels I lifted him up, and threw him over a parked car.

He landed flat on the sidewalk, but got to his knees. "Police," he said. "Do not move."

I said, "I'm sorry as hell about that hand, please know I got nothing but respect for you." Then I got back into my car, and peeled out.

#

After about ten minutes of uninterrupted cruising I'd put a few dozen miles of cool night air between me and that cop, and I started to feel pretty good. Granted, I'd made a bigger mess in the museum than I expected, but I came out of it with some interesting information regarding my case. And I got to manhandle some heavy-handed lawmen. Overall it was a good start to the evening.

Now if I could only be as successful at the morgue...

I aimed my sled towards the hospital and about a half an hour later I was on the road that led to its parking lot. My clock said it was almost ten, which meant I had a touch over two hours of waiting before Lockter left. The smart play was to pull in, and wait until she went home, then slip past security for maximum time with the corpses.

But instead of the smart play I kept on driving.

Chapter 11

Doodle's attitude earlier was one of pure teen angst. That didn't bother me. What did was the mention of a solo meet that had her nervous. She sounded like she needed backup. And I wasn't going to let her go without it. So I stopped three blocks away from Wetlands and waited for her to pop out. I'd stay planted for as long as I could, and while my heels cooled I'd dice up the case.

The official story was that Thermite and Firewall climbed up to the roof, and shimmied through the vents before hacking the door and cutting off the alarms with a filament they shot through the gaps in the lasers. Then, once inside, they turned on each other before getting the diamond: Thermite burning Firewall with his power, and Firewall using the accelerant they brought for the Kessel Glass on his friend.

And I had to admit, it wrapped up pretty as a present.

But the outside wall and the inside vent told a different story. Could the boys have climbed up and down them without leaving a scratch? Doubtful. Plus, where'd they acquire the plans for Wentorf Hall's security system? Both those issues raised doubts.

And then there was the money.

Swamp's hardware cost a bundle. He admitted as much. So where did two boys, fresh from the slammer, get that kind of butter? It had occurred to me earlier that Swamp may not have been entirely honest regarding the depth of his role in all of this, but even so, masterminding a break in, especially one like this, was way outside of his skill set. Which meant that a powerful moneyman, with museum knowledge and access to chemicals, was behind it all. Someone who could plan, organize, and fund the whole job.

Swamp couldn't tell me who that was, or if they harbored ill will towards the boys, but the evidence on Thermite's body could, so long as I-

A slamming door roused me from my thoughts.

I peered out the window. Doodle was standing on the curb in front of Wetlands. She looked almost like a normal teen in jeans, a red sweater, and a big, black purse over her shoulder. She glanced right. Then left. Then straight at my Jalopy.

I slid down until I was just peeking over the dashboard. But it was too late. I watched her confusion turn into recognition.

She jogged towards me, muttering something and pointing sideways.

I leaned out my window. "What?"

"Pull around the corner. Hurry."

I turned down the nearest side street, parked, and got out.

Seconds later Doodle appeared. "What're you doing here?"

"I was in the neighborhood."

"Bull, your office is on the other side of town."

"How do you know?"

"The address is on your card. It's in Falling Rock, the Tanziger building, fourth floor. I even remember the phone number."

My chest puffed up. "Keen environmental awareness. Good memorization. You could be a detective."

Doodle opened her mouth, but didn't say anything. Instead her features softened. "So you're here to keep an eye on me?"

"Both eyes, actually. What you said earlier, it sounded like you could use some backup." I tussled her thick, black hair.

"Don't." She shoved my hand away. "Don't do that."

"Do what?"

"Act like my dad."

"I am your dad, Doodle."

"Dad's are around more than once a decade."

"Hey, you don't think I wanted to be? Your mom took you out of town without so much as a goodbye or an address. I've had no idea where you've been."

"Whatever." Doodle looked at her watch.

"Hey, maybe we could talk about it in the car? You always loved to drive."

"I can't now. I have a thing."

I reached for her shoulder.

And she stepped back.

So with as much sincerity as possible I said, "What're you up to, Doodle? Why're you and Tera really back in town? Why's no one out here with you?"

She sighed. "If it'll get you off my back, we're pulling a job. Tomorrow night."

"For who? Swamp?"

"Yeah." Her eyes weren't scared, but they sure were nervous. "Now will you please go? I was just being silly before. I can handle myself."

"I know you can. But it's not silly being cautious. It's smart. You were always whip smart. And I was just concerned. Sorry," I said, "Sketch."

"Concerned is fine, I guess. And you can call me Doodle. Oh, I have something for you."

"For me?"

"Yeah, here." She rolled her shirt up. Underneath, on her stomach, were a ton of tattoos. There was a stick of dynamite and a pair of pistols, but right above her navel were twin roses. Doodle closed her eyes tight. And one of the green stems pushed out against her flesh. She pinched it. And peeled it away. All that remained was a blank outline of the bloom, but in her hand was a real live bright red fresh cut rose. "These are still your favorite, right?"

I took the flower and gave it a whiff. "Yeah. You've gotten really good."

"This is nothing. Now get out of here. I got a thing." She walked back towards Wetlands.

"Hey."

My daughter stopped and turned to me.

I said, "I missed you."

Doodle's smile hadn't changed a bit since she was a kid. "I... I'll call you tomorrow. I promise," she said, and disappeared around the corner.

I stared at her rose. My daughter, the matter manifester. Able to create physical objects directly from her body.

I placed her flower on the passenger's seat. It didn't look anything like the ones she made as a kid. Those were all thick and chunky, the bulbs too big for their stems to hold up. Though I liked them just the same.

This was no time for reminiscing though. I had to get to the morgue. So I started up my car. But left it in park. Because there was something in Doodle's voice I couldn't shake. I looked at the clock.

It wasn't even eleven. Plenty of time still.

I took a right, drove three blocks, and parked again. Then I slipped out of my ride and padded back to Wetlands on feet so smooth a wolf couldn't hear me coming. Peering around the corner I saw Doodle at the club's entrance. She looked at her watch as a car rolled up.

It was a late model black sedan almost the size of a truck with headlights burning like a sailor's loins ten days after shore leave. But through the twin beams I could see the outlines of three people inside. The driver lowered his window. Doodle bent down. They exchanged muffled words.

And my kid pounded the roof of the car. Both her hands started swinging about. It was like watching her mom get hot. But then the back door opened. And Doodle froze.

I reached into my jacket and grabbed Lois. She doubled in size, but her green glow was contained inside my coat.

Doodle took a big step back. She unslung her purse and held it out. The driver reached through his window and snatched it.

The back door closed. And the car pulled away.

Doodle then slipped back into the club, safe and whole. So I relaxed, and unhanded Lois. With my fatherly duties done it was time for me to rabbit.

"Where do you think you're going?"

I spun around.

Swamp, still wearing the red leathers from earlier, was standing there with his pale boy Vec.

"Through you both," I said, and hurled a fist at Swamp's face.

He transformed into green liquid and my punch passed through him.

I pulled my damp hand back, ready to toss another.

But then Swamp threw a punch of his own. It hit like a fire hose, blasting needle-like liquid between my eyelids and coarse, bitter bubbles down my throat.

I stumbled back, hacking. And wiped the water away. When I looked up Swamp had vanished. But Vec was still in front of me. I reached for his throat. But he grabbed my wrist, and shoved it to the ground. I flopped to my knees with it, and strained myself trying to get free.

"Having problems?" Vec said.

Fighting his grip I said, "What's your power set, super strength?"

"Me? I'm attractive."

"Not for long." I grabbed at his neck again with my free hand.

But he snatched that one, and pinned it too. Now both my paws were stuck on the cement.

"You sure?" Vec said.

"Let me up and I'll show you."

"Ok." Vec released me and stepped back.

I got up and lunged towards him. But a green wave rose up between us. "Son of a-" was all I got out before Swamp, in his purely liquid form, crashed down and swallowed me whole.

I thrashed as best I could. But I was trapped like a bug in a drop of dew. I couldn't see, couldn't breathe. My head burned and tingled. Blackness started to creep in. And from a distance I heard Swamp say, "Damn man, you go down faster than your daughter."

Then everything went black.

Chapter 12

I opened my eyes to a beautiful sunny day. *Day.* I shot up and looked at my watch. Six thirty AM. I punched the pavement, cracking the cement. *God damn you, Swamp.* My window at the morgue was closed. Now what would I do?

What else?

Wait until nine and sneak in, hopefully avoiding Doctor Lockter and a long prison sentence.

I stood up and did the self pat down. My keys, wallet, and hardware were all still in place, so I turned towards my ride. Dozens of pedestrians were on the sidewalk, making their way to work. I plowed through them on the way to my car. But when I got there all I found was ocean air, and a sign that said tow away zone.

God damn it. Again.

I took down the address of the impound lot, then flagged a cab and headed over. The lady behind the caged counter looked like an angry Russian nesting doll, but for a few hundreds she was kind enough to escort me to my sled. I slid in and returned to the office, arriving too early for Mrs. West and whatever barb she had on her cute quip of the day calendar. I ran past her desk, going for a fresh suit, but stopped dead. On my computer screen was Sandtrout's icon.

And it was blinking.

I hit print and out came my report. It filled the whole page, each line representing some way Thermite and Firewall's lives intersected. There were schools both attended and flights they took together. There were a lot of old hotel charges, and a restaurant they worked at. But no current jobs. And no current address. There was, however, something worth knowing at the bottom of the page.

The name Bundy Strong.

He was a fence mostly, buying goods that thieves stole, but sometimes, for a fee, he'd also facilitate the jobs themselves by introducing people who wanted to hire powered thieves with those black capes who possess the necessary might. When I was with Dread Division we never used him. Too small time. But maybe he'd gotten bigger since then. I'd find out, right after I questioned him about how he knew the boys.

Bittenbach Bay resides between two peninsulas that jut out of the north and south ends of town like a crab claw. The upper one is called Highside, home of the fourth busiest port in the world, and North Point, Bundy Strong's shipping dock. It was a squat, ugly building right on the water, and it looked and smelled like a deep forest mushroom.

I walked inside, past the three wide aisles full of heavy boxes, and up the stairs to Bundy's office. He was at his desk, looking like a toad in a red flannel shirt and brown coveralls, lost in deep thought as he stared at a helium tank against the wall.

"Hey Bundy," I said.

He snapped to and grabbed his chest. "Good lord, pal, what're… Oh, it's you. What do you want, turn cape?"

I walked over, snatched his collar, and hoisted him up to my level. "More respect. I don't take guff from regs."

"I'm not a regular person." He pulled back hard, but went nowhere.

"Lifting five hundred pounds don't make you a cape. Not in this burg." I tossed him back into the chair.

Bundy straightened his shirt. "Whatever. Why're you here?"

"Thermite and Firewall. Did you set them up with the Wentorf job, or were you just going to serve as their fence?"

"What, the Coconut guys? I never met them."

"You want to try the truth this time?"

"That is the truth."

"Bundy, a carrot stick'll pass your lips before an honest breath, so I'll give you one more chance to tell me what I want to know before I start snapping things off you."

He leaned forward. And thought about what I could do to him. His imagination must've been vivid because he said, "Ok. There's one thing I got. Here." Bundy reached under his desk.

And he dropped out of sight.

"What the hell?" I circled around the worktable. There was an open hatch right below where he was just sitting. Through it I saw Bundy running across the floor of the warehouse. Then it slammed shut.

I charged out of the office and took the stairs down two at a time. "Stop. You're only making this harder on yourself."

Bundy was already halfway down the center aisle, fleeing towards the ocean. "Yeah, right." He reached the end of the row and turned the corner fast and blind.

There was a loud crash. And Bundy yelled, "Watch where you're going."

Nice. My quarry had run into something big.

I pushed ahead faster and took the turn. But instead of Bundy I found a pile of upturned cans and a puddle of thick, purple liquid. I jumped over the pool. But one foot landed in the goo. It stuck fast. And I fell forward, landing flat on the warehouse floor. Getting to my knees I reached back and yanked my loafer free. But the rubber sole stayed stuck as I ripped the shoe in half.

I smelled my fingers. *Hyper-adhesive.*

No matter. With one socked foot I resumed the chase. Up ahead was the exit to the wet dock. I charged through it. "This is stupid, Bundy. You'll never outrun me."

To my right was a pile of garbage bags, while on the left sat two wooden wharfs. They ran parallel for fifty yards, and floating between them was a sleek, yellow jetboat. Bundy was standing at its helm. "I already have, unless you got gills." He pushed down the throttle and his engine roared loud as it sucked water from beneath the hull and blasted it out the back. Bundy and his ship shot forward, like a bullet in a barrel. "So long, Curse."

I chased it down the dock.

But with the seahorse power under Bundy he pulled away easy. So I stopped running. And the fact that the boat's engine was on its belly meant I couldn't cripple it with a bullet, so I stood there burning, and watched him escape with the information I needed.

But then a rope slid past me.

The other end was tied to Bundy's boat.

I dove. And just got a hand around it.

The line jerked forward, and dragged me face first down the wooden dock like a cowboy who roped a runaway steer.

Bundy glanced back. "What the? Are you kidding me?" He pressed the throttle lower, pulling me faster down the wooden wharf. Jagged splinters ripped through my coat. The searing friction burnt my pants and singed my knees.

I didn't know how much more I could take. Not because my grip would give, or my legs would burn, but because twenty yards ahead at the dock's end, was a large, cement column. And Bundy was dragging me right towards it. If I smacked it I'd lose my grip. And even if I held on I didn't know if I'd climb my way onto Bundy's craft before I passed out from lack of oxygen. So I took the third option.

Mere seconds before impact I swung my legs to the side, pulled my feet out in front of me, and caught the pillar on both heels. The rope in my hands jerked hard. Pain clawed my lower back. But like a two-ton anchor I held tight, and Bundy's boat slammed to a halt. Its engine was still pumping hard though, and it jerked the vessel side-to-side on the end of my line. Meanwhile Bundy was slung over the captain's wheel, kicking both legs in the air.

Gritting my teeth, I pulled the rope towards me, and wrapped that extra line around my wrist. I pulled again. And the boat came even closer. Then, hand-over-hand I dragged Bundy towards me like a fat man sucks in a plate of pasta, until the vessel was only a few feet from the dock's edge.

But then Bundy straightened up. "You son of a bitch. You're not taking me."

I gave the line another yank. "You… want to bet?"

"Sure." Bundy pulled a knife, and ran to where the rope was secured. He leaned out over the edge and hacked it. Once. Twice. On the third slice the rope frayed. "Ha. See you around." He lifted the blade high. And brought it down fast.

Right as I let go.

I fell to the dock as the boat fired forward like a torpedo, sending Bundy tumbling over its back and into the ocean.

Getting up I grabbed the column, leaned way out over the bay, and reached into the water. I wrapped my fist around Bundy's ankle and pulled him out like a prize marlin. "Hey Bundy," I said. "Glad I caught you."

Chapter 13

I dragged Bundy down the pier, and threw him head first into the pile of garbage bags. "Now tell me everything you know about those boys."

He looked over his shoulder. "Get bent."

Putting my socked foot on the back of his skull I stomped down deep. The bag below him burst sending up the sickly sweet smell of whatever mystery moisture it held.

I covered my nose and said, "I hope you like the idea of facing Saint Peter with a mouthful of whatever that is, Bundy."

Bubbles came out the sides of his half submerged head. I enjoyed the sound for more than a few moments. Finally I let up, and he rolled to his back, sputtering like an old Ford.

I said, "Now talk."

Bundy wiped the brown liquid off his face and said, "Right. Thermite and Firewall. The Burn Boys. We shared a cell in Impenetron for a year or so. When they got out I offered them my services as a fence, but they declined, said they wanted to stay legit. Then a few weeks ago, out of the blue, they called me looking for a job."

"What changed their minds?"

"No clue. But a little while before that I got a request from some out-of-towner facet hound, and since the boys pinch gems I lined the two up. I had no idea it was about the Coconut, though. I swear. Otherwise I'd have charged a higher fee."

I looked down at Bundy. "I need more."

"Like what?"

"The name of the person who hired them, you muzzy fiend."

"I don't got it."

"Bad news for you." Maybe it was the fact I got knocked out the night before by my daughter's boyfriend. Maybe it was because I missed my chance at the morgue. Or it could've been being dragged face first down a pier. But whatever it was, I'd had enough. Putting my heel on Bundy's face I stomped down until the brown liquid was up to my ankle.

Air bubbles from Bundy's lungs began popping the surface of

the liquid. He clawed my leg. And thrashed.

I just pressed him down deeper. Soon the bubbles began to slow. Then they stopped. I took a few deep breaths. And enjoyed the silence. Along with the fresh, salty air. It really was a beautiful morning.

But then I eased off. And pulling Bundy from the muck, I flipped him over, and smacked his spine. He came to life, retching up a can of motor oil. When it was all out he said, "Please. Stop."

I pulled one arm behind his back, and shoved his head back down, inches from the garbage. "The name," I said. "Now."

"I..." Bundy gagged. "I don't have one. I don't work like that. I don't want names, I don't want details. You tell me what skills you want, and I pass your phone number over of who's got them. It's that simple."

"And when do you get your fee?"

"The agents drop off half up front, the principal does the rest after the job's complete."

"So," I said, "when're you getting the second installment?"

"Tomorrow. She calls me tomorrow to set up the meet."

I spun him over and dropped him in the pile. Then I pulled out Rico, and pressed the muzzle into Bundy's forehead. "And what will you do when she does?"

His eyes went cross staring at my Thumper. "I'll call you right after."

"Good. In the meantime give me the boys' address. And anyone they've been known to hang around with."

Bundy stopped staring at my pistol, and looked up at me. "Are you serious? In the can it took them three months to even talk to me. You think they gave me an address? Or the names of their friends? Now you're just wasting both our time."

Ugh. Even over the stink of his garbage breath that comment smelled true. "Fine. But one more thing."

"What?"

I plunged my fist into Bundy's pocket and pulled out his wallet. Inside were a few crisp hundreds. I took three.

"No," he said. "That's mine."

"I'm keeping the drachmas for a new outfit. I'll be wearing it when you call me tomorrow. And Bundy, if I got to come back." I pointed Rico at the garbage. "You're the one who better have gills."

"Good God, you look awful." Mrs. West was in her ultramarine suit, looking aghast. "And where's your other loafer?"

"I lost it at the-"

"It doesn't matter, I'm just happy you're not late for once. There's a change of clothes in your office. I'm stepping out."

"Don't rush back on my account."

Mrs. West gave me one of her not-so-happy smiles before snatching her purse and departing. Her last day was fast approaching and I couldn't help but be excited. Being able to walk into my office without a smart mouth greeting from an acid tongued dame seemed like heaven. But when I got to the mirror in my bathroom I could see she wasn't joking. My pants were shredded. My shirt, too. If I showed up at the morgue like this I'd turn every head in the place. No good.

So I shaved, ran a comb through my hair, then donned a fresh gray suit, and by the time I looked respectable the clock on my wall said eight forty-five.

Right on time.

Then behind me the office door opened.

"Hey Mrs. West, you back already?"

"I'm not Mrs. West," a now familiar voice said.

I turned around. And standing in my doorway, with his pistol in hand, was the blond cop from yesterday. "Now put those flippers sky side, pal. Like I told you last night, you're under arrest."

Chapter 14

"How?" I said.

"It wasn't easy. I ran your plates, but got a bogus address. So I put a BOLO out on a matte black Jalopy, and what do you know? It turned up at an impound lot one day later."

"Yeah, ok. So you followed me here, but what about the deceit device? The dead end hologram in front of my door?"

"That's clever, but I'm patient. And thorough. Now enough with the hoo-ha, you're coming with me."

I looked at his pistol. "Not unless you've got a bazooka blast chambered."

"That's right. You're invulnerable. And kind of strong. Is there anything else I should know about your skill set?"

"Nope," I said.

"By golly that's swell." And he pulled the trigger.

The slug hit my chest. But I barely felt it. "See, bullets don't work."

"That wasn't a bullet."

"What?" I looked down. A dart was sticking out of my shirt. Its tail was blue. Or was it purple? I couldn't tell. Because suddenly everything was fuzzy. The room pitched back and forth. And I fell into my chair. "How?"

"That's a specially designed Trumite needle. It barely breaks through skin like yours, but it's deep enough to get a sedative into your thick veins."

"Since when. Do cops. Have Trumite. Darts?"

"Since a bunch of black capes backdoored Team Supreme and took Top Tower. Now we got all kinds of toys like shockproof vests, viper vapor…"

My tongue started to go numb. "Oh. So we really are going downtown?"

"Didn't catch a word of that. Now relax."

I took a deep breath.

"Good boy." He walked over, holstered his piece, and pulled a set of cuffs. This cop was brave. And smart. But he didn't know that invulnerables like me have supercharged livers, capable of handling sedatives as easy as whiskey.

My head was already clearing.

So when he grabbed my shoulder I jumped up.

"What the?" He pulled his gun.

And I ripped it from his hand, then shoved him onto the chair in front of my desk.

I slipped his piece into my pocket and pulled Rico. "You're one sharp lawman, so keep being sharp and don't move. Otherwise I'll blast away with this Thumper, and spoiler alert, it doesn't spit darts."

The cop froze. But his eyes rummaged around my room.

"Don't do that," I said. "You got a better chance of spotting a unicorn on the sofa than a way out of this that doesn't run through yours truly."

The cop stopped searching, and put his eyes on me.

"Ok," I said, "you're reasonable. That's good. Now let's talk."

"About what?"

I sat in my chair keeping the pistol on him. "About your thoughts on the Coconut. I'm not entirely sure the boys killed each other."

"What?" he said. "Why do you care?"

"I was hired to find out. Didn't you read the door?"

"You're not a detective, you're a black cape."

"I was a black cape. Now I-"

"Help people?" He looked doubtful.

"No." I pinched the bridge of my nose. "I solve cases."

"But last night at the museum you were breaking and-"

"Investigating. I wanted to see if the boys could get in by themselves. I had no intention of putting my spats on the glass floor of the Amphibia Theatre until your Special Forces squad made that decision for me."

The cop did the math in his head. And to his credit he came to the correct conclusion. "Right. No gear. You seemed like a really bad burglar. But everyone's saying the Coconut kills are open and shut, what makes you think otherwise?"

I reached for my top drawer, but stopped. And looked into the Viking's baby blues. I never trusted a cop in my life, but this guy lacked a lick of subterfuge. If Leo and Tony were murdered he might just care. Maybe even help find the real killer, if they existed.

So I grabbed the pics from my drawer, and spread them out. "Tell me how this happened."

The cop leaned forward and used a pen on my desk to shift the photos so the X-ray prints surrounded the bird's eyes. "Alright. Best I figure is Firewall hacks the outer door, then disables the inner defenses-"

"With the filament," I said.

"Uh. Yeah. So then they get inside, but before they can use the chemical in that canister on the Kessel Glass they get into a tussle over the diamond. Firewall sprays his pal, and Thermite blazed him back."

"Right. So two guys who spent five years in Impenetron because they wouldn't rat on each other go up a stone wall, and down an air vent, without leaving a scratch, then beat an impossible defense system they couldn't know anything about, only to burn each other alive next to gear they can't afford?"

He leaned back, and came up with Widow's answer. "You're thinking third man."

"I sure am. And you just nicked my pen."

The cop looked at his breast pocket. "Force of habit. These things are like gold in the station." He pulled out my felt tip and put it back on the desk.

"Don't worry about it. But as to the third man, I don't know if he actually killed the boys or just planned and funded the job. Either way I'd like to ask him."

The cop leaned back, chewing on what I just said. Honestly. He was actually thinking it through. "So how do we do that?"

"Trace the accelerant," I said.

"We couldn't. The canister's inner walls are lined with a glaze that repels any residue. It was completely empty."

There was another way, but before I revealed it I had to know something. "Listen, how come you came to a powered perp's lair to slap a pair of tin cuffs on him solo?"

"Those cuffs are Trumite," he said, "and justice is its own reward."

"That's sweet. Now tell me the rest."

"Ok. Remember those storm troopers you tangled with last night? They're the Special Powers Extraction Commission, a new unit that deals with powered crime. I want in, but they're only taking battle hard ex-military, and all I am is a homicide detective. I figured if I brought in the black cape that slipped them all by my lonesome they'd reconsider."

A unit pitting regs against black capes? This cop was nuts. But...
"Well, if you're really interested in bagging a black cape help me
look into this third man. If he's out there we'll bring him in together.
Then I close my case and you get promoted. What do you say?"

After a fair bit of thinking he said, "Ok. It's a deal. The name's
Laars Monday," and extended his hand.

I shook it. "Dane Curse."

Chapter 15

"So where to?" Monday said as he started the car.

"The morgue. I need to test Thermite for residue."

"You really think that'll lead us to this mystery man?"

"If we can find out which chemical accelerant they used, and where it came from? Definitely." I remembered Bundy said mystery woman, but there was no reason to share everything with this cop just yet. He tried to arrest me twice now, and it's always wise to keep some things to yourself, so I said nothing for the entire ride.

By the time we arrived at the morgue it was nearly nine thirty. Sitting at the entrance was a short technician with brown hair and big ears. "Can I help you?"

Monday flashed his shield. "Where's Laura?"

"Who?" the guy said.

"Doctor Lockter."

He shrugged. "No clue. But I'm sure she'll be here any minute."

"Great. We'll wait inside."

I followed Monday into the morgue. Everything was the same as yesterday. The cold smell, the white tiles, and the two rows of black clad bodies.

"Thermite's this way." I led Monday down the aisle towards the boys who were now out of their bags and under a sheet like the other guests. When I got to Leonard I uncovered him. "Here he is."

Monday glanced at the corpse. "That isn't Thermite."

I looked down. The body was firm, pale, and raw. I grabbed his toe tag. "No kidding, it's Landslide."

Monday checked the last cadaver in the other row. "This one's Slugfest."

"You take that side, I'll take this one." I walked back down the aisle, this time reading off the names of each cadaver, but reached the end without finding either boy. "Where'd they go?"

"Let's find out." Monday turned to the door. "Hey tech, get in here."

The guy from outside strolled in with a clipboard under his arm. "What's the problem?"

"The two bodies from yesterday's jewel heist," Monday said,

"where are they?"

"I'm not authorized to give out specifics on black cape meat. You'll have-"

"Black cape meat?" I snatched his jacket and lifted him a foot off the ground. "Listen pal, every last one of these people is somebody's somebody, so answer the Aryan's question before I tear off your jaw and use it as a doorstop."

Dangling in my hand he looked Monday's way. "Officer?"

The badge didn't twitch.

"Ok, so that's how we're doing this." He flipped through the pages on his clipboard and said, "Oh. Those two were released ten minutes ago. They're probably halfway to Ayers Cemetery by now."

I dropped the guy and ran for the door.

Monday was already there.

#

"Doesn't this thing go any faster?" I said.

"Yeah, much." Monday laid on his horn as we ran a red light. "But I want to conserve gas."

"Cute. You got a siren in this thing?"

"No, it's undercover."

"Great." I searched for the hearse that transferred black capes. Its armed escort would make it hard to miss. "You know if those bodies get buried we got nothing. They don't exhume-"

"I'm aware of the Fletcher Act."

I pointed to the next on-ramp. "Take the highway."

"I-93's under construction."

"Right. Well at least give her some gas."

Monday mashed it down dutifully sending the car screaming into high gear, and even though we were at least twenty minutes away, thanks to the swift wheel work we turned onto the road to Ayers Hill in less than ten. I looked out my window. The sun was still climbing. It was pretty early. But black capes don't wait to get planted. They go in the moment they arrive.

I started bobbing my knee. "Come on come on come on."

Monday said, "We're almost there. Look."

I followed his gaze to the top of the hill where the bone yard's green grass was framed by white clouds. "We're going to make it."

"Maybe not." We skidded to a stop in the middle of the next intersection. "Road work."

Monday was right. Halfway up the next block a team of four workmen were snaking a manhole.

I looked left. "Turn down there."

"That's Red Forge Road, it doesn't run to Ayers."

I turned to the right. That way was worse. It was like looking down a ski jump. We were at the top of Hillimanjaro, Gold Coast City's highest, longest, and most treacherous incline. And at the bottom was Bittenbach Bay.

"To hell with this," I said, "let's ditch the boat. We might make it if we run."

"Great idea, while we're at it why don't we-"

An explosion from Monday's side sent glass flying across my brow like buckshot. I turned away and covered my eyes as our car pitched over and rolled onto its roof. When we came to a stop I was still in my seat, thanks to the belt, but now I hung upside down like a side of beef. It took a few seconds, but when my bearings returned I looked out my window. And was staring at the bumper of a massive, black truck. The thing was maybe a foot from me, with its engine still idling as it sent the thick smell of gasoline into our car.

I turned to Monday. "Hey, you alright? I think this pickup T-boned us."

He just hung there limp as a thick line of blood wormed its way from behind his collar. It slithered down his face, and dripped onto the roof.

"That looks serious," I said. "We got to get you to a-"

The truck's engine growled. Then it roared. And the metal brute lurched forward, plowing into us for a second time. My door crumpled in. And the roof ground against the concrete as we slid sideways. Towards the edge of Hillimanjaro.

I reached out and jabbed the truck's bumper. "What the hell you doing, Jack?"

But it kept coming. And pushed us right over the peak.

Monday and I took off down the hill like a greased toboggan with the beast shoving us fast. One block flew by. Then another. And the smell of burning metal filled the car as our roof spat sparks in our wake. Reaching through them, I dug my fingers into the road to slow our descent. But the asphalt may as well have been warm chocolate cake for all the good it did.

At this pace we'd be at the bottom in seconds.

Unless…

If I could just get ahold of the truck and latch on, I could use it as an anchor. So I reached out my window as far as I could. And grazed its bumper with my fingertips.

Just a little closer. Another inch tops, and I'd have him.

Grabbing the side of the door with my free hand I pulled myself farther out. And felt the truck's cold metal. I clamped down on it with everything I had, tethering us to our attacker. But the truck hit its brakes. It slid to a halt.

While we kept going.

And all I had in my hand was a small piece of jagged metal. Then our car shook. We'd hit the pier, and were skittering across the wooden planks towards the bay.

But suddenly everything turned peaceful. Floaty. There was nothing outside my window but blue ocean horizon. While the inside was filled with a gentle breeze.

Then dark water burst through our windows. I thrashed against that white, roaring surf and tried to scream, but the bay, cold and brackish, filled my nose and mouth. Desperate to taste the air I fought for a breath. But before I got a single one the sea had swallowed us whole.

Chapter 16

The icy water's pressure built as our car raced, grill first, towards the bottom of the bay. I struggled against my belt. But it had me locked in. So I grabbed the latch and ripped it free.

Right as we crashed into the ocean floor.

I lurched into the dashboard. And spat out what little air was left in my lungs. Then our car toppled forward onto its roof. We were upside down again. Only now it was on the seabed.

If we didn't get moving fast this crappy car would be our tomb. So I tore Monday's seatbelt off with one hand. And grabbed his jacket with the other. Then I drew my legs in, put my heels on his seat, and launched us through my window like a pair of torpedoes.

A few straggling bubbles came with us, and made a break for the surface. As fast as I could I followed them up.

The pressure eased. The water became clearer. But then a pair of talons clutched the back of my eyes. I needed air. Or we were going to die. But the surface was easily forty yards away. I kicked harder. And looked back. Monday's limp body dragged behind me like a corpse. It was slowing me down. If I dropped him I might have a chance. All I had to do was let him slip away. Nobody'd blame me. Nobody would even know.

Instead I tightened my grip and kicked as rough as I could while clawing with my free hand towards the surface. It was thirty yards away now. My temples were burning like lumps of coal. The shallow water blackout was creeping in.

And we were still so far. We weren't going to make it. Not on my strength alone.

Reaching into my jacket I pulled out Lois. She brightened right up and lashed herself to my arm. I didn't know if this would work but I had no other options. So holding Monday tight I aimed my Kapowitzer at the bottom of the bay. Then I said a prayer.

And fired.

The pistol exploded loud and bright, even underwater. And it launched me and my anchor upwards. We breached the surface like a pair of dolphins, and came crashing back down in a cold splash. Floating there on my back I sucked in as much air as I could.

Monday was bobbing nearby like a buoy. Lois was now glowing bright red. She wouldn't be ready to fire again for another six minutes and forty-seven seconds. So I holstered her, then swam to my pal. Snaking one arm over his shoulder I looked to the dock where a group of people were waving and pointing. I yelled to them, "Toss me a line."

One said, "We need rope."

Another asked, "Where can we get one?"

"Maybe if-"

"Hey!" My voice stopped them. "There's a life preserver on the corner of the dock. Get it."

The nearest man ran towards the flotation device and snatched it from its perch. He hurled it towards me, and brother, that guy must've thrown discus in college because even with a nylon rope fluttering behind it the white donut landed mere inches away.

Keeping Monday tight I slipped my free arm through it and said, "Now pull."

The land dwellers got in a hasty line and started to yank us towards the shore, and we were under the edge of the dock in seconds. The topside team kept pulling, but their plucky grit couldn't hoist all four hundred plus pounds of us out of the drink. Not completely.

So I said, "That's enough, anchor the rope."

A bald guy peeked over the edge. "How?"

"I don't know, loop it around something." I looked over at Monday. "Hang in there copper, we're... uh, that ain't good." The water around us was an unnatural purple, with swirls of crimson here and there. Wherever Monday was bleeding from it was bad. And getting worse. I yelled, "Hurry up."

Another second passed and Clean Dome poked his head out again. "You're good, we got you anchored."

Holding the rope tight in one hand I put my foot inside the life preserver like it was a stirrup, and stood up. Everything above my knees was now out of the bay. With my free hand I grabbed Monday's belt, and lifted him up like Lady Liberty's torch. "Here, take him first."

A dozen hands reached down, grabbed Monday, and pulled him over the ledge. Then I jumped up, got ahold of the dock, and pulled myself out.

Monday was lying still with some dame's ear on his chest. She said, "He's not breathing."

"Out of my way." I pulled her off and knelt down next to the cop. I pinched his nose, stuck my mouth on his, and pushed a breath into his lungs.

But it didn't stay long. And it didn't do much.

So I gave him two more, then placed a hand on his sternum and pumped. Once. Twice. Three times.

But Monday wasn't moving.

I breathed into his mouth again. And hit his chest. Again.

I was cold from the dip, but the sweat on my face was as hot as rain forest dew. I wiped the warm slick off my brow and put an ear to his heart, listening for a healthy beat. More nothing's all I heard. "Come on," I said, "I don't need another dead cop on my sheet."

Then a gusher blasted from his mouth. And Monday rolled to one side, retching out a barrel's worth of Bittenbach Bay.

The crowd cheered loud.

That bald guy slapped my back. "Nice work."

"You saved his life," another said.

I leaned over Monday. "You ok, copper?"

He sounded a little froggy. "First rate."

"Good. Stay here. I'm-"

"Hey look," someone said. "The cops."

I looked up to see that, just a few yards away, a couple of GCCPD cruisers were inching by. I waved to them. "Hey, over here."

But they drove past. And took the turn up Hillimanjaro. There was a black van tight on their tail. With Gold Coast City Morgue painted on its side.

"Monday, that's them," I said, "that's Thermite and Firewall."

"So go already."

I took off running after the van. *How would I stop it without causing a ruckus?* No clue. But I'd think of something. Maybe if-

"What's that in his hip?" a woman said.

I glanced back as I ran.

"It looks like a pipe." One of the Samaritans was pointing down at a stumpy, hollow tube that poked out of my pal's flank. And from the open end poured a whole lot of blood.

Damn it.

In all the excitement I'd forgotten about that cherry punch in the bay.

"Hey lady," I said, "how long until the ambulance gets here?"

"We called when you guys went in, so five minutes I guess. Maybe ten."

Five maybe ten? The van was already halfway up the hill. Meanwhile Monday looked like a tapped maple. Who knows how much blood he'd already spilled? But lots of guys lose a few pints and survive. And if I let that van leave then the evidence I needed to save my agency would be buried. Everything Carl built would be gone. Besides, I just met this cop. I owed him nothing.

"What're you doing?" Monday said.

I knelt down next to him and tore off a piece of my jacket. Then I wrapped a hand around the hunk of shrapnel. "Hey," I said, "you think the Prospectors'll make the playoffs this year?"

"Huh?" Monday looked up at me. "Why're you asking-"

In one smooth motion I pulled the metal from his body.

Monday screamed and twisted like the Chubby Checker fan club as more blood gushed from his open wound. But I clamped the torn cotton from my jacket down on it, turning the stream into a trickle.

Monday struck my shoulder. "You shouldn't have pulled that out, it was acting like a plug."

"It was acting like a spigot," I said.

"Whatever. Let one of the citizens handle it now, and get up that hill."

"Unless one of these regs can press a few tons I don't think they'll have the strength to Dutch boy this dam, so I'm not going anywhere until the ambulance arrives."

"But the bodies."

"There'll be one more if I don't hang back."

"That means…" He winced. Then lay still. "Never mind. Thanks."

I stole a peek up Hillimanjaro. The police cruisers were nowhere to be seen. Neither was the van. I looked down at Monday. He was a good man. An honest cop. I said, "Shut up."

Chapter 17

A few minutes later the paramedics arrived and had Monday field dressed quicker than a lawyer tells two lies. But as they loaded him in, three patrol cars pulled up and five cops got out.

"Get moving," Monday said from inside the ambulance, "they're going to want to question you."

"I'll let you know what I find."

The medic inside shut the door and they pulled away.

I turned towards the hill. I could still make it. Maybe. But I had to rush.

"Where you going? You're a hero."

I spun around.

It was Clean Dome. He was pointing at me and jabbering to the nearest cop, a tubby bag of bear claws who looked like he hadn't chased a criminal since hoop skirts were raging.

"It was nothing, really." I started walking backwards. "I was doing some laps when-"

"Hey you," the cop said. "Get back here, now."

Three other peace officers looked my way. One grabbed his radio. Another, his pistol.

I stopped where I was. I could blast away with my stunners, or knock each of their chops, but I doubt I'd do either before they raised a ruckus. And whatever backup they got would make getting to Ayers impossible. So I sighed, and returned.

"Is this true?" the cop said. "Did you save that guy?"

I looked at his badge. "Yeah, Officer Heralds. And that guy's Detective Laars Monday."

His face lit up when he said, "Son of a bitch, that was Monday? I always knew he'd end up at the bottom of the bay."

The cops around us traded some smiles before going off to interview the other witnesses.

"Yeah," I said, "Detective Monday. But I got to go."

"Sorry pal, no can do. I need a report before you shake out." Heralds pulled out a pad and pen.

"Sure thing. Monday and I got stopped by roadwork when a black truck T-boned us up there." I pointed to the top of the hill.

"The impact flipped us over and the pickup plowed us into the bay. I got to sign something or what?"

"Slow down," Heralds said as he scribbled. "When did all this happen?"

"When?" *You've got to be kidding me.* "Early last week. It's just with the road so dry we didn't make it to the bottom until today."

"You want to make jokes?" He poked my chest. "Or give me the straight dope?"

"Hey Heralds," one of the other cops said. "We're heading out. You got this?"

He looked me in the eyes. "Yeah, I can handle it."

Both pairs of cops got into their cruisers and took off, leaving me and Heralds alone.

"Ok, so what's your name?" he said.

"My first name's Ow."

Heralds stopped writing. "What?"

I grabbed his left ear and squeezed it like a lemon.

He dropped his pad and pen, and clamped down on my wrist. "Ow!"

"That's right," I said, "O. W. Last name's He-tore-my-ear-off. You want I should spell that, too?"

His eyes were full of fear and anger. "Let me go."

"Don't think I will," I said, and lifted him off the ground.

"Arrg." He tightened his grip and jabbered, "Please drop me, I'm sorry, I won't bother you no more."

"Oh, you're sorry, well in that case it's fine." I shook him some.

"Oh God oh God, let me go, I promise you can leave."

I obliged, and dumped him on the sidewalk. "Now remember, you promised. But just to be sure." I grabbed the radio on his belt and crushed it. "Now be a pal and sign that report for me. And if I every hear you bad-mouthing Monday again I'm going to squeeze both your ears, only this time I won't stop juicing until I get a full glass."

I turned from the cop and ran to the curb. A taxi was coming up fast. Putting two fingers in my mouth I let out a whistle that hurt every dog ear for miles. The cab screeched to a halt, I hopped in, and threw the driver a soggy hundred. "Ayers Cemetery, and don't spare the whip."

#

It didn't take long before I was legging it through Ayers' wrought iron gate and onto the vast, green field of fresh cut grass. All around were the gleaming, white angels and markers of everyday citizens. I ran past them, and took the long, sloping path of small rocks that led to the tall hill in the back. It was covered in tombstones that, unlike the ones around me, were identical, gray, worn down by time, and so tight knit there was barely an inch between them.

And instead of upright citizens the bodies beneath belonged to cattle rustlers, cowboys, and hooch happy mobsters, though all the fresh tenants wore the black cape.

I sprinted towards the hill, searching for grave men on the job. About halfway there I ran into one coming my way. He looked fiftyish, had on a pair of overalls, and was carrying a dirty shovel.

I stopped and said, "Hey buddy, any work left up there?"

He looked me up and down. "Who's asking?"

Sighing, I ran five fingers through my wet hair. "A guy who's one second from just beating the answer out of you."

He put both hands up. "Whoa, you can't blame a guy for being cautious."

"I can't blame him, but I can sure as hell see how much dirty shovel can fit in his mouth." I took a step forward, ready to make good on that promise.

He jumped back. "Ok, yeah. All the work's done. The shockcrete dried about ten minutes back. I got the soil over them both. It was real respectful, I promise."

I looked up the hill. "How many you plant?"

"Just those two." He looked nervous. "Thermite and that other one, the computer guy."

"Firewall?"

"Yeah, sure, that's the one."

I pushed him out of my way and walked towards the graves. I needed to see for myself. And sure enough I found two fresh mounds of dark dirt. The tombstones weren't there yet, but they'd arrive soon.

Thermite and Firewall.

They shared a childhood, then a cell, and now they'd share this field for eternity, along with the evidence I needed to save my agency. I took one last look around. The stones on Ayers Hill were all worn and cracked. They made it look like a pile of broken dreams.

I could almost see where mine were lying.

Chapter 18

After my thwarting at Ayers I felt, and smelled, awful. So before returning to the office I stopped at my place for a hot shower. First I scrubbed the remnants of Bittenbach Bay off. Then the thin film Swamp had left behind the night before. And by the time I washed the layer of standard city grime from my skin I was ready to think about the case. Or more importantly, what just happened.

Someone tried to kill me. While I was with a cop. That wouldn't have happened if I wasn't actually onto something. But what that something was still eluded. So I tried to figure out who wanted me dead. There was Swamp and his pale friend Vec. Neither one loved me, but they could've killed me last night if they wanted me stiff. Bundy was suspect, but he's not the type to get his hands dirty. Which meant that whoever the unknown driver was, he probably killed the boys. That meant-

My front door slammed.

I turned off the water and pulled the shower curtain aside. "Who's there?"

No answer.

Stepping out of the tub I said, "Hello?"

Still nothing.

Was that the guy who shoved me into the drink, come to finish the job? How'd he find me? Only Carl Cutter and Mrs. West have this address. No time for thinking. I needed my pistols.

But they were hanging on my coat rack next to the door. Which meant I'd have to use my fists. I wrapped the nearest towel around my waist, ran through the kitchen, and into the living room. The intruder was standing between me and my iron, defiant and familiar.

I said, "God damn it, Tera."

Doodle's mom looked like she was on the way to church in a bright yellow sundress and matching hat. Her hands were on her round hips. She looked down with a smile, and in her island spiced accent said, "Couldn't of picked a smaller towel?"

I followed her gaze, and saw she was right. The thing barely wrapped around my waist, and hardly reached halfway down my thighs. "You got no right to complain about how you're received when you break into my house."

"The door was unlocked. And I'm definitely not complaining. You've taken care of yourself. Same knobbly face, but that big body's still firm. Still hard. But is it still susceptible to sonics?" Tera opened her mouth.

"Don't." I dropped the towel and clamped both hands on my ears.

But no sound came from between her lips. Instead she gave my lower body a not so quick once over. "Yeah," she said, "still firm."

"Cute." I grabbed the towel off the floor and wrapped it around me. "Wish I could say the same. That skin tight stuff doesn't suit a mom your age."

She scrunched up her nose. "That's a lie."

Looking at her body all I could say was, "Yeah. I guess it is. Now why are you here?"

"To tell you to leave Sketch alone."

"It's been nearly ten years since I saw her last, and you're asking me that?"

She smiled in a way that happy people don't. "I'm not really asking."

"Then I'm not really listening."

"Dane, you know I-"

"You're here on a job, and you got our kid in the mix."

She snapped to me. "Of course. And I need Sketch's head in the game, not full of your silly dreams."

"Yeah. Silly. As opposed to the serious life of crime you're priming her for."

"Stay away from her. It's too late for you to act like a dad."

"And it's never too late for you to act like a mom. Do you want her in jail like that scumbag brother of yours? Or your uncle? Jeezus, tell me you realize the road you got her on leads to Ayers or Impenetron."

"I'll die before that happens."

"If you'd live for her, that would be better."

"Stay away. You don't want to know what I'll do to keep us on track." Tera walked over. And I got a deep whiff of her flower perfume as she grabbed my jaw and kissed me hard. Her open mouth was sweet and wet. Sucking on it was like biting into a ripe pear. And I took it all in as my brain soaked in that old familiar hormone that makes men do dumb things.

Tera slid her hand over my chest, down my stomach, and inside the towel. But I grabbed it.

And pushed it lower.

Then I shoved her away. "Quit it."

"I would." She licked my spit off her lips. "If you didn't like it so much."

"What I'd like is for you to let our kid live a life like a normal person."

That got the smile off her face, and she moved away from me. "What you mean is average. Weak. Too scared of her own power to use it."

"It's called being careful."

"A fancy term for cowardice."

I stepped to the tiny islander, lording my size over her. "How come you always want me to hit you?"

She stared up at me without fear. "How come you've never been man enough to try?"

I grabbed her arms and shook her once. "You damaged bitch, I won't let my daughter turn out like you."

Tera opened her mouth and let out a scream. The sonic blast hit my chest and knocked me over the sofa. I landed on my back, but jumped up quick. Grabbing my end table, I threw it towards her. And ran right after it.

Tera screamed again. The table exploded in midair.

I charged through the cloud of splinters. And clamped my hand around her mouth. I didn't squeeze hard, but my seal was tight enough to muffle her wail.

"Stop it already," I said. "I won't hurt you."

Tera's eyes had some of that old fire, but now it was burning on a lower heat.

"I know you love Doodle. I do too. And I just want what's best for her. Can you really say that's what this job is?"

My ex glanced down. Her shoulders relaxed.

"Good. Now I'm going to let you go. No more sonics." I eased up on my grip.

Tera rubbed her jaw. And emitted a high-pitched shriek.

Pain shot through my head. I covered both ears. It didn't help. Scrambling backwards I clipped my coffee table and tumbled onto the carpet. I struggled to get away. But Tera's voice got worse. I pulled into a ball like a dead armadillo. It felt like my skull was expanding.

And the thing is, she still didn't let up. It took another couple of painful seconds before my world finally went quiet.

By then Tera was standing at my open door. She said, "Sketch is like me, and we're doing this job whether you like it or not. Afterwards, we're leaving town. But until then stay away, or things will get much worse." She turned to leave.

I got to my feet and lumbered towards her. "Stop."

Amazingly she obliged. "What?"

"Don't you want a life for that kid where she doesn't have to commit crimes in order to eat?"

Tera looked around my apartment. "You know, even if it all goes to hell whatever's left over will look a lot better than this."

Then Tera walked out my door.

This time I didn't try to stop her.

Chapter 19

After Tera left I threw on a clean suit, hailed a cab, and headed to the office where I found that Mrs. West had returned from her errands. "You smell like soap," she said.

"That's because I showered."

"Is it Thursday already?"

"If so then you should've been gone for a week."

She cut a spoiled milk smile. "Someone's waiting in your office."

"They have a name or do I got to guess?"

"It's Dastard Lee." Mrs. West opened the door for me and said, "He's here."

Lee was sitting on the sofa in her usual cammo pants and striped shirt. "Thanks Wags. So when're you moving east?"

"Tomorrow. I just wanted to make sure I did all I could for this agency before I left."

I walked into my office. "She should be long gone already."

Lee shot me a glance that could split oak, then looked at Mrs. West. "You always did fret too much. It never helped before, and I doubt it'll do much now."

"I guess it's in my nature. You two have a good meeting. Afterwards we can-"

I shut the door on her. "I didn't know you knew my girl."

"I knew her back when she was a girl. And you should show her more kindness. She loves this agency and what it's done. Almost as much as she loved Carl."

"We all loved Carl."

"And Carl loved some of us back more than others."

I took a seat behind my desk. "That's not my fault."

"No, I guess not," she said. "Listen, I'm here-"

"About that furniture I busted? I can cut you a check."

"What?" Lee looked confused. "You mean with Slamazon and Kalamity? No, don't worry about that. But be warned, if this noise with Dread Division doesn't die down I may have to ban you."

"Great." Henchmen's was the most valuable asset a PI like me had. I rubbed my face and tossed my hat on the desk. "So why are you here, you got news on Thermite and Firewall?"

"Sorry, strike two. No one I know heard the names."

"More good news. First a big, black truck shoves me into Bittenbach Bay, then-"

"Someone in a truck took a swipe at you?" Lee looked at her lap and got all solemn on me. "So I'm too late."

"What do you mean?"

She looked up and said, "I came here to warn you, Scourge's back in town."

I straightened up. "How could you possibly know that?"

"One of my bar boys, Psy-ball, spied him this morning, near the docks. Next to a nighttime colored pickup."

"God damn it, that was him?" I jumped up. And drove a fist through my desk. The strike left a nice hole in its center. "How long? How long's he been here?"

Lee had both hands up. "I don't know. All I-"

"And that nervy bastard tried to cadaverize me?" Fire jumped into my throat. I savored the burn. "The guts he's got, if that's-" I stopped dead. "Wait. He wouldn't move on me without muscle. Who's in his back pocket?"

She took a big breath of air, and let it out slow. "Gunmetal."

"He hired Gunmetal Gray?" You know that fire in my throat? I swallowed it and fell back in my chair. "You're certain?"

"Yeah. Psy-ball spotted them both." Lee leaned forward and rubbed my arm. "Sorry kid. I hate to bring the bad news. But it could be worse."

"How? How could it be worse than Gunmetal Gray?"

"I don't know. It's something people tell each other." A silence thick like Georgia air in summer settled over us. We soaked in it for a while until finally Lee said, "Anyway, that's all the news that's fit. I'm going to catch up with Wags. Let me know if there's anything I can do to help with Scourge."

"There is. If you see him let me know."

"Sure thing." Lee got up, opened my door, but then stopped. "Hey, I know you're a big boy, but do me a favor and be careful. These days black capes are dying like fruit flies in winter."

Not looking up I said, "I will."

"I'm serious. I've had enough with the corpses in my place. Hell, that dame Widow from the Spinnerettes dragged another one in this morning for a final drink. I don't want that to happen to you, so be smart, huh?" She walked out to my waiting room, pulled up a chair next to Mrs. West, and the two started clucking like happy hens.

Meanwhile I looked out my window. And thought about the news that just fell into my lap.

Scourge was back in town. And he tried to kill me. That meant I was onto something. It also meant I knew who Widow's third man was. But what I didn't know-

Wait. What did Lee say?

I got up and walked into the waiting room. Both dames clammed and turned to me.

"Hey Lee," I said, "what'd you say about Widow?"

"She just lost a relative. I could tell it was someone special the way she was clutching that urn."

"Urn?" I said.

"Yeah. She's dumping the ashes at Jutter's Mill. Apparently it was a special place for her and whoever's in there."

My mouth went dry. "You know who got planted on Ayers today?"

Lee looked at Mrs. West, then back at me. "No clue. I mean Hard Drive went in, or what was left after Al Mighty, but I don't know who else-"

I charged into my office, grabbed my hat, and raced back out.

As I passed the girls Mrs. West said, "Where are you off to now?"

"The beach."

She looked out the window. "But it's not sunny out."

I flung open the door. "Oh yes it is."

Chapter 20

I ran down the stairs, aimed my car towards Jutter's Mill Beach, and stomped on the gas so hard I nearly put my heel through the floorboard. The buildings outside flew by, and for every blurry mile I reflected on that cryptic crypt keeper and what he said. *Thermite and the computer guy...* He meant Hard Drive, not Firewall.

Normally I'd be fighting the urge to track him down and pulp him raw, but this was, in every way, great news.

See, Thermite and Firewall had been fused together when they died, so tightly that they had to be pried apart. But the cops weren't too careful with the process, and Firewall left a hand on his partner's arm which Thermite traded for a couple of fingers. Fingers that would've survived the crematorium flames, thanks to their fireproof nature, and might still be coated with some residue from the accelerant that killed him.

If that was the case then they'd be inside Firewall's urn. Or they would be until Widow dumped them into the ocean blue.

I arrived at Jutter's Mill twenty minutes later. The parking lot was nearly deserted. In the corner sat a pair of dumpy vans, and a row of rusted bikes. But on the other side was one very nice dark blue auto with a longer than normal hood full of chrome exhaust ports, and an ornamental silver spider on its nose.

I charged past it, and scanned the beach. Widow, still in black, was fifty yards down the coast, ankle deep in the surf. In one hand was an urn.

In another, the lid.

I yelled, "No, don't."

But she didn't acknowledge me.

So I leapt onto the beach. My feet dug into the dry sand and I spilled forward. Getting up on one knee I cupped both hands around my mouth and screamed, "Stop."

The wind kicked up. Widow held the urn out. And began to tip it over.

I took a deep breath and yelled, "Mandy Marcus, stop right there."

Widow snapped to, and turned my way. She put a third hand on her forehead.

I got up and ran over. "Don't dump those ashes."

"Why not?"

"It's about your brother. I…" Didn't know how to phrase this. "I have to look in him for a second."

"You. What?" Widow walked out of the water with a look on her face that screamed duck.

"It sounds bad, I know, but-"

"No you ghoul, it doesn't sound bad, it is bad. I assume you mean to…" She swallowed. "Sift through his ashes."

"Yes, that's what it means. Or more importantly, I want to see if any bits of Leo are in there." I continued with my reasoning as quick as I could. I tried to be clear. And I tried to be kind.

Widow listened intently. When I finished she stood there chewing it over.

I knew she would acquiesce. This was the best, and maybe only, way to find her brother's killer. I was still prepared for a fist or three to fly my way though. But instead of splitting my lip, Widow's shoulders went weak and she held out the urn. "Sure. It's not like Tony'll care."

"Thanks." I grabbed it.

But she didn't let go. "That's my brother you're running your fingers through. So be gentle."

"For certain." I took the urn and spun around. Then I dipped my paw into the ashes like a bear with a honey pot. I was expecting them to be coarse, with bigger parts still un-burnt. But the remains were fine like sand. I pushed deeper, all the way to the bottom, and searched for thirty seconds. It was twenty more than I needed. There was no one inside but Anthony.

I removed my hand, making sure I didn't take any bits with me, then turned around and handed him back to his sister. "I'm sorry."

Widow nodded. A tear broke free, ran down to her chin, and leapt to its fate among the grains of sand below. "That's ok. Now if you'll excuse me." She turned and walked back into the ocean as a cold breeze came in soft.

I removed my hat, held it over my heart, and bowed my head.

She knelt down and gently upended the urn, pouring her brother out with care, and the water, blue and clean, scooped up Anthony "Firewall" Marcus and took everything he ever was, and everything he'd ever hope to be, out with the tide.

Widow stared at the sea, and murmured her goodbyes. They were soft and sweet, and when they were finished we walked back towards our cars. Halfway there she took my arm, and leaned on me a bit. "I guess I should thank you."

"What?" I said. "Why?"

"Because yesterday you had doubts, but today you obviously think my brother was murdered."

"I always thought he was murdered, but now I know it wasn't Leonard. And not because they were valentines."

Widow snapped to me. "You know?"

"Of course I know. People don't see that much of each other unless they're stuck sweet like crème brûlée crust."

"And it doesn't bother you?"

"Why would it? Ten percent of the black cape community twists that way. Twenty percent of the white capes." *A difference I've never been able to account for.*

Widow squeezed my arm. "So then what changed your mind?"

"Got a lead on a guy by the name of Scourge who I'm certain was hired to alter how Tony and Leo were found."

We got to the asphalt and headed towards Widow's ride. "I've never heard the name."

"Most people haven't. But he's one of the best thieves I've ever seen. And also an unhinged lunatic."

"How do you know him?"

I scanned my memory. And stifled a shiver. "So you're aware I used to roll with Dread Division."

"Everyone knows that."

"Right, of course they do. Anyway, most people think we were a thug squad, but our real profession was burglary. And we were great. Loyal to each other, and always on the lookout for new talent. A couple years back, one guy that got our attention was Scourge."

"What's his power set?"

"He has heightened senses. His eyesight, hearing, and smell are all insane. And he used them to scout, plan, and execute jobs with unmatched precision, but he was especially good at hiding, destroying, or altering evidence to throw the cops off his trail. We wouldn't take him on fulltime though, or introduce him to the whole team, until we had a trial run. So me, Subatomic, and Acid Green went on a gig lifting art from a mansion down in the Foothills with him. And it went off hitchless. Except on the way out we got made by the owner's eight-year-old daughter. Normally, we'd leave it at that, I mean who believes a kid's testimony, but like I said, Scourge was dynamite at concealing evidence, so the three of us split while he hung back to-"

"How do you cover tracks when a witness is involved?"

"Oh, there're lots of ways. He decided to torch the place so it looked like the haul was destroyed instead of stolen."

"Sounds smart."

"Yeah. But he put the place to flame with the family still inside."

"Good lord." Widow covered her mouth.

"But before that he spent an hour with them. And his knife."

If Widow was going to say something it got stuck deep down in her chest.

"Listen, I'm not trying to make us out as noble, but we didn't kill children, or murder their parents for fun, so naturally when the three of us found out we felt responsible. And told the rest of Dread Division. The consensus was to spread him over the street like butter on bread. So a meeting was set to introduce him to the whole crew, and split the take, after which Scourge would get the treatment he deserved. Only he failed to show. I guess he got wind of it and skipped town."

"What did you do?"

"Cursed our luck, and made it clear he was never to return."

We got to Widow's sleek, blue number and she opened the door. "So, do you think he's the killer?"

"I can't say for certain. But I'd be a fool not to assume he's involved. Just how deeply is something I don't know. Yet."

"Well, if I can help with anything let me know." She got into her car and started it up. The engine sounded fission powered.

"Thanks. But I think I got it... Wait."

"Yes?"

I leaned down. "You run with the Spinnerettes, right? Can you contact Redback for me? I need some potent anti-venom."

"Sure. Can I ask why?"

"Because Scourge's got some muscle. Gunmetal Gray."

Widow's eyes got real big. "Goodness. You must be shaking."

"No." *A little.* "Not really."

"Ok. I'll reach out and see if she's amenable to parting with some. If so, I'll drop it by your office."

"Sounds swell," I said. "Thanks."

"I'm glad to help." She closed her door and drove away.

I walked back to my ride. Behind me I dragged a sack full of questions. Some were about the boys. Most were about Scourge. I needed help to sort it all out. Only one person came to mind.

Chapter 21

I pointed my wheels towards Gold Coast General Hospital, partially to see if the cop was ok, but mostly to find out if he or his pals had any info on, I assumed, Scourge's truck. I figured maybe they found some traffic footage of him fleeing, and we could trace it back to whichever doorway he was currently darkening.

When I arrived I found Monday in a private room on the third floor, propped upright in a surgical gown. His breast pocket had a big, blue stain.

"What the hell happened?" I said.

Monday looked up at me. "You were there."

"I mean the scrubs. You stealing pens again?"

He glanced down at his chest. "Yeah. Force of habit."

I tossed my hat on the foot of the bed and took a seat next to him. "So how's the flank steak?"

"Healing steady. That piece of shrapnel went deep, but all it poked was meat and skin. The docs say I can leave tomorrow."

"They're not afraid you'll pop a stitch?"

"Negative. They used this stuff called liquid skin. It acts like a cork until you heal." He pulled the sheet aside and showed me the wound. It was red and angry, but instead of sutures holding the flesh together it was filled with a pale plug.

"Convenient," I said.

"Yeah, it's great." Monday dropped his sheet. "And that's all the foreplay I need. Did you stop the burial?"

I leaned back and sighed. "Afraid not. By the time I got past your inquisitive Officer Heralds it was too late."

"Heralds? No wonder you took so long." Monday drummed his fingers on the bed. "So then there's no way we can identify the accelerant."

"Not that I can think of. But it's clear we're onto something considering someone tried to kill us. And I think I know who that somebody is."

"Really? That's great. Our traffic cams lost him after a few blocks. Who?"

"A guy who goes by the name of Scourge."

"Scourge? Tell me, how come you guys always choose evil sounding handles? I mean, I'm not trying to give you ideas, but Perry Mortem? Manfred Mayhem? Those aliases push you to the top of the watch list. Now, if a black cape called himself Johnny Justice, and wore stars and stripes, he'd probably rob banks for years before anyone caught on."

I wanted to respond with a clever one liner, but all that came out was, "That's really smart. But you know there's sort of an unwritten rule with capes that the name reflects the power."

"Yeah. I guess." The cop shrugged. "Still, it's never made sense to me. Anyway, who's this Scourge?"

I explained his abilities and how he used them, leaving out our history.

When I finished, Monday said, "So he's a murderous super thief who uses super senses to commit and cover crimes?"

"No," I said. "But yeah. Sort of. Though questions still remain. Like how do we find him? Who hired him? And did they want the boys dead, or was it an accident after the job went sour?"

Monday said, "I'm leaning towards the latter."

"Me too. Otherwise it was an assassination, and those two boys never did a thing to warrant something like that."

"True. They were the very definition of small time," Monday said. "Except for the Shelly theft."

That got my attention. "What's the Shelly theft?"

"It's what got them tossed in Impenetron. About six years back the boys broke into a big time penthouse owned by a woman named Margaret Shelly and made off with a small fortune in stones."

Interesting. "Did they recover the loot?"

"Oh yeah," Monday said. "Those two traded every carat for a lighter sentence."

"Well then that's hardly a motive for murder." I thought about Wentorf Hall. "Especially one this complex."

"You're not kidding about it being complex. I still can't figure out how they got as far as they did."

"Really?" I looked over. "Firewall opened the outer door and then launched the filament across-"

"Right, the filament." Monday was looking three breeds of sheepish. "I'm sorry, but that's a red herring. I talked to the curator and she says the security system's set inside the wall too deep for any filament to have worked."

"What? The filament didn't work?" *Add that false evidence to the absence of clues in the vent, and Scourge had to be involved.* "Of all the cats to keep in the bag why'd you choose that one?"

"I wasn't showing you all my cards," Monday said. "It was only a few hours after you busted into the museum."

I turned away and crossed my arms. "A lack of trust doesn't suit you."

"Really, did you tell me everything?"

"In fact I did." I turned back to him. "Except that the moneyman we're looking for is a moneywoman, and Bundy Strong gave them the job."

"Bundy Strong? Why didn't you say so?"

"I wasn't showing you all my cards," I said. "It was only a few hours after you tried to bust me at the museum."

"You're a laugh riot."

"I know this. But Bundy's low level, why your concern?"

"Just some things I've heard, like he's a true dirt bag, worked with the Feds squealing on other fences, but then double crossed the G-men, too."

"Why didn't they arrest him?"

"No idea. It could all be rumorous hearsay, but either way I wouldn't trust anything he says."

"If you ask him questions like I do you'll get honest answers."

"And what answers did you get?"

"When I asked him the name of the woman who hired the boys?"

"Yeah." Monday shot up. "What'd he say?"

"Please stop, I can't breathe, you're killing me."

Monday stared at me.

I said, "I don't know yet. He'll give it to me tomorrow."

And he eased back onto his pillows. "Let me know how that works out. But just so you know a name alone won't be enough. We'll need physical evidence that links her to the robbery. Something on par with the chemical accelerant."

"Understood. But that path's a dead end. Unless you were also lying about the container and the residue found near the bodies." I pushed my eyebrows up as high as they'd go.

But Monday shook his head. "Alas I wasn't. The only place that had a sample was on Thermite's body. God damn Heralds. If only you'd stopped them from getting buried."

"Yeah." I thought of the beach. And Tony's urn. "Actually only one of them got buried. Firewall's sister had him cremated. But don't worry, I stopped her from dumping his ashes, and rooted through them."

Monday looked like he smelled something awful. "Why'd you do that?"

"To see if some of Thermite was in there with him."

He threw his head back and laughed.

"What?"

"After a body's cremated it's pulverized to a fine sand, that way if the family spreads those ashes a hip joint won't flop out like a soup bone. Although... That's not bad thinking. Heck, it might be genius. If some of Thermite did get mixed in with Firewall, and it's not in the urn, then it might still be in the crematorium. Downstairs."

I looked at Monday. *A bit of Thermite still stuck in the oven?* Without a word I charged down to the basement. No one was guarding the doors to the morgue, so I burst in.

And stopped. "Doctor Lockter?"

The red headed white cape looked my way and said in that wavy voice, "What're you doing here?"

My body went chilly slack as I froze in place, and against my will I said, "I'm here on official police business."

"You can tell it to them. From prison. March yourself there."

My body turned to the door. But I bore down against it. The tendons and bones ground against my will to stay put, like a millstone on grain. And I wrenched open my mouth enough to say, "No." The word came out loud. And set my throat aflame.

"Stop." Lockter paused. "Why is this so important to you?"

"Me and Detective Monday need-"

"Detective Monday? You mean Laars Monday?"

"Yeah. You know him?"

The Doc stepped aside, and in her common tongue said, "If you're working with Laars go ahead."

My blood felt like it jumped three degrees as she returned control of my body. I said, "Thanks?" and charged past her, through the door on the far wall, down the hallway, and into the last room on the left.

Inside was a large, steel oven. And the tech with the big ears and brown hair from earlier. He stopped dead. "How'd you get in here?"

I grabbed his jacket and pointed to the oven. "How many got cremated today?"

"It's uh… This is the second."

I shoved him aside and opened the door. Heat poured from the oven like a volcanic rent. I stepped back and covered my face.

"What're you doing?" the tech yelled.

I pointed at the corpse. "Who's that?"

He looked at his clipboard. "Slugfest."

"But he's invulnerable. Will he burn?"

"Yeah, the oven's set on high, and it may start slow but it'll build up quick so we got to get that door shut now." He took a step past me.

And I shoved him back, then leaned down and peered inside. Sure enough the body of Slugfest was still intact, but beneath it, about halfway back, was a small pile of charred chunks.

"How often do you clean this thing?" I asked.

The tech said, "After every time."

I grabbed the back of his neck, pulled him to me, and pointed at the pile. "Then what's that?"

He looked down and said, "Ok, not every time. But always at the end of the day. Doctor Lockter checks nightly."

"So those nuggets are definitely from Firewall?"

"Yeah. Please don't hit me, I didn't-"

"Hit you? Pal, I could kiss you. Now where's the emergency cut off?"

He pointed to a big, red button on the oven. "It's there, but-"

I couldn't believe my luck. There were actual pieces of Thermite still here. I finally found the physical proof that would lead me to the killer, and all I had to do to retrieve it was shut the oven down. I walked over to the kill switch and hit it.

But the red flames kept licking the corpse.

I looked at the tech.

He was full of fear. "I tried to tell you, that button's busted. The oven won't stop until it's run its course."

I looked back at the flames. This was bad. If it got toasty enough inside to crisp Slugfest then those bits of Thermite would probably burn too. And even if they didn't, any residue left over would be compromised. If it wasn't already.

I searched the room for something to scoop them out with. I saw a sink, a painting of a field, and a terrified reg. That left me only one choice. Tossing my jacket aside I rolled up my sleeve.

"What are you doing?" he said.

I thrust a hand into the oven. Flames licked my skin, but I pulled out a handful of cinders before it got bad. I joggled them, and the gray ash slipped through my throbbing fingers, leaving nothing behind.

I looked back in the oven. That spot I cleared was barely a foot in. If I wanted to reach my target I'd need to go deeper.

A lot deeper.

"Are you insane?" he asked.

"No." I reached in again. Further this time. And the flames didn't just lick me, they bit deep. My nerves seared. And muscles baked. When I yanked my paw free it was bright pink and shaking. But I had another handful of soot.

I sifted through it. And found a small chunk of body the size of a briquette. "Yes! You can close it up."

"Sure thing." The tech leaned over. "But what do you want that bone for?"

"Bone?" I looked at the lump in my hand. "You're sure?"

"Yeah." He grabbed it and wiped the ash free to reveal some white. "See?"

No good. Even if this was Thermite the accelerant wouldn't have soaked in so far. I dropped the bone and looked back in the oven. The pile I was aiming for was only six inches deeper than I'd just gone.

So taking a deep breath I cocked my fist back.

And the flames inside doubled in size. Their heat pushed me back and I covered my face.

The tech yelled, "Hurry. You got ten seconds before that heat starts lighting stuff up out here."

I grit my teeth. And threw my hand in. This time as far as it would go. It was like the skin from my shoulder down was being peeled off. I screamed. And grabbed every bit of ash and soot, pulling it out in one clean swipe. The black cloud fell to the floor and the tech slammed the oven shut.

I dropped to one knee. My arm was bright red. There were bubbles on my hand and wrist. I could only feel throbbing pain.

"You," I said. "Go through that."

The tech joined me on the floor and sifted through the charred crumbs. He smeared them this way and that. Mostly it was just dark embers.

But then he held something up. "Is this was you want?"

I leaned forward. In his hand was a human thumb.

And it was still a little pink.

Chapter 22

"Is that what I think it is?" Monday said.

I was standing at the foot of his bed, holding up my prize in a plastic bag. "If you think it's Thermite's finger, then yes. Now let's test it." I opened the bag, pulled out my hand scanner, and waved it over the digit. A few seconds passed before I had its answer. "Damn."

"What?"

"My scanner can't identify it. But something's definitely there."

Monday raised a hand. "Toss it here. I can have one of our lab boys give it a go."

"Why not?" I threw the bag to Monday.

He grabbed the bedside phone and dialed. "Hey Cress, I got something that needs to be analyzed, how fast can you swing by the hospital? Great. See you then." He hung up and turned to me. "We should get the results by tomorrow. Give me your number, and I'll let you know what they find."

I jotted down my office line and handed it over. "Here. Now, can you do me one more favor?"

"Sure, what?"

"Call the nurse. I need some heavy duty burn balm."

#

The topical cream I slathered on my arm quelled the burning just fine, but it wasn't the only reason I left the hospital in a pretty good mood. If there was residue on that finger, then Monday's lab could trace it to a supplier, and if that person was truly Scourge then I would not only settle a long standing debt, but I could also close Widow's case and maybe save my agency.

It was all good news.

So when I got to my apartment I went to the kitchen to celebrate with a two-pound side of beef. Once it was fried right, I brought it over to my desktop computer and booted up Sandtrout. Taking it off the advanced hunter setting, and clicking on the normal search engine stuff, I typed in the name of the woman Monday mentioned earlier: Margaret Shelly. He wasn't so interested in her, but I was intrigued for two reasons. First, the boys stole her jewels, and second, Sandtrout missed her on its first sweep.

Both bits had me curious.

Moments passed. I took a bloody mouthful of beef. And a stream of articles came up. The first few were about the robbery, and the rest outlined her work history.

I decided to start with the theft. And immediately saw why my software didn't register it as a place the boys' lives crossed. The Fletcher Act, able to suppress information regarding black cape trials, kept their names out of the papers, though from the descriptions of their powers it was evident who was who.

It was almost six years ago to the day that the boys broke into Margaret Shelly's penthouse suite. Firewall disabled the security system and Thermite burnt through the safe. It seemed cut and dry, but on the way out they triggered an alarm that locked the place down. Firewall used his power to override the defenses and the boys escaped, but not before they got caught on film.

Hmm. If the system was disabled how'd they get their picture taken?

It didn't say, so I looked up the police report to see what was stolen. There were a couple of diamond tennis bracelets, some ruby broaches, and assorted emeralds, all totaling fifty thousand dollars. Not a tiny job by any means, but considering everything was returned I didn't see a motive for murder.

So I looked at Margaret Shelly's work history.

And let out a long whistle.

She was an architect whose resume contained every high profile skyscraper built in the last fifteen years. There were also a few banks tossed in, and even a Federal law enforcement agency. But despite her lengthy list of achievements I could only find one company she was attached to: a firm called Stronghold that specialized in security systems.

Interesting.

I cross-referenced the name with the museum. Nothing came up.

Then I checked it against flammable agents. Nothing came up.

Finally I looked for a connection to gemstones. And still, nothing came up.

Nuts. Maybe Monday was right. A six-year-old crime with the take returned wasn't a motive for murder.

Still, I turned to her finances. But then, across the bottom of my screen, the news ticker flashed in big, red words: Mayor Greenie Survives Assassination Attempt.

I spun around and clicked on my TV. A blond spitfire in pink with soot on her face was jabbering into a mic. "-in this shocking turn of events, a single terrorist, dressed as catering staff, attempted to assassinate the mayor at tonight's Save the Finch gala in the Gold Coast City Museum. But thanks to the quick response by security only one partygoer, head curator Ms. Alice Johan, was injured. For now, the terrorist has eluded police, but our News Channel Three camera caught what we believe is her picture. We must warn you, the following footage is shocking."

The screen popped over to a video of the incident.

Mayor Greenie stood at a podium before a field of black tie clad socialites. He makes a joke. They laugh. Then behind him the stage explodes. A single woman in a black party dress is swallowed by the jagged hole. Everybody screams. Then they scatter. And someone knocks the camera sideways. That's when the picture freezes, capturing the culprit. It's a little blurry, and she's standing a ways back, but I can clearly make out Doodle. And her twin pistols.

"As of yet her identity is unknown, but she's considered armed and extremely dangerous. If you have any information regarding this young woman's whereabouts, the Gold Coast City Police Department request you contact them immediately. At the museum, this is Peppermint Jones, back to-"

I clicked off the set.

But couldn't believe it. Tera had my kid try to murder the mayor? God damn that bitch. The next time we'd meet I'd thump the accent out of her.

The telephone on my coffee table rang and I grabbed it. "Hello?"

"Dane," a quiet voice said, "I need help."

My antennae jumped up. "Doodle? Are you ok?"

"I'm fine. Can you come and get me?"

"Yeah, of course, tell me where you are."

"The corner of Flint and Little Rock."

"Don't move. I'll be there in twenty."

I bolted down to my car and in less than fifteen minutes I arrived to find Doodle cowering inside a shoe store's darkened doorway, still wearing her crappy tux.

Leaning over I popped the lock. "Get in."

She slipped inside. "Thanks, this isn't-"

I jammed the gas and we jumped forward like the trunk was full of stolen bank notes. "Put on your seatbelt and tell me what the hell's going on."

She clicked the shoulder harness into place. "I'd rather not."

I took a sharp right. "I didn't ask what you'd rather do."

"Dane…"

"Hey, this isn't a taxi, but I still charge a fare, and this ride costs that explanation."

She crossed her arms. "That's not a fare."

"A cop recently told me that life's not a fare. Now spit."

Doodle looked out the window again. "It's nothing, I was just at the wrong place at the wrong time."

"Really?" The light in front of me turned red, and I came to a stop. Reaching over I grabbed Doodle's shirt and pulled it up. The spot on her stomach where the twin pistols were tattooed just last night was now blank. As was the stick of dynamite. "Then how do you explain this?"

She yanked her shirt down. "It's nothing. Damn it."

The light turned green and I pulled forward. "I must be the first dad in history angry that his daughter doesn't have a tattoo."

"Calm down. It's no big deal."

"No big deal? It's no big deal that you… Wait. Guns have moving parts. And dynamite's an explosive. How'd you manifest them?"

"For the guns I tattoo the schematics one layer at a time. The chemicals are harder, but so long as I understand their molecular makeup I can swing it."

"You know how to draw schematics? And who taught you chemistry?"

"I just read a bunch of books."

"Wow." Doodle could design machines. And she understood atoms. That took skills. Smarts. "So you could be an engineer or something?"

"I'd rather be an artist, but yeah. Sure."

I stopped at the next intersection and looked at my daughter. She was beautiful. And brilliant. I've never been so proud of anything. If I could just get her off the criminal's path, she would have a good life. A normal life. All I had to do was keep her out of trouble.

Then a police siren lit up behind me.

Chapter 23

"Pull over!"

I looked in my rearview. A black and white GCCPD cruiser was so tight on my tail we could've been sharing an axle.

Doodle spun around. "It's the cops."

"You sure? Might be a volunteer firefighter." I crushed the gas and we ran the red. But the next block had a line of cars three deep all waiting for the light to change. Still, I kept the pedal on the floor.

"What're you doing?" Doodle said. "We're trapped."

"Settle down." I pulled the wheel to the left. We drove over the curb and onto the sidewalk. Where a lot of people were strolling. I laid on the horn. Two women leapt into a doorway. A deliveryman sprang onto the hood of the nearest car. Glancing in the rearview I saw the cop was following close.

"Watch out," Doodle yelled.

I retuned my attention to the sidewalk in front of us. A woman was there. Pushing a stroller.

"I see her," I said, and jerked the wheel to the right.

We missed the pram by inches and drove off the curb into the intersection.

"Truck truck truck," Doodle said.

To the right was a mighty Mac. The behemoth's horn boomed as its brakes screamed.

"On it." I veered left. My back bumper kissed the truck's nose as it spun out, blocking the intersection.

Doodle looked back. "We got away. Great driving."

I gave her a sideways glance. "You always loved to drive."

"Well it's funner when-"

Another cop car pulled behind me.

I said, "Hold on."

"No," she said, "keep it steady."

"Why?"

"Because." Doodle rolled up her sleeve. On her forearm, above a king cobra tattoo, and a clutch of blue butterflies, was a rendering of one dozen jacks, the kind kids played with before I was born. She closed her eyes. And the sharp, metal toys pushed out against her flesh. Then, one-by-one, they fell into her waiting hand, and when all twelve were manifested out her window they went.

A few loud pops came from behind as her metal toys punctured the patrol car's tires sending it into a spinout.

But another black and white zipped past him, and clamped onto our tail.

"This is getting tiresome," I said.

"So what're we going to do?"

"I got an idea. We're ducking into Tunnel Town."

"Really?" Doodle turned to me all bright eyed. "You're kidding?"

"Nope. But we'll need to take the expressway to get there." Ahead was an on-ramp. I turned up the steep incline and we were on the highway in seconds. But I immediately regretted it.

"It's like a parking lot up here," Doodle said.

And boy was she right. All seven lanes were slathered with cars as far as I could see. "Damn it, the construction. Seven interstates run through this burg and I choose the I-93."

"The what?"

"Five miles up there's a bridge where they've removed one of the sections. Now this damn road's a traffic causing cliff." Keeping my gas pedal horizontal I swerved onto the shoulder, kicking up dust and stones in my wake. But behind me, through the cloud, red and blue lights were still flashing. They were getting smaller. But still, we were on a highway's shoulder. There was nowhere to hide, and nowhere to go but straight ahead to the next exit. If I got there though, we'd be home free.

"What'll we do now?" Doodle said. "There's no way to lose him."

"Don't worry," I said, "I got an idea. But we'll need something big."

She pointed ahead. "Will that do?"

I followed her finger to an SUV in the closest lane. "No. Bigger."

"How much bigger?"

"A lot." I kept looking. There were some minivans. A pickup truck. Another SUV.

Then I finally saw what I needed. "That's it. Hold on." I stomped the brakes and we slid to a halt. The cloud of stones and dust rolled in from behind, covering us like late night fog. "Be right back." I jumped out, and ran back a few yards past my rear bumper.

In the closest lane, rolling my way slow, was a massive cement truck. I stepped in front of it. The mighty vehicle stopped. Its horn bellowed deep. I crouched down. Reached beneath its bumper on the driver's side. And grabbed the frame. Taking a deep breath, and putting everything I had into my lower back and legs, I pulled up. Slowly the truck lifted off the ground. But I could only get it up to my waist. And if this was going to work, it had to go a lot higher.

"What the hell?" The driver jumped out, and hit the ground already running. It made the truck lighter, but not by much.

I knew I couldn't curl it the rest of the way, so quick as a cat I dropped down and slipped my right shoulder under the frame. The mammoth weight pressed me lower. Beads of sweat formed on my face.

Then the police cruiser pulled up on the shoulder, stopping behind my Jalopy, right next to the cement truck. The front door opened and out came the cop. "This is the police, vacate the car with your hands up."

Peering under the truck I could only see his feet, but the look on Doodle's face said he was aiming his pistol at her.

I sucked in as much air as I could, and pressed. Pain ran up my lower back like wildfire. Both knees shook. But the colossal truck pitched over some, towards the cop. I grabbed the frame with both hands. And pushed some more. My elbows nearly buckled. But now the truck was leaning over even farther. Just one more shove. That's all it needed.

I took a deep breath. Harnessed everything I had in reserve. And put it into my arms.

Finally, gravity claimed the truck for its own, and the large vehicle toppled sideways. The cop screamed, "What the hell?" and dove to the ground, barely dodging death as the truck flattened his cruiser. Wet cement poured from the spout in the back, covering the street like thick, gray oatmeal.

I jumped back in my Jalopy and pulled away. "That'll slow them down."

Doodle looked back. "That was incredible, he'll never catch us now."

I wiped the sweat from my forehead. "Not unless he grows

wings."

"I got a pair of those on my back," Doodle said. "They don't really work though, just-"

A spotlight lit up the car and a loud voice boomed, "Pull your vehicle over now."

Doodle leaned forward and looked up. "Great, they got a chopper."

"Fat lot of good it'll do. Hold on." I pressed the gas down and took the next exit. As I bombed down the off-ramp I could see cop lights flashing to the distant right. So at the bottom I turned left.

"How are we going to lose them all?"

Tightening my grip on the wheel I said, "We're almost at Tunnel Town."

Doodle turned towards me. "Really? Where is it?"

"Right there." About a hundred yards ahead our road ran under a bridge.

As I raced towards it the chopper above us picked up some altitude. He was planning on flying over the bridge to pick us up on the other side.

But as we drove beneath it I clicked off my headlights and pulled the emergency brake. The Jalopy spun out forty-five degrees, and we came to a stop facing the wall.

Doodle said, "What are-"

"Get out." I pointed to a yellow wrong way sign. "And pull that thing to the right."

"Why?"

"Do it now!"

Doodle jumped out, grabbed the sign, and yanked. Then, directly in front of my bumper, a section of the wall lifted up like a garage door, revealing an inky, black tunnel.

I said, "Let's go already."

Doodle hopped back in and we drove through the opening. Behind us the door closed, while a few feet above, on the ceiling, a small orb lit up and bathed the rough-cut, red tunnel in a soft, yellow glow. We drove forward, and as we went new lights clicked on as the old ones behind us died.

I turned to my kid and said, "Welcome to Tunnel Town."

She looked out the window in wonder. "This is so cool. How many tunnels like this are there?"

"Dozens. Hundreds probably. Nobody knows them all, but this one leads to an old club called Crush. It's where Tera and I spent a lot of time." I smiled at the memory.

Doodle said, "Neat."

"Not always." I looked her way. "But it was worth it."

After a ways the tunnel opened up and I laid on the gas. It took about half an hour but we finally came to a fork. I turned right, and when I got to the tube's end, the wall sensors that worked the lights had the rock face slide open. We drove out through Speedy's abandoned garage, which served as the false front, and behind us Tunnel Town sealed tight.

Doodle looked around. "Where are we?"

In both directions ran block after block of run down buildings. "The Outskirts. Way north of town. Where're you staying?"

"With Swamp. But after tonight I'm not sure. I'll call mom's answering service and leave a message, and in an hour or two she'll get back to me on where to meet." When we stopped at the first red light Doodle leaned over, kissed me on the cheek, then opened her door. "Thanks, I can find my way home from here."

I snatched her arm. "In the Outskirts? No. No way you're roaming these streets. Or any streets. You need to lay low."

"Ok." Doodle shut the door. "I guess that's smart. Where're you thinking?"

"Someplace special." I cut a smile. The dewy kind. "But first, are you hungry?"

Chapter 24

A few blocks from my office was Eggs Am, a twenty-four hour diner with a checkered formica floor so dotted with scuff marks you couldn't tell which were the white squares and which were the black. My usual spot was at the lunch counter in the front, but we required cover, so I led Doodle down the row of sparkly, blue booths to the spot in the corner, and slid into one side while she took the other. Holding a hand up to my mouth I yelled, "Acouste."

A big, burly Greek came out of the kitchen wearing a white shirt, black pants, and an apron as dingy as his smile was bright. He waved, grabbed two cups of coffee, and brought them over. "I'm sorry, Dane. I didn't hear you come in. Two of the usual?"

"Please." I motioned to Doodle. "Got my daughter with me."

"This is your little girl? She looks just like you."

Doodle's gaze was a bone breaker. "Thanks a ton, pal."

The big Greek chuckled. "I mean it in the good way. You both have the same soft eyes. The same warmth. Anyway, I'll leave you to chat." He turned on his heels and teetered off.

Doodle said, "Listen, I didn't-"

"One second." I waited for Acouste to make it all the way into the kitchen. "So yesterday when you said you'd call, I didn't think it would be right after you tried to kill the mayor."

She leaned back and said, "I didn't try to kill the mayor. I just muled an explosive through the metal detectors and planted it where I was told."

"Take it from me, that won't hold up in court."

"Whatever, I'm not going to get busted."

"That's what everyone thinks right before the cops knock. Which they'll do, once your accomplices get snatched. Speaking of which, where are Tera and Swamp anyway?"

"I went in there alone."

"What?" I squeezed the table so hard I left imprints.

"Calm down. It's no big deal. Swamp and Mom said the job would go smoother if it was just me."

"Swamp said that?" I shook my head. At least now I knew why he and his pale friend were so jumpy when I stopped by. "When a man loves you he gets you a diamond, not into trouble with the law."

"Like the one you got mom? You know, she told me all about you guys."

"Hey, twice I asked Tera to… Wait, what'd she say?"

"That you were always setting her up for jobs like this, and if she declined you'd rough her up some."

The mercury in my thermostat jumped to Jupiter. "She said what?"

"Don't worry about it. I'm not mad. I just don't want a lecture."

"I… I…" I didn't know what to say. Or which was worse, that Tera filled my daughter's head with such tales, or that Doodle simply accepted them as part of life. Either way I wanted to shake the lies from her. Explain what really happened between me and her mom. But I sensed it was too late. The untruths had taken deep hold. And besides, even a guy with a skull as thick as mine knows badmouthing the other parent is the dumbest move you can make.

So instead I sat there. And stewed.

Fortunately, mere moments later, Acouste arrived. He dropped off our grub, and when he got back to his spot behind the counter, Doodle scrunched up her nose and said, "What's this?"

I said, "Scrambled eggs and hash browns."

She took a nibble. And brightened up. "This is great."

"Right? Now eat. And while you do tell me how you hooked up with Swamp and his pale boy in the first place."

Doodle took another forkful. "We were living in New York, working for Big Six when he and us had a falling out over money, so me and Mom pulled roots and left town. A few days later she got wind of a job that needed my skills from a friend out here, so we came to Gold Coast, met Swamp at Wetlands, and he hired us for tonight's gala."

"Do you know why he wanted to kill the mayor?"

"I didn't ask and he didn't say."

"Do you mind telling me what the plan was?"

"Sure. I went in, manifested that single stick of dynamite, and put it on the helium tank they used for the balloons. I set the timer for fifty seconds, but I think Mom tattooed it wrong, so it blasted in five."

"And that was it? No exit strategy? Wow, that plan has Tera written all over it."

Doodle rolled her eyes. "Anyway, that wasn't the only thing that went weird. The explosion was bigger than anything I can produce."

"But you can make gunpowder."

"Only a quarter stick's worth. And that takes more energy than I can consume, so Mom injects me with a high calorie fatty sludge to supercharge my output. Speaking of which, are you going to finish your plate?"

I looked down at my eggs. They were barely touched. And my gut was growling like an angry guard dog. "No. Here," I said, and passed them over.

"Thanks. So like I said, making explosives is real difficult, physically. Gunpowder's as potent as I can get. Anything more than that and the human body can't contain it. I think there were other explosives in that helium tank. But either way I have no clue. Now I've got some questions," she said, "about you."

"Really? Go ahead. Ask me anything."

"Why does everyone say you're a turn cape?"

I leaned back and sighed. "Because my old crew, Dread Division, got sent to Impenetron for a ten-year tour two weeks after I left the group for good."

"All of them?"

"Yep. All fourteen."

"Fourteen? Are they black capes or a basketball team?"

I laughed. "Dread Division had a deep roster for two very good reasons. First, it gave us a large talent pool. There wasn't a job that came our way we couldn't do. And second, if something did go sour, and we encountered white capes, they'd never know how to deal with us."

"What do you mean?"

"Ok, think about it like this, the win-to-lose ratio between white capes and black always favors the heroes, right? Why?"

"Because they're stronger?"

"Nope," I said. "We're pretty evenly matched."

"Oh, so you guys had power in numbers."

I shook my head. "No. Don't ever believe that. Teams who rely on numbers to win are teams that bleed a lot."

"Alright then, why do we lose so much?"

"Because the only thing that white capes train for is to fight black capes, and they train as a team. As a team, not just a group, like us. They have bonds. Loyalty. If one of them's injured their partners help, and they battle accordingly. But with us, well, when a black cape hits the street we leave them where they lie, and save our own skin.

"Also, they practice their strategies. They have techniques they use in tandem whereas we fight as individuals. Thus, when a black cape squad shows up to steal a nuclear warhead or kidnap the president, the opposition fights together, as a unit, and are prepared for any of the thousands of methods we may employ."

"Like in basketball," Doodle said, "when the Prospectors play the Emperors they strategize who's the most dangerous offensive player, the best passer, and change their plays according to who's on the court at the time."

"Good girl, yes. That's exactly right. So whoever Team Supreme fights, if they know who they're facing, they'll instinctively know which strategy's most effective. And it doesn't matter, The Boo Boys, Fearsome Foursome, Bloodlines… They all lose for that very reason. But not Dread Division. Were we a flamer, a speedster, and a teleporter? Or a strongman, a telepath, and a waterman? The white capes never knew because the four or five players in the field wore the same uniform and always rotated. It's why we never got busted."

"Until that last time."

I sat back. "Yeah."

Doodle thought about what I said, mulling over the wisdom. Finally she arrived at the question that Tera once asked. "If only five capes are on the job at one time do you still split the take fifteen ways? That seems dumb."

"Two thirds went to those who did the job. The rest to the others. And it wasn't dumb. It made us tight. Loyal. Which, since I'm the only one breathing free air, is why everyone hates me so much."

"Well, you had to expect they'd come for you after that business with Top Tower."

I sat up straight. "You heard about that?"

"Are you kidding? When a squad of black capes lay siege to Team Supreme's headquarters for over twenty-four hours, and escapes without a trace, deaf men on Mars hear about it. For an entire year the whole world's law enforcement agencies wanted you bad."

"Yeah." I remembered the day fondly. "But that was years back.

And nobody pinned it on us. If that's what Dread Division got picked up on, the news would've been all over it. So whatever crime they were convicted of was something else entirely."

"That sucks." Doodle took a sip of coffee and thought about it. "But if the white capes never ID'd you guys, then how'd they arrest all of them? I mean some, that I get, but all?"

"I wish I knew."

"So, uh, did you? Rat them out I mean?"

"No," I said. "But nobody believes it, which is why my business dried up. Except for this gig about the two guys who died trying to steal the Coconut." I got all nonchalant. "You know anything about that?"

"No. Nothing. Just what I read in the paper."

"Really? I know Swamp sold them their gear, maybe he had more of a hand in the actual robbery?"

"Not likely. He was with me that night."

"You're sure?"

"Positive. The whole night."

Ugh. "Ok. Come on, it's time to motor. Here, take my keys and hop in the car while I pay the bill."

"Sure thing." Doodle snatched them and ran outside.

Acouste was behind the counter, reading a paperback.

I walked over and said, "So?"

He looked out the front window. Doodle was in my passenger seat. "Whatever you asked her, she's telling the truth."

"You're sure?"

Acouste pointed to his ear. "I know I'm old, but I can still hear a heartbeat from across the room. A couple of times she was concerned, or surprised, but when a person lies their pulse is very specific. I'm telling you, every single thing she said was on the steady level."

I couldn't help but sigh. This time from relief. "Thanks a heap. Here." I handed him a wad of hundreds.

"No, this is too much."

"Not for that news. You have a good night. The eggs were excellent as always."

He laughed and looked down at his book. "How would you know?"

I walked out. Doodle leaned over and unlocked my door. I slid in and started it up. "So I was thinking, how about we head to my place. No one will be looking for you there. You could spend the night and call your mom in the morning."

She thought about it. "Sure. That sounds good."

"Good." *Actually it's great.*

We drove back to my apartment and found a spot a few feet from my front door. When we got out Doodle said, "Hey, do you got any food? I'm still kind of hungry."

I remembered the state of my fridge. "No. But there's a twenty-four hour market around the corner."

"Great, let's go." Doodle walked past me.

And I grabbed her arm. "No. You head up to my place where no one can identify you. It's number 310." I handed her the keys and started down the block.

"Got it. Grab something with lots of sugar." She ran up the stoop and into my building.

When I got to the market I filled a cart with a few cereal boxes full of bright colored marshmallows, a gallon of milk, and three frozen pizzas. Then I paid for it and headed home. And on my way, I swear, I actually hummed a happy tune.

My kid was staying over. We'd spend the night talking. I'd steer the conversation to art school, convince her to apply to one. She'd meet a nice boy there. Maybe we could all have dinner once a month. She'd graduate, and have a normal life.

I know it was a tall order for a single night's work, but I was hauling two tons of can-do attitude, and that's why, when I got home, I practically floated up the stairs and through my unlocked door.

But the lights were off.

"Doodle? Where are you?"

She didn't answer.

I put down the grocery bags and hit the light switch next to the door. My bulb made a popping sound and the room remained dark. So I walked to the far wall and clicked on the lamp there.

My living room was cold and empty, but on the coffee table lay a fresh rose. Underneath it was a note written in feminine scrawl.

Hey Dane,
Sorry but I had to run. I called Mom

and we're leaving town tonight.
Thanks for everything.
-Doodle

I went to the kitchen and grabbed a bottle of whiskey, then plopped down in my chair. Sitting directly in front of me on the coffee table was that big lump of meat I'd cooked earlier. It was cold, and the blood had congealed. Nobody in their right mind would want it now.

I knew exactly how it felt.

Chapter 25

When I woke up around ten I was still in my chair, as upright and stiff as the empty bottle on the floor. I got to my feet and stretched, popping all the vertebrae back into place that got knocked around by last night's truck lift. As I did something fell from my lap.

It was Doodle's bloom.

I picked it up, took a deep whiff, then tossed it on my coffee table. I was going to miss that kid. But at least she was safe. And away from Swamp. Plus, now that she knew how to get in touch with me maybe she'd call.

As I finished that thought the phone rang. I snatched it up, full of hope. "Hello?"

"Morning." The voice was gruff.

I recognized its owner immediately. "Bundy Strong. I knew you'd call. You got my name?"

"I do, but before I hand it over I need a favor."

"A favor? Every breath you've taken since last we met is one I've thrown your way."

"And I need one more. I told you my principal was going to drop off my dough. What I didn't anticipate is that she's sending a proxy."

"Who?"

"You don't know him. He's from out of town. Goes by the name Scourge."

I looked at the phone. "Scourge?"

"Yeah. Stupid name, I know, but he's got A-1 dark urges. He'd probably peel my cap and keep the dough for himself rather than do what he's told and pay me my fee. But I figure with an ape like you on my elbow he won't be so apt to go sideways. Then, after he slides me the green, I'll slide you the name."

"Wow. Great plan. But I got a better one. Why don't-"

"Hey. This isn't a negotiation. I got a line on the info you want, and you got muscle I need. Let's do something here."

I thought about the pitch. And said, "Alright Bundy, that all sounds swell. Just tell me when and where you're meeting this Scourge."

"Limestone Rock."

"That's a big spot. Where exactly?"

"On the roof of Blackstone's Hubcap plant, off Old Access Road. He'll be there at two, so I say we arrive by noon."

"Got it. Blackstone's at noon. See you then."

"Hey Curse," Bundy said.

"Yeah?"

"Don't forget your hardware. This might not be as easy as all that."

"Thanks." I hung up the phone and thought it over.

This was perfect. Scourge was expecting to deal with Bundy, but instead he'd run into me. Assuming, that is, that Bundy was on the level. I remembered Monday's warning about trusting him. And it was advice I'd take.

So, instead of putting my faith in that half cape I'd head out right now, and be there two hours early. That way, if Bundy was setting up a double cross, I'd see it coming a long ways off, making it duck soup to blast Gunmetal, and catch Scourge unawares. Then I could beat the name I needed out of him and close Widow's case without having to worry.

I grabbed Lois and Rico, and slid them into my shoulder holsters. However this shook out, it was bound to be a big morning.

Chapter 26

Limestone Rock was an island that jutted out from the south part of town. Along with Highside, it's what made Bittenbach a bay. But while the northern peninsula's got the ports, Limestone Rock's the hot ticket for manufacturing. Or at least it was until the lure of low cost labor and warmer climates became too much for the executives to ignore. Now Limestone Rock's sort of a ghost town, a new old west boom burg that's all but deserted save for a handful of active places and a whole lot of empty ones.

The building I was going to, The Wild West Glove Depot, was one of the empties. It sat beside Blackstone's abandoned hubcap plant, and at five stories it was the island's tallest building. From on top of its roof I'd have a panoramic view, so I could spot any creeping adversaries from a ways off.

I parked down an alley three blocks away, slapped on my mask, and crept towards the Glove Depot. I didn't see a soul the whole trip. Unusual. But not unwelcome.

When I arrived I climbed the fire escape and got to the top in seconds. The roof was as clear as the street below, save for the far corner where a couple of oil drums sat next to a pile of wooden pallets. If need be they might make good cover, but before I went rearranging my aerie I wanted eyes on the target.

I turned and stared down at the top of Blackstone's Hubcaps. Nobody there, either. I was completely alone. Now all I had to do was wait. It would be a few hours, but eventually they'd show. And then I'd open-

"Fire," someone yelled.

I spun around.

Two cops were standing behind the barrels in the corner. One had a shoulder mounted rocket launcher. It roared loud, and sent a yellow fireball towards me. The blast hit dead center so hard I could feel it in my teeth. It launched me off the roof. I twisted around as I plummeted to the ground. And struck the concrete.

I got to my knees and looked around. The blast had knocked me over the road. I was right next to Blackstone's. Across the street was a cop. He was running his mouth, but all I heard was ringing. I got to my feet. And stuck a finger in my ear and wiggled.

The cop kept rambling. All I caught was, "-move."

Then I noticed a dozen more lawmen. I couldn't tell where they were coming from, but it looked like someone had tapped a well full of them.

"I said don't move," the first cop yelled. "Fire."

Gunshots popped all around as twelve projectiles struck my chest. And the world went gooey. I slumped backwards, into the wall. Leaning against it I looked down. My shirt and tie were burnt away. The skin beneath was ashy and black. And sticking out of the seared flesh like a feather duster were a dozen Trumite tranquilizer darts.

I swatted them off, and went to take a step, but stumbled and fell. Two canisters landed next to me. The label on their sides read: Viper Vapor. They belched out blue smoke that stunk like brimstone. It spread thick around my hands and feet. And my head got heavy as I wretched.

The cops started chattering. "Suspect has been neutralized."

"Wait until he passes out, then slap on the cuffs."

"Tell the backup he can stand down."

The smoke was all around me, and rising higher. Despite my tolerance for knockout sedatives I knew that a few more mouthfuls of this haze and I'd be too numb to fight my way free. But still, I pinched my nose, and closed both eyes tight. Then I flattened out, plunging myself completely into the noxious cloud.

"Where'd he go?"

"I can't see him."

"Wait until he comes out, then blast him again."

I gave it a couple more seconds. Then I sprang from the mist, and launched into the wall behind me, blasting through it head first. Bricks and plaster skittered across the cement as I spilled onto the floor of Blackstone's Hubcaps. It was dark inside. And the hard ground was cold. The only light was from the hole I just made.

Back on the street the cops were yelling.

I got to my feet. And pulled out Rico. Aiming high up, I fired off a few explosive tips at the part of the wall that was still standing. Some of the building gave way and crumbled, putting a pile of rubble between me and my attackers. I turned from it, and sprinted across the warehouse floor.

My head was still soggy, but with each step my vision got a little sharper. My thoughts, a touch crisper. And I was almost one hundred percent when I reached the far wall. I tossed my shoulder into it and crashed through to the other side, as easy as long division.

Now I was on the street again. And there was no one around. I charged back towards my car, taking a wide arc over a few extra blocks to avoid any cops. It worked. I made it without seeing a soul.

There were a total of three bridges linking Limestone Rock to the city, and I was driving fast for the nearest one. But with only one block behind me I ran into a problem. Around fifty feet beyond my bumper a single cop stood in the middle of the road, pointing a pistol at me.

No. Not a pistol. His hand was empty. And open.

I couldn't believe it, but he was standing there like a traffic guard, telling me to stop. That was either intense courage, or suicidal optimism, but either way I wasn't slowing down.

The thing was, even though I raced straight at him, this cop didn't move.

So I did. With only twenty feet to go I pulled into the right lane so I'd drive around him. Fortunately he stayed put. Good thing. I'd have pulped him raw if-

No.

At the last second the officer sprang in front of me. I squashed the brakes. My tires locked. But it wasn't good enough. I plowed into him at full speed.

My whole body jerked forward, and I bashed my skull against the steering wheel. Sitting back I rubbed my crown. And stared ahead at what had to be the impossible.

The officer, looking whole and hardy, was holding the front end of my car a few feet off the ground.

I jammed on the gas and my rear tires shrieked and spun. The smell of seared rubber filled the car like corpse rot. But I didn't move. Not one bit. So I eased off the petrol and got out. "What the hell?"

The cop dropped my ride and stepped around it so we were face-to-face. I didn't notice it before but he was massive, both wide and tall. And he had a gas mask on. Through it he said with a voice as deep as Nietzsche's thoughts, "You don't recognize me?"

I said, "No."

"Maybe this'll help." With one hand the cop tossed his mask aside, while the other ripped his blue uniform off. Underneath was the orange and white getup I'd seen just two days before.

And my heart dropped to my guts. Both fell to the street.

Because I'd just tried to run over Al Mighty.

Chapter 27

He put both fists high on his hips and said, "So which way you coming, quiet or bloody?"

"Kicking and screaming." I cracked all my knuckles. "This won't go down like your dance with Hard Drive."

Al said, "I sure hope not." And I swear, underneath that blood red beard, he actually licked his chops. Then he charged me like a longhorn.

I whipped Lois out and aimed. But Al moved quick for a big man and dropped a meaty hand on my arm. Lois fell to the ground. Before she hit, Al had his other fist in my chin. The blow snapped my head back. And lifted me up.

I sailed backwards and hit the street, grinding to a halt. Then I sat up. And rubbed my jaw.

Al came strolling over. "You know, Hard Drive lasted a lot longer than this."

Lumbering to my feet I said, "Stow the sugar report and let's get on with it."

Again Al charged.

I shuffled back with my fists up.

When he closed in he tossed a hook, high and hard.

This time I slid the punch, and dug a right cross into his chest. Al folded over. But not as deep as I'd hoped. So I dropped my left fist onto the back of his skull. He fell to one knee. And I hit his chin with a fast uppercut.

Al sailed back the way he came. But flipped midair. And landed with both feet and one hand on the ground, in the perfect three-point stance.

I shook my head. "You know how God damn stupid you heroes look pulling that stunt?"

"Shame. It'll be the last thing you see." Al launched towards me again.

But I was quicker this time, and had Rico out. I blasted a few high-velocities into his thigh, knocking him to the ground.

Then I turned and ran. As fast as I could. Away from him, and my car. It wasn't the safe direction. But it was my only choice. I couldn't beat Al hand-to-hand, so my only hope was to lose him, then double back to make my escape.

So I turned down the next corner. And before Al could catch up I ducked into an alley. Sliding behind some garbage cans I crouched down and froze.

A few seconds later he came charging by.

Skulking to the corner I poked my head out. Al was at the end of the block. He looked both ways, then disappeared around the building to the right.

So long, you big, red moron.

I popped out of my hiding spot and started back down the street towards my car, taking the corner at full speed.

And ran into something hard.

I tumbled backwards. And a tooth jumped from my craw, cutting a sloppy line across the blacktop. I sat up and blood poured down the back of my throat like a cup of warm copper.

Standing before me was a five-foot woman rubbing her knuckles. She had on green pants, a tight fitting black, long sleeve shirt, and her brown hair was in a ponytail. Then I saw her face. And the two shiny Trumite fangs that stood out like polished chrome in her smile.

My heart jumped into my throat, making it so tight there that I could only push out two words. "Gunmetal Gray."

"Hey kitten," she said, "bet you wish you hadn't snooped around our clean sneak now."

I crab walked backwards.

"No patter? From what I hear that's ominous." She charged towards me. And pounced.

I pulled out Rico.

Just in time for Gunmetal to grab my hand. We rolled twice, and when we stopped she was straddling me. And had both my wrists tight. I shoved up against her. But she stayed planted. And opened her mouth wide. I could see my reflection in her sharp canines. That, and a single drop of green venom. It flopped free and fell on my cheek. The burning was a lot like acid.

She chomped down quick.

But I turned my face away, and all she bit was ocean air.

So Gunmetal tried to get closer. But I pulled both arms in, and kept her at bay. She snapped at me twice more. Each chomp was nearer than the last. "Almost there," she said. "I've almost got my mouth on you."

"Thanks, I'll pass."

"It's not up to you." And a bad day got worse as an electrical charge, red and thin, ran from her right thumb to my wrist. It stung. Worse than a normal shock.

"No," I said. "Don't."

Gunmetal smiled. And from the tip of each finger a crimson bolt leapt. All ten ran down my arm, and through my chest on their way to the ground. Every muscle I had locked, including my heart. It felt like I was being cooked from the inside.

When finally her electricity stopped I went limp, putting up as much of a fight as Vicky Taylor did on our first date. Which is to say, not a lot. Now nothing would stop her from using those Trumite fangs to puncture my meat and inject venom that was more poisonous than Chinese milk. She'd done it before. To dozens of mugs like me.

After all, she was an assassin who specialized in murdering invulnerable black capes. And that market was one she had near cornered.

Gunmetal leaned in. Real slow. Savoring the bite. Her teeth were almost on my throat. I could feel her breath. It was getting faster. Hotter.

Then two long horn blasts blew loud enough to summon a kraken.

And Gunmetal paused. She looked over her shoulder.

"That's enough," a voice I never thought I'd hear again said. "We have to leave the rest for Mighty."

She nodded. And ran off, leaving me flat.

With great effort I sat up, and watched as she jumped into the back of a pickup truck. It was the same make and model as the one that pushed me and Monday into the drink yesterday. There was even an identical hunk of metal missing from its bumper. Only now it was covered in bright red paint. Behind the wheel was a man in a black suit and derby. He studied me with a left eye that was noticeably bigger than the right, and sat above a cheek cluttered with deep scars.

It was just like Lee said. *Scourge had returned.*

He waved. "Give Al my regards."

"You son of a bitch." Rico was lying a few feet away. I snatched him up and turned to Scourge.

But he and Gunmetal were gone.

Which was a wise move.

Those damn horn blasts would bring every cop on the island. Every cop, and every cape.

So I got to my feet, holstered Rico, and moved back to my car.

"Where do you think you're going?" Something grabbed my coat from behind and flung me into a nearby wall.

I turned and caught a shot to the jaw. Both legs clicked off and I crumpled to the ground. More blood, all hot and wet and mine, cascaded down my chin.

"We weren't through," Al said.

Looking up I wiped my mouth. "Haven't had enough yet?"

"Nope."

"Ok. But don't say I didn't warn you." Quick as I could I drove an uppercut between Al's thighs. He grunted and bent over. I jumped to my feet and swept his leg. The big bearded strongman fell onto his back. I dropped my left fist on his face like a sledgehammer. Then I dropped my right.

I stomped his chest.

Then his gut.

And finally, I leapt into the air, raised both knees, and pounded my heels into Al's face, driving his head through the concrete. Standing there breathing hard I said, "You should stay down."

Al looked up at me with an unmarred face. "You think?" Then, like Slamazon, he ignored my advice, jumped to his feet with the grace of a cat, and threw an uppercut into my chin.

It exploded loud, shattering the nearby windows. But then a sort of quiet peace settled around me. The ringing in my ears was replaced by the soft hum of a quiet breeze. I was floating weightless. I spun over. And looked down.

It was then I realized that Al had launched me thirty feet into the air.

Buildings passed beneath me. Three in all before I tipped forward and began my descent. I landed on the roof of a building, and plowed through its ceiling, crashing inside.

I lay still for a few moments, looking through the hole I'd just made at the clouds above. I could've done that for hours, but instead I got to my knees, gathered up my scattered wits, and looked around.

There were dozens of rusted hubcaps littered about the place. Two large holes were in the walls to my right and left. And straight ahead hung a crooked Blackstone's sign.

I was back in the hubcap factory.

Al knocked me back the way I wanted to go. Of all the lucky breaks, I was only a few blocks from my car. All I had to-

"Still standing, huh?"

Al was in the hole I'd made earlier, looking fresh.

I turned and ran the opposite way.

But he was on me quick. The big man grabbed the back of my collar. And punched a kidney. I screamed and thrashed. But he gave me another one. I tried to collapse. But Al flung me across the room backwards. I crashed through one of the still intact walls, rolled a few times, and settled in a heap on my knees.

For the moment I was alone, outside. A breeze came in from behind me. I looked back. The Pacific waves were licking the shore not twenty feet away.

I thought about making a swim for it. But breaststroke's never been my strong suit.

"Going somewhere?" Al was outside now, ambling my way like a man without a care.

I looked up at him. "It was stupid to think I could outfight you."

"Yeah." He grabbed my coat's lapel, and hauled me to my feet. "It was real dumb."

I said, "Should've tried to outthink you."

"Is that right?" Al lifted up his fist. It looked as big as a ham. But he paused. And lorded his deathblow above my head like it was the Sword of Damocles.

I took the moment to suck as much blood into my mouth as I could, and spit the glob in his eye.

He dropped me, and wiped his face clean. The blood was now gone. Replaced by murderous intent. "You son of a bitch. I'll kill you!"

I shuffled back towards the sea. "Come on. I'm going to spank you like I did your sister last night. Let's see if you enjoy it as much as she did."

Al's eyes got huge. He grit his teeth so hard I thought they'd shatter. And he lunged at me. His heavy right led the way. I sidestepped it. Barely. And grabbed his wrist with both hands. Then

I spun him around like an Olympic hammer tosser. Once. Twice. Three times.

But on the fourth pass he began to pull himself towards me. His eyes were wild. The skin around them twisted like old bark. He yelled, "Let me go."

And so I did.

I threw Al Mighty at a perfect forty-five degree angle over the ocean. He sailed high for a spell before gravity remembered to pull him down, and he plummeted into the white foam over four hundred yards out.

Which is a pretty good toss for a white cape his size.

But there was no time to mark it. Instead I turned tail and ran back to my Jalopy. Lois was right there next to it. I scooped her up and drove towards the nearest bridge. The cops had pulled back, probably to give Al some room, so I found an unguarded on-ramp and fled back to the city without further delay.

Normally after a fight like that I'd go to Henchmen's for a pint of whiskey. But it didn't seem wise considering how much blood I just lost.

Chapter 28

Once I got back to my office I headed upstairs to patch up my mug. Mrs. West was behind her desk in a coral suit, and she looked up at me like I was beating a puppy to death with a bagful of kittens. "What happened to you?"

"Al Mighty," I said. "And if it's all the same, I don't need any-"

"To the couch, now." She leapt up like a spring chicken, instead of the old bird she was, and threw a wing under my arm. For a small dame she dragged strong, and got me on the sofa quick. "Now don't move. I'm getting the kit." She ran into my bathroom and came out with a white toolbox.

"Why're you being so sweet?" I said, and pointed to my face. "I would think this might cheer you up."

"Oh, you're thinking now? Probably should've started that before you went knuckles-to-nose with Big Al." She looked my mug over. "You got some cuts to seal, but first I got to fix that busted beak. Now hold still." She grabbed my schnoz, and jerked it to the side. It slid back into place with a hot crunch.

I sat up and said, "That hurt."

Mrs. West shoved me back down. "Less whining, more reclining." She tore off some medical tape and fastened it over the bridge of my nose. Then she cleaned the gash above my eye and clamped it shut with more tape.

"Are you done yet?"

"Well, since that split lip is caked with dried blood, and only time will heal your shiner, I suppose I am." She grabbed the kit and returned it to the bathroom.

I got up, walked to my desk, and pulled a bottle of rye from the bottom drawer.

"That's more tea," Mrs. West said.

I looked at the whiskey. "But the seal's unbroken. How-"

"I have skills you're unaware of. Now sit down." The batty dame shoved me back with both hands, herding me onto the sofa like a brittle, old collie. "So, Al Mighty? Was it about the case?"

"Sort of."

"You want to talk about it?"

"Not really." I leaned back, and put both hands behind my head. "Carl always talked things through with me."

"Carl had more patience than a city full of hospitals."

She kicked my foot. "Don't be rude. Or, since it's you, try to be less so. Now do you want to talk or not?"

I looked at her from the corner of my eye. "I guess it couldn't hurt." Taking a deep breath I sorted the facts and prepared to lay them out flat. "So, you know I'm investigating how Widow's brother and pal were killed on the job in Wentorf Hall. Well, they got said job from Bundy Strong, who shared a cell with them in Impenetron. The thing is, he doesn't know enough about Wentorf to crack its defenses, or have the skills to plan the strategy itself. For the former, I got no clue how he pulled it off, but for the latter he hired Scourge."

"So he's the one who killed the boys?"

"Not necessarily," I said. "I'm sure he planned the heist and the cover up, but those dead kids were smart thieves, they wouldn't have attempted the heist without a third man who could've gotten the stone from behind its display, and Scourge doesn't have that ability."

"Maybe they didn't know that. Maybe it's like Ms. Marcus says, an assassination."

I looked over at Mrs. West. "You mean someone paid Bundy to put together a team all in the hopes of murdering two boys?" *Interesting. But,* "No. Nobody hates them that much. Though I do believe a woman's behind all of this. Bundy said so."

"But Bundy Strong's a liar. Isn't it possible he's the one pulling the strings?"

"Very possible," I said. "But that would mean he had enough money to hire Gunmetal Gray to protect Scourge from me, and I don't think he has that kind of dough."

Mrs. West snatched my arm. "Hold it. Gunmetal Gray's involved?"

"Yeah, she knocked loose a tooth before Al put my nose on the back of my head."

"Wait." Mrs. West squeezed. "You fought her? And survived? That's amazing."

"Not really. She only spared me because Scourge wanted Al to finish me clean."

"Still, Gunmetal Gray…" The old dame sat back and chewed on

the fat I just cooked up. Finally she said, "So Bundy's probably underground now, right?"

"Yeah. But I'll swing by North Point later anyway, see if I can't locate him. Maybe get some payback for the second suit he's damaged."

"If he's not there how will you find him?"

I thought about it. "Only two things can help, the chemical that burned Thermite, or maybe if I could find, and search, the place the boys lived for a clue. Not that I'm in any shape to do either." I tipped my hat over my face. I didn't want to say it out loud but my body felt like a bag of broken pottery.

"I'm certain you'll figure it out." Mrs. West got to her feet, and slid my hat off. And then, I kid you not, she laid both lips on my forehead.

I popped my peepers. "What was that?"

"A kiss."

"I didn't know you gave those out."

Putting her hands on her hips she smiled. "I know we don't get along, but you're a good egg. Harder boiled than most, and currently scrambled, but a good egg. Carl chose you well, former black cape helping people-"

"I don't help people, I-"

"Work cases. I know. But that can be the same thing sometimes. And maybe I'm too hard on you because of how much more time you two spent together, or how things worked out between him and me, but I want you to know, before I leave, that Carl chose the right man to keep this place going." Mrs. West walked to the door.

"Hey."

She stopped and looked at me.

"You got a lock of hair out of place."

Mrs. West winked. "We both know this bun's perfect. Now let me go get you some real booze. We'll say it's my going away present to you. In the meantime, lie down."

She left, and taking her advice, I kicked my feet onto the couch, and tipped my hat over my eyes. Truthfully, I was done for the day. And it was barely eleven. I needed some rest. So I closed my eyes. It took no time at all for the sleepy wet heavies to settle in.

But then, because fate has an extra large mean streak, my phone rang.

I glanced at it sideways from under my hat.

And the bells tolled again.

I willed them to stop. But they chimed twice more with no sign of fading, so I reached out and picked up the receiver. "Hello?"

"You're supposed to say 'Dane Curse Detective Agency.'"

"Monday?" I said. "You out of the hospital yet?"

"They're discharging me now."

"So they got a free room?"

"They do," he said, "but how about an adventure instead?"

"I'm still sore from my last one."

"Sorry to hear it. I guess that means you don't want to follow up on the accelerant we found on that thumb. Turns out it's a rare chemical called nitro-tri-phosphorus. And only three places in town are licensed to sell, store, or produce it."

I sat up and pushed my hat back. "Just three? You're sure?"

"Just three. Now come on," Monday said, "you want to go shake some trees?"

Truthfully I wanted to crash on the sofa and sleep until my body knit itself back together. But there was no time to rest. No time to heal. I had things to do, and those things didn't include waiting around for Scourge or Gunmetal Gray to come find me. Instead I had the chance to find them, and the person paying their fee. And this time I'd truly have the advantage of surprise.

"Shake some trees?" I said. "No. I'm going to uproot them. Now make sure your car's got a siren and pick me up."

"Good man. I'll swing by your office in thirty minutes."

Pushing down the pain from my beating I stood up and grabbed my coat. "Make it ten."

Chapter 29

Scooping up all my tools I went downstairs to wait for Monday. He arrived fifteen minutes later in a white sedan. I slid into the passenger side and said, "The Ritz, and step lively."

Monday pulled into traffic. "You weren't kidding about that hospital bed. What happened?"

For obvious reasons I kept the dance with Al to myself. "Fell down some stairs."

"What, all of them?"

"No." I laughed. It hurt. "Anyway, I'm surprised you're free. I thought for sure you'd be investigating the whole Mayor Greenie thing."

"There's enough cops on that beat."

"Any leads yet?"

"I hear the only thing they got is that picture, and the fake name she used on the catering sign in sheet."

"Interesting."

"Not really. Let's focus on the task at hand. Here." Monday pulled a piece of paper from his jacket. "I got it from the Center for Biotechnology and Information. They're the spots that have nitro-tri-phosphorus."

I took the sheet and read the names. "Chemi-Labs, Panier Solutions, and Allen-Fox. Who's first?"

"The furthest one out," Monday said. "Chemi-Labs."

Monday aimed our car east, and after thirty minutes of freeway cruising all the glittering buildings turned into rolling, green hills. A little further out and those hills melted down to flat fields. Past them, rocky outcrops grew into mountains. And finally, when Gold Coast City was so small it looked like a drop of mercury on green felt, we pulled up to Chemi-Labs, a six-story building made of dull glass and cement.

We walked into the lobby, past a few plastic plants, and up to a receptionist who could've passed for Mrs. West's mother. She gazed at us over her thick glasses. "You were expected twenty minutes ago, officers."

I said, "Then you should've opened this plant closer to town."

Monday pulled off his hat and stepped to her. "I'm sorry for the delay. We're here to meet with a representative from the chemicals department."

She looked at me before turning to Monday. "I'll show you to him." The lady stood up, led us down a long hall and into an office. "Pete, your twelve o'clock is here."

We walked into an artwork-free room where two chairs sat in front of a cheap desk. The man behind it had black hair, a thick mustache, and a white short sleeve dress shirt with no tie. As the secretary closed the door he said, "Hi guys, I'm Pedro Jimenez, but everyone here calls me Pete."

"Nice to meet you. I'm Detective Monday. This is Dane."

Pete smiled and motioned towards the chairs. "Please."

We parked and Pete said, "I'm sorry, but the person who contacted me was vague, what's this about exactly?"

"Earlier this week some nitro-tri-phosphorus was used in the commission of a crime," Monday said, "and since you're one of the few sources in town…"

"Ni-tri in a crime?" Pete leaned back and whistled. "That's interesting, but I guarantee it didn't come from us."

"How can you be so sure?" I asked.

"Because nitro-tri-phosphorus is one of the most volatile chemicals known. It takes a trained, experienced engineer just to keep it from igniting during transport, and none of our men have removed any in weeks. And if a layman did, well, you'd have heard the explosion. All the way in Oregon."

I said, "So you can't just skim some off the top with a spoon?"

"Uh, no," Pete said. "It requires a specialized level nine canister." He looked back and forth between us. "Tell you what, why don't I take you on a tour of our warehouse? That way you can get a better idea of how this stuff works, and why we aren't the source your looking for."

"Is that possible?" I said.

"Of course. And besides, you came all this way, we wouldn't want to bore you. Just give me one quick moment." Pete grabbed his phone. "Hi Stella, could you let the warehouse know I'm heading over there now for a ni-tri demo? Thanks." He hung up and said, "Follow me."

Pete led us from his office, down the hall, and outside. There was a cement walkway that hooked right, and led to a larger building with a silver door and a keypad. Pete swiped his ID across it and the readout turned green. Then he entered a six-digit code.

The door opened and we followed him into a small, silver cage. To our left, behind a pane of bulletproof glass, stood a security guard. He leaned over, pressed a button, and through the speaker said, "Name and purpose for visit."

Pete pressed his ID to the glass. "Pedro Jimenez, plus two for inspection."

The guard clicked off the mic, then grabbed his phone. After a terse exchange he nodded, hit a buzzer, and the door in front of us popped open. We walked through it and into a chilled, bright changing room that smelled like hospital soap. On one wall was a series of lockers, while on the other hung half a dozen HAZMAT suits and helmets. Pete pointed to them and said, "Put one of those on."

"Why?" I said.

"Because we're heading into an atmosphere that's nearly devoid of oxygen."

"Yay." I slid my suit on, careful to ensure I didn't snag it on anything, and once we were all geared up Pete led us to another door, and swiped his card over another pad. Just like outside it turned green and unlocked. He put the card in his breast pocket, and all three of us entered the chemical storage unit.

The place was big, and mostly made from stainless steel. On the far wall were five giant vats. Pete brought us to the one in the center. On it were dozens of red and yellow warning signs like it was some shiny, modern King Tut's tomb.

"This is it, our complete collection of ni-tri. See here?" He pointed at a slim line of glass that ran up the tank with different numbers marked off in red. "This is the gauge that tells us how much we have. And this." He pointed to a screen on its side. "This is who takes it out and when. A drop can't be removed without it being logged, and you'll notice nobody's gotten any in over a month."

I looked at the dates and the volumes. They matched up. "Would it be possible to switch out the liquid somehow?"

"Not from our tank. Watch." Pete swiped his card again, and entered his code on the pad. The nozzle hissed. There was a row of metal tubes hanging off the vat to our right. They were smaller than the one found at the crime scene, but otherwise fairly similar, and Pete plucked one. "Now we're ready to extract the liquid."

"You're going to do what?" I said.

"Come on now, I don't want to bore you." He pushed one end into the vat's nozzle, then gave it a half twist. The slim tube clicked, and the vat gave a quick blast, like it was trying to get my attention on the sly. Pete pulled it free, and the vat powered down. He pointed back to the gauge. "See, the nozzle and the indicator are linked, and it records my ID and the amount extracted. Now, follow me."

Pete led us to the center of the room where a table sat. On it was a silver thermos and a metal bar. Looking at me Pete said, "You hold the bar out, and I'll spray it."

"Whoa," Monday said. "Is that safe?"

"It'll be fine. That canister there is filled with a gas that'll kill the fire before it really gets going. You ready?"

I grabbed the bar and held it out. "Go for it."

Pete aimed the small metal vial at the iron bar. "Watch this." He clicked the button on its side and a mist sprayed out, lightly coating the end of the pole.

A few seconds passed.

Nothing happened.

Then a few more ticked by.

I pulled the rod up to my face for a closer look.

"No." Pete stepped forward right as the steel burst into blue and orange flames. A wave of heat passed through my suit and I smelled plastic burning as Pete grabbed the bar and held it as far from himself as possible.

"Damn that was hot." I looked at my hands. "Am I on fire?"

Pete looked me over. "No. We're just a little singed."

"Thanks," I said.

"No problem. But look." The metal bar he held was burning like an Olympic torch, its tip engulfed in flames.

"Amazing," Monday said.

Pete nodded. "And how. You want to hand me that thermos?"

Monday grabbed it from the table and passed it over.

Pete traded him the vial of ni-tri for the thick canister, then pointed it at the glowing metal and pressed a button on its side. A white gas flowed from its end, covering the fire and killing it like bleach on daffodils. Then he placed both the rod and the container on the table.

"So that's that." Pete turned to us. "Ready to go?"

Monday held up the vial of ni-tri. "I'd like to look at this for a moment."

"Sure. When you're finished just put it with the rest."

Monday studied his new toy as I walked towards the exit with Pete.

"What exactly was in the spray?" I said.

"Argon. Inert gasses kill the flames. It's what's in our atmosphere right now."

I thought it over. "How come the iron burned in the first place?"

"The low percentage of oxygen in the air isn't enough to completely quash the fire, but it does weaken it significantly. Now if the ni-tri was in an oxygen rich room that reaction would've been ten times as powerful."

"Really?"

"Oh yeah. That's why this place gets flooded with argon in case of an earthquake."

"Makes sense, one big ruckus and it'd burn like a candle."

"A candle? If one of these vats went up it would be on par with Hiroshima. That's why when you remove it you need a grade nine container."

"Like that vial." I nodded back towards Monday.

"No, that's a grade six."

"Six?" The hairs on the back of my neck all jumped up. "Is that safe?"

Pete chuckled. "Not outside. Not even a little bit. But in here, it's fine."

"So whoever used the ni-tri in our crime had to know what they were doing?"

"That's correct. It can't be safely handled by just anybody."

"Thanks for the tip. Hey Monday, you ready?"

The cop was at the table, holding up the metal bar. "Yeah, let's motor."

Pete grabbed the knob and pulled the door open, and all three of us walked back into the locker room. Then the seal shut and Pete said, "Go ahead and disrobe, it's safe."

I unzipped my suit and stepped out of it.

Pete did the same. "So where's your next spot? You must be

going to-" He stopped and stared at Monday with huge eyes. "Don't. Move."

Monday had his front zipper halfway down. "What's up?"

I looked over and froze. Inside Monday's breast pocket was the vial of ni-tri.

He looked down. "Damn it. I think I just slid it in there, force-"

"We got to get it back inside right now." Pete snatched the thin canister and sprinted to the storage room's entrance. He ran his keycard over the pad. But it glowed red. "What the hell?" He tried again. But the screen kept its crimson gaze.

"What's the problem?" Monday said.

Pete spun around. The cool middle manager demeanor was replaced with a look of terror. "My key card. Its magnetic strip was damaged by the heat."

"So?" Monday said. "I thought a grade nine container could hold it safely."

"That's a grade six," I said. "It's safe inside the lab, but not out here."

Monday's smile melted off. "What do we do?"

"We have to get this outside," Pete said, "and as far away from here as possible."

"So open the exit already," I said.

"My card's not working."

I pointed at the exit. "Try anyway."

Pete charged to the door that led to security. And ran his card over the lock. It glowed the same reddish hue as the one to the lab. "I told you, we're locked in." Pete lashed out and hit the large, red button on the wall. The lights flashed above us. A loud siren screamed.

"No we're not." I pulled out Lois. "Stand aside."

"What's that shoot?" Pete said.

"Hot light."

"Don't. An energy blast inside here could be just as bad as the ni-tri igniting."

"Fine." Sliding my pistol back home I threw a shoulder into the door. And bounced back. Then I grabbed the knob and pulled.

"That lock can handle ten tons," Pete said.

Monday said, "It was an accident."

I punched the door. Again and again. Without leaving a dent.

"Don't worry about it," I said. "We're getting out of here."

"No," Pete said. "We're going to die."

Chapter 30

"Maybe," I said, "but not today. Quick, what's the difference between that vial and the grade nine type?"

Pete searched his memory. "The metal, the casing, the gas intake-"

"That last one," I said. "Explain."

"Grade nine pushes the chemical out with internal pressure. This vial, when it sprays, exchanges gas with the atmosphere as it clicks off. And since ni-tri ignites in oxygen…"

"So if I cover the nozzle after I spray it?"

"Impossible," Pete said. "It'll take a couple hundred pounds of force to-"

"Got it." I snatched the vial, aimed it at the lock, and sprayed a stream of ni-tri on it.

"No!" Pete ducked down and covered his head.

I capped the tip with my thumb, then clicked it off. And the vial stayed whole. But the lock burst into orange and blue flames. Along with my thumb.

It was like someone drilling through the bone. There was no time to cry about it though, because the lock melted and fell to the ground. I kicked the door open and ran into the next room. Sirens were screaming all around as red lights flashed. The guard was gone. But he left the exit open. I charged through it. Drew the vial way back. And with my thumb still smoldering I threw the ni-tri as hard as I could.

The metal tube sailed through the air.

And it exploded.

A wall of fire came rushing at me. Orange, red, and roiling, it hit like a wave. Everything on my body turned hot as I flew through the air. And back into the building. Monday slammed the door. The flames hit it hard, and shook the walls. While all three of us froze, waiting for the second explosion that would end our lives.

But it never came.

Pete opened the door and walked outside. "How did you… That was amazing."

I joined him. "Thanks."

Then Monday came out. "Great toss, Dane. Sorry about that. It was-"

"If you say force of habit," I said, "I'm going to slug you."

The cop nodded. "Anyway, sorry Pete."

I threw my arm around our host's shoulder and pulled him to me. "It's no biggie. After all, it's not like we were bored."

#

Pete led us to our car without another word, and we headed back to the city. It took about forty minutes to hit the Welcome To Gold Coast City sign that's painted with twenty-four carat dust, and fifteen minutes after that we were in front of the giant silver donut that housed Panier Solutions.

Its lobby was as wide as an airplane hanger, and smelled clean like mountain air. It was also empty, save for some leather sofas, and the reception desk, which was a large semi-circle built into the far wall. Inside it were three smartly dressed kids, and a thirty-foot statue of twin winged women.

As we neared it, one of the receptionists, a blond girl in a black suit, smiled at us like she was hawking toothpaste. "Good afternoon, gentlemen."

Monday pulled his badge. "I'm here to speak wi-"

"Oh yes, I know. Vice President Spinner. We were informed you'd be coming." Her smile may've stayed bright, but it got a bit brittle as she motioned to the closest leather sectional. "Please take a seat, the VP will be here shortly."

Monday said, "How long until he gets here?"

And her brittle smile dimmed some. "I'm sure Ms. Spinner won't be long."

"Got it," I said. "Thanks."

We walked over and plopped down on the couch. I grabbed the nearest magazine, but barely got past the second page when a woman said, "You're the detectives, yes? I'm Laura Spinner."

The VP stood a few feet away looking down at me with something less than respect. Her soft, dark skin matched her long, black tresses, and whoever cut the green suit she had on tailored it in such a way that it inspired wicked thoughts, but then judged you harsh for having them.

The cop jumped to his feet. "Thank you for seeing us. I'm Detective Monday and this is Dane."

I sat back and crossed my legs.

She cocked an eyebrow at me before turning to Monday. "My office told me this was about a recent theft involving nitro-tri-phosphorus."

"It is," he said.

"Then this will be a short meeting. We haven't had any here for some time."

"But the Center for Biotech and Information said-"

"The CBI is not mistaken. But early last year we ceased its production and transported all of our stock to the facilities in Mexico."

"Old or new?" I said.

Spinner kept her eyes on the cop. "Old."

Monday said, "Who oversaw transport?"

"Myself."

"And how can you be sure that none went missing?" I said.

"Since we crossed the border with a volatile substance we dealt with auditors from two Federal governments." She held up a folio. "You can check all three of our reports. Now, is there anything else?"

"Nothing," Monday said, taking the folder.

I nodded. "Thanks for your time."

We took the long trek back across the lobby, and when we finally got to Monday's car he said, "That was quick."

"But do you believe her?"

He looked down at the folder. "I find governments and companies all make mistakes. But I doubt these three would all make the same one."

"Agreed," I said. "So Chemi and Panier are off the hook."

"Yep. But we still have Allen-Fox." Monday opened his door and slid behind the wheel.

But I stood my ground. And stared at the big, silver building. Fighting the urge to grab my guns.

Monday got out, and looked over the roof at me. "We going?"

"In a second," I said.

"What're you looking at?"

"Can you see the reflection of that blue soccer mom SUV? The one in the upper parking lot?"

Monday didn't move his head. "Yeah."

"I think that's the bastard who tried to kill us yesterday."

"Are you serious?" Monday's eyes clicked over. "But you said Scourge drove a black pickup."

"He did. But as we slid down Hillimanjaro I tore a piece off its bumper, which is the exact same damage I saw on a red truck he used to run me down this morning. And it's the same on that SUV up there."

Monday snapped to me. "This morning? Is that what happened to your face? Why didn't you mention it earlier?"

"Because… it's not important. Now I'm telling you, that truck can change its color and shift its hide, and if we look in it we'll find our killer."

Monday gave it some thought. "Ok. Let's go get him. But you don't make a move until I do, got it?"

"I promise."

We got into our car and drove towards the compound's exit. There was only one road out, and on it, about twenty yards ahead, was a left turn that led to the upper parking lot. At the last second Monday turned up it, and gunned the engine.

But the SUV stayed put.

Monday pulled behind it and stopped. He hopped out and held up his badge. "Police, don't move."

And still, the SUV just sat there. As did the two people inside.

Creeping towards the front of the vehicle Monday put a hand on his pistol.

Then the blue vehicle roared to life. It drove forward, over the parking block, and bombed down the grassy hill towards the building.

I jumped out of the car. "I knew it."

The SUV hit the lower lot we'd just come from and turned towards the exit.

I pulled Rico, aimed over our hood, and fired a high-velocity slug. It bounced off Scourge's rear window.

"Stop shooting," Monday said.

"Ok." I ran around the back of our car.

Scourge was now out of the lower lot and rocketing towards the exit. I fired off a target seeker at his front tire. But despite it hitting dead center the vehicle kept rolling.

"What're you doing?" Monday yelled. "I said stop."

"I know." I replaced Rico and pulled out Lois. Clicking off the safety my Kapowitzer doubled in size and glowed green. I depressed the trigger halfway and twin ribbons whipped out from the handle, crisscrossing down my arm.

"What the hell is that?" Monday asked.

"Retribution." I aimed at the truck's engine. And pulled the trigger.

As Monday tackled me.

The discharge was loud. The blast, bright. Lois' kick sent me flying back. I landed flat, and when the spots vanished from my eyes I could see I was lying on the street, with Monday on top of me. Below us Scourge was almost at the gate.

"Why'd you do that?" I shoved Monday off and got up.

He staggered to his feet. "You blast them with a God damn Kapowitzer and we'll both end up in jail."

Lois was now glowing red. I knew how she felt. "Jail? Performing jail worthy acts is a part of my business model." I holstered my gun, then slid behind the wheel, and slammed the door as Scourge crashed through the front gate's wooden arm. "Come on, we're losing him."

Monday grabbed the handle. "Move over, I'm driving."

"Not this time." Reaching through the window I snatched his collar. I pulled him in, head first, and tossed him onto the passenger's side.

Then I gave chase.

Chapter 31

For an SUV, the black-then-red-now-blue beast was moving swift. But thanks to my heavy foot we were only seconds behind it when our white sedan rocketed out the busted gate. Scourge had put some distance between us though, and about a half dozen cars occupied it.

"I'll grab the screamer." Monday opened the glove box, pulled out a siren, and fixed it to the roof. The thing let out a banshee's wail, and those vehicles that separated us from our target moved aside.

"Here we come," I said as we passed the last car and got on Scourge's tail.

Monday said, "How're we getting them off the road?"

I held up Rico in my right hand. "I can start throwing more harpoons any time."

"Don't," Monday said. "Unless you can guarantee you won't hit any citizens."

I put the pistol out the window, aimed at the sky, and fired off five shots.

"What are you doing?" Monday said. "We're-"

All five slugs cut a wide arc in the air, turned towards the SUV, and bounced off its side. "Those are target seekers. The first in each clip has a homing tracer the rest follow. Not like they did any good."

Monday looked impressed. "What else you got loaded?"

"Explosive and high-velocity. But they just fly straight."

He looked at my piece. Then scanned ahead. "Go for it."

I leaned out the window far enough to aim with my right hand while still holding the wheel with my left. It was awkward, but I was going to make it work. Clamping one eye closed I lined up Scourge's rear windshield with my muzzle real nice.

But he veered right. And clipped a station wagon. The smaller car fishtailed left. Then spun to a sideways stop in the middle of the road. I slid back into the driver's seat, dropped Rico on my lap, and jerked the wheel to the right. We missed the wagon by inches as our back end pulled out too far. We squealed sideways. I jammed on the gas and forced us back on course. Though now Scourge was further out.

"You're losing him, I'm calling in backup." Monday grabbed his radio. "Dispatch, this is Detective Monday, I'm… wait." He released the transmitter. "Are they slowing down?"

I looked ahead. Monday was right. The blue SUV was easing off the gas.

We closed the gap quick and got right on its rear. But then its back window slid down. And out poked a black rod.

"What the hell is that?" Monday said.

A pipe? Maybe a- "It's a cannon, get down!"

The muzzle let fly a full dose of lead. Monday ducked as the slugs ripped a dozen round holes through our windshield and shredded his headrest.

"Son of a bitch." Staying low the cop barked into his squawker. "Dispatch, this is Detective Monday. I'm in pursuit of a blue SUV on Palladium road, heading west into the city. The suspect has opened fire. Request immediate backup."

The dispatcher came back with, "Roger that, backup on the way."

The cannon fired a fresh round of bullets. They punched a crooked line across our hood. Thick, dark smoke seeped out each hole. The cloud blocked the windshield. I couldn't see through it.

"Not good," I said. "It's time we go on the offensive. Take the wheel."

"On it." Monday reached over and held it steady, then peeked over the dash.

With a heavy foot on the gas I pushed myself out the window until everything above my belt was hanging in the breeze.

The cannon turned to me. It loosed more rounds. Two whizzed past my right ear. The third hit my shoulder. "God damn it."

"You ok?" Monday said.

"Yeah," I said. "That and angry." Holding Rico steady I aimed at the cannon. But then the wind shifted, and the black smoke from our engine flowed my way. The smell of burnt motor oil choked my nostrils as the dark smog blocked my sight.

Monday yelled, "You going to shoot some more or what?"

"In a second." I cocked the pistol. "Just one second." And the wind shifted again, sending the smoke in the opposite direction. Now I could see the cannon clearly. Its Cyclops gaze was upon me. But I stared right back. And laid my sights straight down its maw. Then I pulled the trigger.

An explosion, bright and red, lit up the interior of the SUV. Scourge swerved right, then left, as smoke billowed out his rear window.

I slid back into the car, but left my head in the wind like a happy collie.

Monday sat up. "Nice shot."

I yelled, "Yeah, now how about doing something about this smoke?"

"Give me a second." Monday clicked open the heating vents in the backseat. The black cloud stopped seeping from the hood holes, and instead flowed directly from the engine into the rear of our car. I could see better now, but the air inside was getting thick, fast.

Monday said, "Now roll down-"

"Already on it." Without taking my eyes off the road I pulled my head back in, then aimed Rico behind me and blasted out our rear windshield. The dark, gathering cloud blew right out the hole, and into our wake.

Monday was glowering. "I was going to say roll down the windows."

"That's what I did."

"We'll discuss it later, look." Monday pointed ahead.

Scourge was pulling onto the crosstown expressway.

"I see him," I said, and followed his trail of smoke up the ramp.

And glory be, there was nearly no traffic, just five broad lanes of side-by-side room in which to maneuver. I floored the pedal again. Outside my window buildings were flying by. We were now inside the city proper.

"Go faster," Monday said.

I looked at the speedometer and the tachometer. It was three o'clock in both time zones. "This is as fast as it goes."

"Then how's he doing that?"

Monday was right to be amazed. Our speed was rubbing up on triple digits like a buzzy showgirl on a diamond dealer, but the blue SUV, a much larger and clearly armored vehicle, was putting distance between us, and not the kind you measure in inches.

"Never mind," he said, "it doesn't matter. Backup's arrived." On the other side of the highway, coming our way fast, were a pair of black and whites. They slammed on their brakes and pulled a U-turn through a gap in the dividers. We passed by them in a blur, but since they were GCCPD cruisers they caught us up fast, and whipped by in pursuit.

"Now we got the advantage," Monday said.

"How do you figure?"

"There's power in numbers."

Glancing at Monday I said, "I've never found that to be true."

Ahead, one of the cruisers pulled up on Scourge's left, while the other took the right, flanking him in. But then, Gunmetal leaned out of the SUV's rear driver's side window. She extended her arm and sent a bolt of red lightning into the cop car there. Its engine erupted, flipping the vehicle sideways onto its roof.

Gunmetal then slipped back in, and popped out of the other side. She tossed another bolt into the remaining cop car. It exploded too, then rolled to a stop.

As we zipped past the smoking wrecks I looked at Monday. "You were saying?"

"Never mind," he said. "They're getting off."

Scourge got into the right lane and disappeared down the exit ramp.

"That's residential," Monday said. "What's he thinking?"

"He's thinking he's going to switch the car's exterior and get lost in traffic." I moved to the right to follow them down. It took a few seconds to get there, and by the time we were at the top of the ramp Scourge was already at the bottom, turning right.

Monday snatched his radio. "Dispatch, the blue SUV is taking the Strontium Avenue off-ramp, we-"

"It's not going to be a blue SUV for long," I said.

Monday turned to me. "Yeah, but what am I supposed to tell them to look for? Any car of any color?"

"Anything with a busted bumper that's blowing smoke."

The radio chattered, "Detective Monday, come back. We're looking for a blue SUV on Strontium, correct?"

Monday stared at me. "That's correct. Or any vehicle with a..." He rubbed his face. "Busted bumper that's also trailing smoke."

"Repeat?" the radio said. "Any vehicle-"

"Yeah," Monday said. "You heard right."

"Copy that." The dispatcher's eye roll was practically audible. "All units be on the lookout for a blue SUV on Strontium. Or any vehicle at all with a damaged bumper emitting smoke."

We hit the bottom of the ramp and turned right. Strontium Avenue had way more cars than the turnpike. But it only had two lanes, both going the same way, and there wasn't a single side street to hide down.

The cars ahead of me heard our siren and pulled over. I gunned it past them.

Then Monday said, "Son of a bitch. I don't believe it."

And neither did I.

Blocking both lanes were three parked cop cars. Standing in front of them were six officers with their guns pointed at a blue SUV that had stopped in the middle of the road. And it was spitting smoke from its tail.

"They got him," Monday said.

I pulled to a stop and we jumped out.

Monday drew his gun. "Gold Coast Police. Vacate the vehicle with your hands high."

I yanked out Rico and Lois. My Thumper's hammer stood poised to strike while the Kapowitzer was looking froggy and bound to my bones. And neither one was shaky. They were steady floating, ready to deal out doom to Scourge and Gunmetal before either one had a chance to shoot me a nasty look.

Then the driver's door opened.

"Hands up," a cop on the far side yelled.

"Stand fast," I said.

Scourge slipped one leg out. Then the other. And he stepped away from the vehicle.

I lowered my hardware. "What the hell?"

Monday said, "I don't think that's Scourge."

And he was right.

The driver was standing there, with his hands up, in a green sweater and tan slacks. And he was clearly Asian. Behind him the back door opened and a little girl got out. Throwing both arms around her daddy, she plunged her face into his side.

"Son of a bitch." I powered down Lois and slipped her and Rico into their holsters.

"Get on the ground," one of the cops yelled. "Now." He charged forward.

I moved to intercept.

The cop ignored me and leapt at the duo like an angry jungle cat. Reaching out I snatched his belt and jerked him back.

Dangling in my hand like a suitcase he said, "Release me now."

I said, "You sound a lot like Officer Heralds."

Another cop with chevrons on his shoulder ran around the auto and aimed his piece at me. "Hands up."

I looked at him. And didn't move.

"Stand down." Monday had his badge up high. "All of you. These aren't the perps, and he's with me."

"Got that, Sarge? Now catch." I tossed the cop to him, then turned to the civilian. "You. What just happened?"

The Asian pop held his kid close. "We were... we were parked at the light when a crazy truck drove by and shot up our car. I thought we were dead for sure, but then the police arrived and we-"

"Yeah yeah, I got it." I looked at the SUV. Scourge laid the holes perfect. They were blowing as much black smoke as the ones he put in ours.

"What kind of truck was it?" Monday said. "I'll put out an APB."

The guy looked at him. "Sorry. I was too busy praying to notice."

Monday stared at the guy. Then he looked at the closest boy blue. "Officer, get their statements. Dane, let's go."

As we walked back to our car Sarge called out, "Monday. Consistency's only a virtue if you get the right guy."

I turned around and walked towards him. "Keep waggling that tongue and I'll use it to shine my shoes."

He stepped back. "Easy big fellow. If you're working with Monday you'll need a better sense of humor."

Monday said, "Dane."

I spun his way.

"Let's go."

I turned back to Sarge, gave him two stink eyes, then headed to Monday's car. He was already behind the wheel when I slid in and said, "What'd the law hog mean by that?"

"It's nothing."

I slammed my door.

Monday pulled away and said, "You realize Scourge's been tailing us for two days now, right?"

"Yeah."

"You know why exactly?"

"Let's find out who got him the ni-tri," I said, "and then we can ask him directly."

Chapter 32

Allen-Fox's office took up three of the topmost floors in one of City Centre's sky scratchers, and like the last two stops it had a helpful receptionist who pointed us to their representative, Mr. Errol. He was a silver haired man behind a walnut desk sporting Italian cotton from his shoulders to his shoes. And while the room was clearly decorated with a hefty corporate budget, the most expensive thing in it was Errol's rich man's expression, the kind he thought would protect him from the rest of the world. "Gentlemen," he said with a gleaming smile, "please, have a seat."

Of course Monday obliged.

But I remained standing.

"Thanks for seeing us," Monday said. "I trust you know why we're here."

"I do," he said. "This is about stolen nitro... something."

"Nitro-tri-phosphorus," Monday said.

"Yes. That's correct. We produce and store it. But our entire stock lies in the facility in North Dakota."

My heart dropped. "North Dakota?"

"Yes. And I can assure you, it's quite safe."

I said, "When did you last ship any to the city?"

"Gold Coast? Never. There's not much use for it within a populated area like this."

Monday looked to me, then to Errol. "Where's the closest location you've delivered to?"

Errol turned to his computer and typed in a few words. "Vancouver. About one month back."

"Canada," I said. "Great."

"Could some have been stolen from that shipment?" Monday said.

"I seriously doubt it. Our technicians are very careful, and in order to syphon any off, the thief would have to be extremely knowledgeable in chemistry. That particular compound is very-"

"Volatile," I said. "Yeah, we're aware."

Monday said, "Can you send me a list of everyone in your company who has access to that plant?"

"Of course, but that'll take days to compile. Hundreds of workers are stationed there, but I'll send it over when it's done. Is there anything else I can help you with?" He looked back and forth between the two of us.

"I suppose not," Monday said.

"Glad to hear it," Errol said. "Have a good day."

The cop left. I stayed for a second, and stared at the wealthy man. I wanted to grind him into paste. But not because I thought he was a liar. So I followed Monday to the elevator. He pressed the down button and a few seconds later the doors slid open. We stepped in, and began our long descent.

"Do you believe him?" Monday said.

"I don't think he was lying, but he's probably wrong. Of all those we talked to today he seemed the least plugged in. If we want to be certain though, you could subpoena all his records."

"Oh, I will. But that's going to take a week, at least. There're parking violations that'll take precedence over running that kind of interstate paperwork for black cape bodies."

"We could always swing by the Badlands."

Monday said, "I don't have jurisdiction."

"And I don't need it."

"So when're you leaving?"

I studied my loafers. "I'm not. Even if I could comb through their whole warehouse it would probably take forever to find the man who pinched that juice."

The elevator kept sinking, faster than my hopes, and I was deep in gloomy thoughts when we stopped on the twentieth floor. Its doors opened and a young man, all smart and clean cut, got in. Behind him, on the wall, was a name I'd seen before.

"Hold it." I shoved the kid aside, grabbed a sliding door, and pushed it open.

"What's wrong?" Monday said.

I pointed at the big, beautiful logo. "Stronghold."

"What?" Monday said.

The kid turned to me. "Hey, I got a very important-"

"You work here?"

He looked me up and down. "What's it to you?"

I grabbed his tie and lifted him up until he dangled. "You guys ever do any deals with Allen-Fox up on the fortieth?"

He grabbed his tie tight. "Jeezus pal, let me go, I can't breathe."

"If that were true you couldn't speak. Now answer my question."

The kid stopped fussing and said, "Ok. Yeah. We do a lot of work for A-F."

"Thanks." I tossed him against the back wall and stepped off the elevator. "Monday, head downstairs and start the car."

He motioned to the kid. "What's this all about?"

"I'm just shaking some trees."

"And what're you going to do now?"

The door was already closing when I said, "Uproot them."

Chapter 33

I kicked in Mr. Errol's door.

He jumped up from his desk. "What's the meaning of this?"

Crossing the room I said, "Why didn't you mention Margaret Shelly?"

Errol had that indignant look rich guys get. "I'm sure I don't know what you mean."

"Just tell me, when did she work for you?"

"Margaret?" He tapped his chin a few times to let me know he was thinking. "Years now. She was the project manager for a number of our plants."

I reached over that walnut desk, wrapped my claw around Errol's throat, and dragged him to me. Then, holding the VP an inch from my face, I said, "Listen pal, if I thought you were swell, I'd still break you in two for jerking me around, and Errol, I don't like you one bit, so I'm going to ask some questions, and if you don't answer them, I'm going to hurl you through that glass like a cannonball."

"That glass?" The smug around his sneer was so thick it looked like day old stubble. "It's shatterproof."

"Shatterproof? You don't say?" Lugging Errol to the window I jabbed the pane with my free hand. It burst through easy. I grabbed the jagged edge and pulled the whole thing inside.

Cold, fierce wind rushed into the manicured office. Papers whipped around. Over the din I said, "Now, what did Margaret Shelly do for your company?"

Despite the sudden drop in temp Errol was sweating. He clawed at my hand, and scraped his heels against the expensive rug, anything to put some distance between us.

"Stop that," I said. "You're not going anywhere."

"But you can't do this, you're the police."

"Sorry, no shield here." I pulled back my jacket, exposing Lois. "Just a heavy sword and a heart that would swell at the sound of you smacking concrete. So answer quick before I hurl you like a frisbee."

Errol glanced out the window, then at me. And finally, there was respect. Sure, it was the kind that only comes from fear, but I'd take it. "Margaret Shelly was head of our compound project."

"So she did security?"

"Security? No. More like asset protection, she-"

I pushed Errol out the window. And grabbed his tie as he leaned way back. He snatched my wrist, and looked over his shoulder at the long drop. "No. Don't let go."

"Then don't get wise."

"I'm not, I'm not. Security is the manpower onsite, Margaret designed the facility itself. Created the safeguards. She was the chief architect on how to protect our most valuable assets."

"Has she been in contact with you since?"

"Of course. She runs annual audits on everything. The last one was two weeks ago."

I pulled Errol back in and tossed him onto the brown, leather couch. "You're telling me that Margaret Shelly was at your plant recently, and she's in charge of protecting your stockpile of nitro-tri-phosphorus?"

He blundered down the sofa backwards, but stopped when he hit the armrest. "Yes. Of course. Who else would?"

I rubbed my jaw. "Brother, anybody would've been a better choice."

"That's not true."

"What's that mean?" I lunged at Errol.

He flinched, and cowered behind his hands. "I'm sorry, nothing, it means nothing."

I loosened up some. Errol was seconds from jabbering away with what he thought I wanted to hear, and that was never a good way to get to the truth. So I laid a gentle hand on his shoulder and said, "Relax. I'm sorry I almost threw you out the window. But I'm calmer now, and I promise, you're safe. Just tell me why you think Shelly's the best choice."

Errol lowered his hands. And took a steadying breath. "Because. She's the expert in making hard to access buildings. Jewels, money, information…"

I said, "And chemicals?"

"Of course. She's done all the big spots. Napier, Franklin, that big job Chemi-Labs built in the mountains."

"And isn't that a thing?" I looked out Errol's window, taking in both the breeze and the view.

Margaret Shelly.

She was the last person the boys stole from. But that job got them hoosegow bound for five years. Was that not enough punishment to slake her lust for vengeance?

God damn scorned women.

Errol broke my train of thought. "I'm sorry, but did we do something wrong? Margaret Shelly's a respected member of the community, I'm sure this is a misunderstanding."

"No, it's not." I turned and walked towards the door. "And now she's going to jail for a five-year-old robbery."

"Oh," Errol said. "You mean the one that crippled her son."

That stopped me cold. "What did you say?"

Errol wasn't scared anymore. Just sort of sad. "When those men broke into her apartment they cut the gas lines, and when the walls sealed up they got out." He took a deep breath. "But her son did not. He was still there, trapped in his room."

"He died?" I asked.

"No. But the brain damage... Death probably would've been kinder."

"You're telling me that, because of those two thieves, her kid's in a hospital eating through a tube?"

"Yes. It was the teddy bear's nanny cam that caught the whole crime on film. How do you not know this?"

Because the damn Fletcher Act suppresses certain facts on black cape trials. "Don't worry about it. Thanks for the help." I turned to go. "And sorry about the window."

When I got down to the garage Monday was waiting by the car. "How'd it go?"

I said, "Call your dispatch, I need an address."

"On who?"

"The woman who murdered Firewall and Thermite."

I explained everything to Monday and he looked up the address, then we headed over to her condo with me marveling at her patience the whole way. Margaret Shelly. The boys break into her pad, steal her jewels, and harm her kid, so she waits over five years, and takes vengeance.

It was just like Mrs. West said, an impossible assassination.

And it made perfect sense. Bundy didn't have the dough and Scourge didn't have the knowhow to put this into play. But Margaret Shelly, she had both. Along with the greatest motive I could think of:

she'd lost a child. To a God damn flammable chemical. Just like the one used on Thermite and Firewall.

That's what the poets call justice.

But what the rest of us call murder.

Chapter 34

Like most buildings in this burg Margaret Shelly's condo was all steel and glass with a top so high it poked through the clouds. The doorman out front opened up for us and we took the elevator to her penthouse.

Monday pounded the door. "Police, open up."

But a full minute passed and our entry remained barred.

So once again he trounced and announced. Yet the gate stayed shut.

"My turn," I said.

Stooping down, I pulled out my lock pick, and slipped it into the brass knob. I fished it left. Then right. Up, then down. I wiggled and jimmied, and finally Monday said, "Having some trouble?"

"No." I straightened up. And punched the door. Its wood frame splintered as it popped open. "After you."

We walked in and Monday pointed to the kitchen. "You go that way, and be careful."

I pulled out Rico. "Why?"

"Are you serious?" The look of concern would seem out of place on most other cops. "This woman has access to chemicals that burned a flamer. Who knows what she's got on her now? And what she's willing to do with it to remain free. Hell, this whole place could be booby trapped."

I looked at the scorched spot on my thumb. Monday was right. This dame could have a slew of wretched liquids and gasses that would burn, poison, or melt my hide. I nodded, then began my search with a new sense of caution.

I started through the kitchen. It had no place to hide. So I kept going and hit the hall. Three doors ran down it. I got to the first, kicked it open, and aimed Rico inside. Beyond my pistol's sights were a wall of books, a glass desk, and two leather chairs. But no Margaret Shelly.

I moved to the second door, took a moment to focus, and lunged forward, throwing my shoulder into the wood. The oak seemed firm. But I flew through it like rice paper, stumbled a few feet through the dark room, and fell into a wall.

Hot liquid sprayed me. It covered my face like a mist, ran into my eyes, and up my nose. I scrambled backwards, clawing my way out of the room.

I screamed, "Monday. Help." Then I gagged. And wretched. *What was this? What was I covered in?* It burned. My flesh felt soggy, like it was flopping off my skull.

"What's wrong?" Monday said. "What happened?"

"Chemicals." I hacked. "I'm sprayed."

He clicked on the light. There was a long pause. Then, "Ha ha ha, open your eyes."

I did.

I was in the hallway, leaning against the wall. In front of me was the busted door. On the other side, a powder room. With a shower.

"This thing's got no dials, you hit the touchscreen." He pointed to a pad on the wall. "And the mist setting got you good. Lucky it wasn't set on oscillation. You could've lost an eye."

"Hilarious." I wiped my brow clean and stood up. "Did you find her?"

"Yeah. Turns out she's only three inches tall. I slipped her in my pocket so she could call her tiny attorney."

"And the jokes keep coming," I said. "Come on. Let's check the third room."

Monday led the way.

When we got to the last door I stood on one side while he took the other. Monday nodded. I turned the knob, and charged in.

And relaxed.

It was a storage closet.

"Damn," Monday said.

"Come on, let's go."

We walked back into the living room.

I said, "Now what should we- Don't move, lady!" I whipped my piece up and pointed it at the brunette who was now standing in the doorway.

"What're you doing here?" she said. "Get out before I call the police."

"Already here." Monday flashed his badge. "So keep still, Margaret."

"Margaret? I'm not Ms. Shelly. I'm the building's concierge."

"Of course you are," I said. "Where is she?"

She shook her head. "I can't be certain."

"Honey," I said, "you can be all hazy vague. Just talk."

The woman looked at me, then Monday. "I don't like to be indiscreet, but I believe she's visiting her son at the hospital."

"Which one?" Monday asked.

"Mineral Plains."

#

"Take the parkway, it's faster," I said.

Monday veered into the left lane and got on it. "You go to hospitals a lot?"

"Just this one."

Thanks to my topographical knowhow we got to Mineral Plains quick. Monday parked and we rushed in. He stopped at the front desk and hit the bell.

But I sprinted past him. "Follow me."

Monday got tight on my tail. "How do you know the way?"

"Look down," I said over my shoulder. "You see those colored lines? Each one leads to a different wing. The green goes to long term care." Which we got to in no time. Behind the nurse's station, in pink scrubs, was a small, bony gal.

"Hey Mabel," I said.

She looked up from her computer. "Dane. It's good to see you, Beatrice will be so-"

"No," I said, "I'm not... I have to see another patient. A young man by the name of Shelly."

"I know him," Mabel said, "but you're not family, I can't let you in."

"Which is why I brought this." I motioned to Monday.

He pulled his shield. "Police business. I need to see that patient."

"Alright," she said. "Robby's this way."

We followed her down the hall, past the vending machines, beyond the bathrooms, and right by room 244 with the chart that had the same name as mine, to find Robby Shelly. He was under a sheet with so many tubes and wires running out of him he could've been a surge protector.

"Where's his mom?" I asked.

"Margaret? She was here earlier." Mabel looked at her watch. "But she left about an hour and a half ago."

"You know where she went?" Monday asked.

"As a matter of fact I do." The tiny nurse beamed. "The airport. She's spending a few days in Brazil and then over to Mexico for a conference. But first she's going to Argentina. All on a private jet. I hope she enjoys it, that poor woman deserves a bit of fun."

"Argentina?" My heart dropped. "You're sure?"

"Positive. I think it's a work thing, though she didn't really say."

Monday's shoulders slumped. "Great." He turned and plodded out.

I stared at Robby. He looked handsome. Peaceful.

Mabel said, "So when are you going to see your mom? She's doesn't have much time left."

I looked down the hall and said, "Honestly Mabel, which one of us does?"

#

Monday and I went downstairs and took stock of the situation at a small table in the area they call a restaurant.

"So that's that," he said. "Again."

"But at least this time we got our man. I mean woman."

"Do we?"

"Yeah. It was Maggie Shelly. She has the money, access to the chemical, a rock solid motive, and probably intel on the Coconut's security system. She hires Bundy to lure the boys into Wentorf Hall with the promise of diamonds, and pays Scourge to kill them both in a way that makes it look like they did it to themselves. Then she runs to a non-extradition country. The whole thing wraps up watertight."

"I guess." Monday looked around. "Everything you say stands tall, but I don't know about the foundation. I'd like to see a money trail, or a confession. Anything that could pass as hard evidence of her guilt because as of right now I find this deeply unsatisfying."

I thought about what Monday said. Would Widow be satisfied with nobody punished, and no hard proof? Maybe. I know I wouldn't. Monday was right. It wasn't satisfying. "You know, this is my first solo case. I mean real case."

The cop looked me over. "Really? You wouldn't know."

"Well, I did a lot with my old mentor." I thought about Carl. About his agency. And about the black capes and their families who wouldn't be coming to it anymore. "I doubt he ever had one this disappointing."

"If he did this job for any length of time, I'm sure he did. Hell, I have."

I had nothing else to do but call Widow with the bad news, so I said, "Do tell."

Monday leaned back. "Years ago I caught this dead black cape on my beat. Shot in the back of the head while he knelt in Grime Alley. It was real gangland execution stuff, but the slug we pulled from his skull was police issued. All of a sudden nobody wanted to find the pistol that spat it, but I followed the trail back to a sergeant with the one-four who lost his brother to that same black cape. That gave me motive and means, but when it went to court-"

"Stop," I said. "You. Pressed charges? Against a cop? For killing a black cape?"

He looked at me, like I was sort of funny. "Of course. And it wasn't killing. It was murder. Anyway, all of a sudden the investigator that collected the evidence claimed she broke the chain of custody, so the perp walked."

"Wait. Are you talking about Mr. Boogety?"

Monday nodded.

I pushed my hat up. "Wow. No wonder you're so popular with the blue boys."

"That's the reason. And since we're talking taboo, the name on the chart up there, is that your mother?"

"It is."

"Sorry to hear it. How long does she have?"

"A month tops."

The cop gave me the socially acceptable silence before he pried. "So how can you afford this big ticket place?"

"If there are no further questions, my former profession provided me with a hefty savings which I passed over to this hospital, in full, for services they're currently rendering."

Monday opened his mouth. But kept his tongue still. Finally he said, "Well, I'm sorry to say it, but the time has come for us to go our separate." He extended his hand.

And for a second time I shook the cop's paw. "It's been real," I said. "Strange."

"Listen, take my number." He passed one of his cards over. "Loop me in if you need a hand in the future. I could always use a pair of ears on the wrong side of the law."

"I will," I said, "for the exact same reason."

Monday smiled. "Cute. Anyway, I'll see you-"

"Gentlemen?" A woman stopped next to our table. "You're the detectives, right? My concierge said you'd be here."

We both turned to her.

And I couldn't believe it. The middle aged brunette looked exactly like she did in the profile pictures I'd seen the night before. Only instead of a suit she was now in a maroon sweater and cream slacks. I said, "What're you doing here?"

"I heard you were looking for me," she said.

Monday looked between the two of us. "Who is this?"

I opened my mouth, which was drier than before, and said, "Detective Monday. Meet Margaret Shelly."

Chapter 35

It was Monday who broke the silence. "Hello Ms. Shelly. Yes, that's correct, we have been looking for you. Would you mind joining us?"

"Not at all." Margaret took a seat.

I said, "We wanted to ask you a few questions about Leonard Thebes and Tony Marcus, also known as-"

"Thermite and Firewall. I'm aware of the nature of this meeting. When I returned to my apartment the concierge explained everything. Though I must admit I expected you sooner."

"The nature of the crime," I said, "precluded a novice from pulling it off."

Her spine went chilly stiff like a double vodka up. "I'm no novice."

"I didn't mean to offend, but… We looked at the black cape community first."

"Probably a wise decision. But as we're finally speaking I'll tell you now what I'd have told you then, I didn't wish those two harm."

"I'm sorry," Monday said, "but you realize why that's so hard to believe."

"Of course. My son Robert was injured when they broke into my home." She pulled a kerchief from her purse that somehow looked more expensive than my shoes, and used it to clean a few tears away. "Tell me, do you have any children?"

Monday said, "No."

I said, "Yes."

Both guy and gal turned to me.

Margaret said, "Then you know. Killing those two wouldn't heal Robert. He'll never be healthy again, so their deaths would do nothing. For me, or my son."

"Forgive me," Monday said, "but if that happened to me, I'd want revenge. And even if-"

"Vengeance doesn't heal you," she said. "It just adds more corruption to the world. And besides, you can't ever truly get even. Not for something like this. How could you?"

I may've nodded, but like Monday, I wasn't sure. Doodle and I weren't close but I'd bash the head in of anybody who harmed her.

Though maybe Margaret had a point. Burning Leo and Tony wouldn't bring her boy back. And she seemed sincere. But like I said, I was unsure. "I'm sorry Margaret, I understand what you're saying, but they took everything from you and only got five years. That had to gnaw like a worm in your core. Hell, it's eating me, and I don't got mud against them."

Margaret reached into her purse and produced a stack of letters. "I brought these from home. See for yourself what kind of boys they were."

I passed half to Monday, then started reading mine. It contained what you'd expect from jailhouse letters: note after note of apologies, explanation, and regret.

But then the tone began to change.

Discussions on the afterlife seeped into one. The next talked about their future. About education. Thermite asked how he could use his gift without a cape. Now I'm not the softest touch in town, but I sensed an honest concern that lacked any undercurrent of self-gain. "Were you writing back?" I asked.

"Yes. Anthony reminded me of my older brother. He was a troubled youth as well, but straightened his life out. Which is why I was so surprised they tried to steal again. I can't imagine why they broke into the museum."

Ever the cop, Monday said, "Did you think they were writing these to get leniency?"

"I know they weren't because I offered to speak on their behalf at the parole hearings, but both declined. They were so torn up by what they'd done. They welcomed the punishment. I think that's why Tony stopped seeing his sister. He couldn't face her, not after what he'd done," Shelly said. "Sad, especially since it wasn't their fault."

"What?" Monday said.

"It wasn't their fault. What happened to Robert. It was mine. When I built the security system I altered the gas main's path, which was illegal of course. I also designed the shut-in protocol. Also illegal. Everything that protected my home was done below boards, and it certainly didn't appear on the blueprints those two used to prepare. And for what? Stones? I even kept Robert from seeing his father that weekend out of spite. Leonard and Tony may have broken in, but if I'd obeyed any number of laws, my son would be whole. It was stupid. I was stupid. It was-" She inhaled sharp, practically sucking the air from the room, and the sobs poured out of her like a quick, crashing wave. Margaret dropped her head into her hands, and shook.

I nodded to Monday.

He returned it.

Nobody would do what we thought she did, then come find us to talk about it. They definitely wouldn't weep real tears like a monsoon. So we waited out the storm. And when the torrent became a drizzle Monday said, "Thank you for your time, and I'm sorry for bringing all this back up. But we had to be sure."

Shelly wiped away the final tear. "Of course. I understand."

"Good. Then you'll also understand that I have to ask, where were you two nights ago?"

"Oh." She exhaled a long, drawn out breath, and transformed back to the executive she was. "Atlanta. There was a breakdown in one of our systems. Normally two technicians are on hand, but one's out with appendicitis and the other's on vacation, so I flew out personally. Contact Stronghold. They'll corroborate my itinerary. Though from what I gather, if I were involved, I'd probably be out of town to cement my alibi. Is that what you're thinking?"

"That's not what I'm thinking," I said.

"But it is very helpful," Monday said. "And I'll contact your office about it."

"Excellent. That way you can move me out of the suspect pile and find out who did this that much faster." She looked to Monday. "Now with that out of the way, can you tell me what the murderer used to burn Leonard and Tony?"

"You don't think they killed each other?" I said.

"I know they didn't. The chemical?"

Monday said, "It was nitro-tri-phosphorus."

"That would certainly do it. Have you traced its source?"

"No," Monday said. "We checked with-"

"Petey Jimenez over at Chemi-Labs, Laura Spinner at Panier?"

"Yeah," Monday said.

"Both outstanding executives. So now you must be on your way to Allen-Fox?"

"No," he said, "we just came from there."

I asked, "How do you know all this? I mean Stronghold doesn't work with chemicals, and those companies aren't on your profile."

"Stronghold? No. But if you'd checked my history with Chemical Storage Solutions you'd have seen them. CSS is owned by Stronghold's parent corporation, and my work there is kept separate. For tax purposes." Shelly smiled. "But back to the case at hand. I'm confused. If the killer wanted to make it look like they murdered each other, then why did they have the ni-tri in the first place?"

"To burn through the Kessel Glass," I said.

Margaret shook her head. "That wouldn't work."

"What?" Monday said. "I saw that stuff burn steel. Not melt, burn."

"Oh yes. And while Kessel Glass is stronger than steel, it would burn too. If," she said, "the ni-tri could pool on it. But as you know the display is vertical, therefore it would run off like rain on a windshield before it could work."

"So," I said, "if there was no way to get to the diamond then it couldn't have been a burglary. That means-"

Shelly's mouth opened. But nothing came out.

"What?" I said.

"It's…" She took a deep breath. "Listen, I don't like talking about this, but I've worked with Alice Johan."

"The curator that got blown up?"

"Yes. Another sad moment in her life, poor woman, but she's why I know a little something about Wentorf Hall, and you're wrong. There is a way to get behind the display."

"How?" Monday said.

"The Kessel Glass can be moved. If Anthony accessed the panel on the wall he could've slipped it out of the way."

"Slip the glass out of the way?" I said.

"Why would anyone put that in?" Monday asked.

"Mostly to access the gems in case of an earthquake, but also for a much more practical reason. Every two weeks Alice audits the stones with a team of insurance and law enforcement agents. In order to do that, the glass must be moved."

"So a thief could just slide it out of the way," Monday said.

"Not really. The Kessel Glass is five tons, and it's attached to a precise pulley system that only has enough power to lift it two inches an hour, so once it's activated it takes about half a day to expand enough for the diamond to be removed."

"Which means they'd still be waiting when the morning crew arrived," Monday said.

"Swell," I said. "So the killer would have to be light enough to tread the pressure sensitive tiles, small enough to fit through the laser light show, and strong enough to heft five tons." I thought of who it could be. Swamp could turn to liquid, his boy Vec was mighty strong, Gunmetal was electric poison, and Scourge was crafty. None of them could've escorted Firewall to the control panel, alone or together. "This seems impossible."

"No one said being a detective was easy," Shelly said.

I glanced her way. When I saw her picture last night I had a feeling we'd have nothing in common. I was right. We didn't. But I wouldn't have guessed that I'd like her this much.

"Well, thanks for your help, Ms. Shelly," Monday said. "If there's anything else we'll contact you."

I said, "And sorry about the door."

"Don't give it a second thought. But in case you do wish to speak again here's my direct line." She pulled out a card and passed it to me. Then she got up. "Oh, and is Toby back yet? I heard he'd taken a few personal weeks. I was concerned it might be health related."

"Toby?" Monday said. "Who's that?"

"The VP in charge of processing, sales, and transportation at Allen-Fox. You spoke with him, right?"

"We spoke to a guy named Errol," I said.

"Sam Errol?" Shelly laughed. "Errol's a good man, but he's also in charge of external relations. Which means he spins more than quality control at a dreidel factory. The man you need to talk with, the one who's in charge of the nitro-tri-phosphorus," she said, and slung her purse over her shoulder, "is Toby Teenie."

And the blood drained from my face. "Toby Teenie?"

"You know him?" Shelly said.

"I do." That God damn reg was my last client.

Chapter 36

Monday hung up his cell phone, and tossed it onto the dashboard. "It all checks out, Shelly was en route to Atlanta when the boys broke into the museum. And her finances are clean. If she paid a hefty sum for this crime she did it with a secret trick our fraud guys don't know."

"Of course it checks out," I said, and clicked my seatbelt. "She's clean."

"Yeah, that was a tight one-eighty you pulled inside. Why?"

"Because she looks so good for it. She's got a sexy motive, connections to the murder weapon, and even knowledge of Wentorf's security system. All she'd need is a weak alibi and you'd have enough circumstantial evidence to bring her up on charges."

"Detective Monday?" the police scanner barked. "We've got that information you requested. Toby Teenie's main residence is on thirty-four fifteen Smelter Road."

"Affirmative," Monday said. "Let's go." As we took off towards Toby's Monday said, "So how do you know this guy?"

"He was my last client," I said. "He was being blackmailed."

"By who?"

"He didn't know. All he had was an address where they showed him the pictures."

"Where was that?"

"Some crappy long term hotel."

"Maybe we should swing by there later."

"It was empty save for the safe, but maybe." Yeah, maybe. But probably not. I wasn't going to be seen in the muck drinking from the same bottle as a cop. I was unpopular enough with the black capes as it stood. "But let's hit Toby's place and see what he can tell us first."

About thirty minutes later we pulled up at Toby's spot on Smelter. It was a landed home, with a small yard and two stories that didn't run up on the neighbors. Nice for any city, but in Gold Coast you'd have to be pulling down a hefty six figures to hang your hat inside these walls. Which meant I should've charged him a higher fee.

We walked up to the door. Monday rang the bell and said, "Police."

There was no answer.

"Maybe he's gone," I said.

"Could be that-"

The sound of crashing glass came from inside.

I leaned over the stoop and looked through the window. There, in the middle of the dining room, was all three hundred pounds of Toby Teenie.

"Son of a bitch." I shoved Monday aside and kicked the door open. Then I ran in and stared down at my former client. "Hey Toby. Long time."

The little fat man was shaking like jello. "Hey Dane, guess you still haven't got the lock picking thing down, huh?"

"Can it. Who'd you give that nitro-tri-phosphorus to?"

"What?" He took a step back. "How do you... I don't know."

"Hear that Monday, he don't know."

Monday strode past me and pulled his handcuffs. "Fine by me. He can wag his tale at the booking sergeant. Toby Teenie, you're under arrest for the illegal transport and sale of a controlled substance. You have the right to remain silent."

"Wait, I had no choice." Toby walked backwards, stumbled over his own feet, and fell to the floor. He was breathing heavy, and sweating harder than when he had a Thompson waving at him a few nights back. "I was being blackmailed. All they wanted was a gallon of ni-tri. And I gave it to them."

"The sergeant's going to be so happy. He loves stories like this," Monday said. "You have the right to an attorney."

"No." Toby pointed one of his ten sausage links my way. "Ask him, he got the pictures back for me."

Monday turned to me and I said, "Yeah. But I didn't know he traded the ni-tri for them."

"So you sent them the juice," Monday said. "Was that it?"

"No. They started asking for more things. Explosives that could make it through metal detectors and fool sniffer dogs. I didn't want to be responsible for anything else, so I got ahold of you."

"Who?" Monday asked. "Who did you give the ni-tri to? What did he look like?"

"I never saw his face. But I know his name's Victor. I met him once when he showed me the pictures."

"You didn't hand him the ni-tri directly?"

"They had me send the canister to a shipping warehouse called North Point, but I got no clue where it went after that."

"North Point." I turned to Monday. "That's where Bundy Strong works."

"Let's go." Monday turned and left.

But I stopped. "Is there anything else?"

Toby looked up at me. "Yeah, I mean, it's… I told them to store it in inert gas for the maximum explosion. But that would actually stifle the blast. Not entirely, but, you know, pretty good. So I didn't just-"

"Inert?" I said. "Like helium?"

"Yeah, it's-"

"Thanks." I ran out the door. Firm in the knowledge that this was all wrapped up with Swamp. And his friend Vec. Was he the guy with the Thompson under the bridge? If so, he had telekinesis, not strength. But TK wouldn't help him cut the lasers at Wentorf Hall, so it didn't link them with the murder, only the tools the boys had, and the attempt on Mayor Greenie. I had the rotten feeling that this changed things very little. There was still someone in the middle of it all, pulling the strings.

"Bundy Strong," Monday said. He was standing next to his open car door. "That's who you're thinking."

"I am. But there might be someone else involved. We'll check it out after we locate Bundy."

"I doubt he's still at North Point."

"Let's go find out."

We put the miles behind us fast. But upon arrival we were greeted by an unfamiliar sight. The warehouse's gate was blocked by a police barricade and two uniformed officers. Beyond them were a bunch of vans.

"Hold up," the nearest cop said.

"What's going on here?" I asked.

"We're holding the perimeter. The Special Powers Extraction Commission have a perp trapped inside."

"Is it Bundy Strong?" Monday asked.

"No," the guy said. "It's the chick who tried to kill Mayor Greenie last night. They're about to go in and skin her alive."

Chapter 37

Doodle? What was my kid still doing in town? And why was she in North Point? Was she wrapped up with Bundy? What the hell was going on?

Monday said to the cop, "Move the blockade. We're going in."

"I wouldn't," he said, "unless you got some serious body armor."

Monday motioned towards me. "I do. Let's go."

The cop slid the barrier aside and we drove down to the lot where six vans were in a semi-circle. Five of them were black with the word SPEC written on their sides, but the last one was larger and red. It had walls lined with Trumite and was used to transport black capes to and from Impenetron. And I couldn't help but feel uneasy. That was a dragon wagon, and no black cape who'd ever been tossed in one came out of their own accord.

Monday parked behind it, and we hopped out to join the SPECs. They were all in black armor, with their rifles pointed inwards.

"Are they packing darts?" I said.

"The SPECs?" Monday said. "No. The blackguard may roll with viper vapor like us, but their bullets are all armor piercers. Commander Waters, what's the sit-rep?"

Waters turned around. "Monday. Great. We got a report on a young girl, brown hair, slight frame. Fits the description of Greenie's assassin. Now we're waiting on the water units. Once baywatch gets here we're going in with both balls swinging and taking that dumb bitch down."

I said, "She was smart enough to slip you guys last night."

Waters turned to me. His eyes got thin. "Who's the ogre?"

Monday said, "An investigator helping with gems."

"A diamond dick?" Waters said. "He looks familiar."

Maybe it was the tape across my nose, the black eye, or the bandaged cheek, but he couldn't place my mug, though I knew his. "I get that a lot."

"Yeah, I bet you-"

"Gunboats are in place," Waters' radio squawked. "You're go for assault."

Waters slapped his helmet down and turned to the rest of the

SPECs. "Team, on my six. Lethal force is a go. Capture if you can, but kill if you must."

The commandos yelled their assent and got behind their leader. Together they charged across the lot to the building, and lined up against the wall with their guns primed. Waters opened the door and peeked in. Then he slipped inside, and the rest of his men followed like a black asp sliding into a rabbit hole.

It would take a few minutes for them to find anything. I took that time to glance around the lot and get the lay of the land. And right behind us, sitting on a nearby hill maybe fifty yards away, was a black sedan with that same chunk missing from its front bumper. "Son of a bitch. Scourge."

Monday snapped his eyes off the building and put them on me. "Where?"

I motioned towards the car. "Up there."

"Well I'll be. Did he follow us here or was he already-"

Automatic fire burst from inside the warehouse. And three SPECs blew through the outer wall. They landed on the concrete rough and stayed still as more gunfire erupted from inside.

"That's my cue," I said.

"Wait," Monday yelled.

I charged across the lot, jumped over the three unconscious SPECs, then pounced through the hole they made.

And landed in the middle of a full swing melee.

Chalky smoke was everywhere. Eight SPECs were pinned down behind two different piles of lumber. Waters, with three men, was on the left, while the other four were on the right. Some were firing around the sides of their cover. Others over top. Whoever they were aiming at was returning it with gusto. The lead was thick in the air. A series of blasts clipped both wooden mounds and sent splinters sailing.

"Stand fast," Waters yelled.

"Is anyone hit?" another screamed.

"No, we're ok."

"What's the order, sir?"

Waters glanced around the lumber, then ducked back down. "On my command, you men follow me, the rest lay down suppressive fire. Now!"

The SPECs on the right started blasting as Waters charged from the cover with his men close to heels. Gunshots rang out.

One of the SPECs who remained behind turned to me and said, "Who are you?"

"I'm-" was all I got out before a grenade landed between us. "Get down," I said, and dove away as it exploded. But the blast was small. And instead of shrapnel it filled the air with more thick, white smoke. I couldn't see much farther than a few feet ahead. But out of the mist staggered a SPEC holding his throat. "That bitch... bit me." He fell to the ground and started to jerk.

I pulled his hand back and there, thick and deep, were twin bite marks.

And I knew. The slight brunette dame they were after wasn't my kid.

It was Gunmetal Gray.

Which meant the SPECs were on their own.

I turned and took a step towards the exit. But then a high-pitched shriek cut the air. The roof started to shake. And it burst open, dropping debris all around.

Wait. That was Tera.

And if Tera was here, then Doodle was too. Along with Gunmetal Gray.

I pulled my pistols and charged into the smoke.

When I cleared the other side there were three bodies on the ground. All SPECs. None moving.

I ran past them and down the same aisle I'd chased Bundy Strong through two days before. When I got to the end I stopped, and peeked around the corner. Standing in front of the exit to the wet dock was a tiny woman with her back to me.

Quiet as I could I pointed my Kapowitzer at her spine. All I had to do was shoot. Then I'd deal with Scourge. I depressed the trigger. And Lois' bracers wrapped tight around my arm.

But before I could fire she spun around, saw me, and raised her pistol.

"Doodle?" I said.

"Dane?" My daughter lowered her gun. "What're you doing here?"

"Saving you from Gunmetal."

"I don't need your help, I'm... Wait, Gunmetal's here?" She searched the room frantic.

"I thought so," I said, and put away Lois. "One of the SPECs-"

"Sketch," Tera yelled from the wet dock. "Let's go."

"Sorry. Got to bail." Doodle turned and ran out the door.

I gave chase. But my daughter was swift. She was already halfway to the same yellow jetboat Bundy tried to get away on. Only this time Tera was at the helm.

And she was already sailing away.

Doodle sprinted down the dock after her.

And I followed fast. Opening my stride and pumping both arms I somehow managed to reach out and grab her wrist. "Stop," I said.

Doodle jerked to a halt and turned to me. "Let go. We have to leave."

"Not until you tell me why you're here. And how do you know Gunmetal? What's going on?"

Tera yelled, "Sketch, hurry." She gunned the engines and her jetboat raced towards the open water.

Doodle yanked. "I said let me go."

"No."

"I'm warning you." The cobra tattoo she had on her wrist sat up and bit my hand.

Even though the fangs did nothing I pulled my hand back. Cursing my reflexes I reached out again.

But Doodle was already out of reach, running down the dock screaming, "Mom, wait."

"No," Tera said, "you hurry."

Doodle listened. She was moving like a gazelle.

I followed like a rhino.

But it didn't matter. Tera was already sailing past the end of the pier. Doodle wasn't going to make it. But she didn't know that. And instead of slowing down she charged by the cement column and leapt. My kid soared through the air like a bird, and somehow managed to catch the edge of the boat. Right in her gut. She folded over the side with both legs splashing into the water.

Tera didn't even look back. But she did speed up.

Doodle kicked at the boat's hull, trying to push herself up, as white water crashed over her knees. The waves sucked her down. But she grabbed the edge of the vessel with one hand and held on. Right as more ocean surged over her. So much that she disappeared. And I couldn't tell if she was still clinging, or floating in the bay.

But then, out from under the surf, my kid pulled herself up. She tossed one leg over the side of the boat. Then the other. And she made it in.

As the boat sped away Doodle turned around and yelled something.

I didn't catch it.

From the left a police cutter ripped through the waves after them. It came up close behind. Tera turned and released a piercing scream. The cop boat shook. Then it fell apart and sank beneath the waves. I couldn't spot any men floating, but-

"Out of the way!"

I turned around to see Monday. He shoved me aside and aimed his pistol at my daughter. Her boat was moving faster now. But he was leading it slow. And while she was way far out I didn't like the way this felt. So I swatted Monday's gun, knocking it into the water.

He glowered at me. "What's wrong with you? That's the girl who tried to kill the mayor."

I watched the yellow boat shrink as it headed north. And once it vanished I turned and walked back down the dock.

"God damn it, do you know what you've just done?" Monday ran over and grabbed my shoulder. He spun me around and got in my grill. "Do you?"

"Yeah," I said, "I just saved my-"

An explosion came from behind, and its blast smashed me into Monday. Together we tumbled down the dock, stopping after a few yards. Rubble began to rain down. The sharp sleet hissed as it fell and sandblasted my exposed skin. I covered my eyes as larger pieces started to land. A softball of concrete crashed to the right. Then, a few feet to my left, an anvil size chunk shredded the dock and plunged into the water.

I scrambled to Monday and threw my body over his.

But then the hard rain ceased. And a loud creaking rose up. With Monday still beneath me I looked back. The whole warehouse teetered towards us and, like a tidal wave, crashed down. I braced against the dock as the avalanche of metal and cement consumed us. It took a long while for the rumbling to stop.

When the deluge subsided, I was surrounded by darkness. What little air I had was dusty and hot. And there wasn't enough of it to go around. I had to move. Putting a whole lot of effort into my arms I pressed up. And some of the jetsam slid aside. It gave me enough room to slip a foot underneath my body. And once I was stable I shoved up, and cleared the debris off us entirely.

I looked around. The building was gone. Dust was everywhere. Below me Monday lay still. That spot on his flank was bleeding again. Not bad, but some. I checked his pulse and found it rhythmic enough to give me relief. But he was definitely taking an extended trip to the land of Nod.

Probably couldn't say that about every cop inside the rubble.

I scanned the ocean for a sign of Doodle. But she was gone.

Again.

Chapter 38

I pulled Monday's car keys out of his pocket. It was time to vanish. Voices were coming from inside the wrecked warehouse, but there was enough smoke, dust, and piles of debris that I couldn't see who they belonged to. And that meant they couldn't see me. Meaning to keep it that way I ran down the dock, and took a left, circling around the outer wall, some of which was still standing. Crouching low I moved fast, and the voices from the other side of the rubble grew louder.

"Get an ambulance down here."

"Are there any survivors?"

"Someone call a K-9 unit."

Confusion. Fear. My old friends. Thanks to them it would take a tick before the remaining men got organized. Just enough time for me to Houdini up out of here.

I reached the end of the wall and peered around it. Everyone was looking for survivors, leaving the SPEC vans and the dragon wagon unguarded. Next to them was Monday's car.

I sprinted to it, with his keys in hand, got in, and drove through the outer gate. As I went I looked to where Scourge's car had been parked.

It was gone.

Turning my wheels south I drove swift, with my eyes on the road and my mind on Doodle.

And I didn't like what I was thinking.

She was wanted for trying to murder the mayor, and was also now a cop killer. She'd lied to me about leaving town, and was obviously wrapped up with the very murder I was hired to solve. But how did she know Gunmetal? Did that mean she was working with Scourge? Was he driving that car the night I watched her? And how on earth did she fool Acouste? Wait, did she? When I asked her about Swamp and the robbery she said they were together the entire night. Was she in on the whole thing?

If so, closing Widow's case meant pinching my own daughter. And I didn't know if I could do that. *Could I?*

The questions about Doodle swirled like a hurricane. But at that storm's center was the woman pulling her strings. Tera.

Was she the mystery dame Bundy was talking about? Tera knew all the players. And Doodle said they had a falling out with Big Six in New York over money before coming here. Did she steal enough cash to put this whole thing together? It made a sickly kind of sense. After all, she was never much of a thief, so a failed attempt at stealing the Coconut that resulted in the deaths of two boys, and her daughter's near incarceration, wasn't out of the question.

If that was the case then it was bad news for my kid. Especially since there was only one guy who could've helped me protect her, and I'd just left him unconscious in a heap, convinced that I aided the mayor's would-be assassin.

The tumult of bad thoughts made for an unpleasant trip back to my office. Fortunately it was a quick one, and when I arrived I parked Monday's undercover sedan behind my Jalopy, slid his keys inside the sun visor, and fixed the siren to the roof so it would get back to him safe.

Then I ran up to the fourth floor. When I passed through the hologram my office was dark. I opened the door and stepped in. Mrs. West's desk was empty save for a few cardboard boxes, and a gift-wrapped bottle with my name on it.

She was gone. Finally.

Promising to find and thank her later, I grabbed two empty boxes and ran into the back. I had to clear out as much as possible before Monday was conscious. He'd no doubt be here with a team of blue boys to gut this place as soon as he woke up, so quick as I could I shoved all my files into the boxes. I added the contents of my desk, and the computer. I stacked them up, slung my spare clothes over top, and hoofed it out, grabbing Mrs. West's gift on the way.

But I had to stop and give the place one last look.

I guess the black capes and their families will have to go somewhere else for the help they need. I meant to keep your place going, I wanted to so bad. But I crashed it hard. Like I crash everything. I'm sorry, Carl. So damn sorry.

Then I closed his door, ran downstairs, and threw everything into the trunk.

I needed a place that was safe from the law. I also needed advice from a friend.

But mostly, I just needed a drink.

Chapter 39

When I got to Henchmen's it was all but deserted save for two gals at the bar. As I took a seat three stools down they turned my way. It was Kalamity and Slamazon, the giantesses I'd traded wallops with a few days ago. I expected the pair would start with me again, but instead all they did was pound their drinks and march out the door.

"Chasing away my business, huh?" It was Dastard Lee. She'd come out of the back room with a case of beer in her arms. "What the hell happened to you?"

"Nothing," I said. "Give me a shot of Octane."

"Whoa, that's not a nothing happened drink. That's a something awful happened drink. Does it have anything to do with the face?"

"It has to do with a dame."

"They'll do it every time." She plopped the beer down, put a rocks glass in front of me, and grabbed a half empty bottle from the bottom shelf. It was black, with an eight-sided skull on the label, and across its forehead were the magic words: Three Hundred Proof.

She poured me two fingers.

"Salut." I took a mouthful of the Octane. And immediately regretted it. The stuff was cinnamon silk in the glass, but when it hit the human tongue it dug in like a jellyfish made of poison tar intent on fighting its way to sweet freedom. With a hard swallow the booze lost that battle, and my head went fuzzy numb.

"You know, I got something aside from a bottle of amnesia that might interest you," Lee said, and poured me another shot.

"Do tell."

"I ran into a squirrel this afternoon who owns a holed-up house in Blackwood, and you'll never guess which two capes he had holed-up there for the past month or so."

I lifted the glass and stopped. "Don't tell me Firewall and Thermite."

"I won't, but only because you guessed right."

I sat up straight. "You're kidding me, you got their address?"

"It's the least I could do. Now sit tight. I'll be right back."

She turned and disappeared behind a door.

From the other direction came her barman, the one with onyx

skin and big, white eyes that served me last time I was here. "Hey Dane."

"Hey. You're Psy-Ball, right? Hocus-Focus' kid? You're the one who spotted Scourge."

His white smile shone like neon next to those inky lips. "Yeah. Lee tell you about that?"

"She did. And I appreciate you passing the info on."

"My pleasure. I heard about-" The phone behind him rang. "One second. Henchmen's." He glanced my way. "Let me check." He cupped the transmitter. "Dane, you got a call. Young girl sounding. You here?"

My fuddled mind cleared and I said, "Yeah, give it."

He handed me the phone.

"Doodle, is that you?"

"Hey," she said. "I hoped you'd be there."

"I'm always here. Are you ok?"

"Yeah, I'm blooming. But I'm sorry about what happened at North Point."

She was ok. Thank God. I wanted to reach through the phone and hug her. Instead I yelled, "You're sorry? People died back there. You could've been one of them."

"But I-"

"How do you know Gunmetal? Did you help Scourge kill Thermite and Firewall? Were you in on the Coconut job? What's going on?"

Doodle gave me some silence. It felt practiced. And lasted just long enough to seem sincere. "I didn't kill anybody. And I didn't know those two guys that died. I met Scourge and Gunmetal through Swamp. They were the ones who had Swamp hire us for the hit on the mayor. And I passed them some of his hardware that night you came to Wetlands. That's it. That's all I know. But now, I really need your help."

That last part sounded bona fide. And not at all mendacious. But then again, over the phone, it's easy to mix those two up. "Of course you need help. You only call when you need something."

"Listen, I'm with Mom. She's buying some weapons. I think she double-crossed Swamp, and he's got Scourge and Gunmetal after us. We have to get out of town."

"So grab Tera and go."

"We have no money. So she's insisting we get the payout from Scourge's boss."

"Bundy Strong?"

"I don't know."

"Listen," I said. "I want you to hang up the phone, and get gone. Tonight."

"I want to. I told Mom that. But she's acting obsessed. She wants cash and I'm scared that-"

"Sketch?" It was Tera. "Where are you?"

"Over here. One second," Doodle said. "Please, I'm telling the truth. I need you to protect me when we pick up the money. Like you did before, when no one else would."

I thought about my baby girl, and the spider web my ex had her stuck in. "Fine. Where's this going down?"

Tera yelled, "Young lady, stop hiding."

"I'm not. I'm over here," Doodle said. "I don't know where the drop is. Yet. But when I do I'll send you a telegram."

What? "A telegram, are you-"

"Yes. Just help me, please," she said. "Mom, I'm coming right-" And the line went dead.

I handed the phone back to Psy-ball.

He hung it up and said, "Everything ok?"

"Not at all."

"Sorry to hear that." He finished polishing the glasses in front of him. "Anyway, what's up with Dread-"

"Here you go." It was Lee. She was back from the basement with a piece of paper in her hand.

"Thanks, this could help," I said, taking the address. "Now I got to be going." I sucked down my Octane and stood up.

But Lee grabbed my hand. "Before you do, I got one last bit of news. And this time it ain't good."

I froze. "You couldn't have told me first?"

She looked at her feet. "You know, I mentioned that if this rage about Dread Division didn't die down…"

"No." My skin went cold and clammy. "You're banishing me?"

"I have to. Nobody wants to talk business or be around a turn… Well, you know. I mean, you may drink a ton, but it's not enough to keep the lights from going out, and I got to eat too."

"But I need this place, for access, for info. Carl used to

practically live here. And…" I heaved a deep sigh. "And it's not like I'm a PI anymore so whatever. Don't worry about it." I reached into my pocket and pulled out a crisp hundred from Widow's shrinking pile. "Here, for the hooch."

"No way," Lee said. "That drink's on me."

"Thanks, then it goes to the kid." I put the bill on the bar and slid it to Psy-Ball.

"You're a class act," Lee said.

"And a laugh riot," Psy-ball added.

I turned to him. "How do you mean?"

"This bill," he said. "It's marked."

Lee grabbed the note and held it up. "No it's not. Take it."

"No thanks," the ebony barman said. "There's irradiated material on it."

I looked at the bill. "You're kidding?"

"Nope." Psy-ball closed one eye while the other flickered static like an old TV set. "There's a thumbprint here. Ultraviolet ink. The kind that cops use. If they catch this on me they'll think I stole it, so thanks." He slid the rotten dough back my way. "But no thanks."

I pocketed it and said, "I'll be sure to take it up with Widow."

"Widow." Lee snapped her fingers. "That's who hired you. Firewall's her brother."

"Well, if you figure out how he died let me know."

And with that I put my hat on and walked out of Henchmen's for the last time.

Chapter 40

I got in my car and sat for a second. The Octane was still doing its thing in my veins, but that's not the reason I wasn't turning the key. I figured it was possible I'd be tossed in Impenetron. Maybe beat Glory Anna in a fistfight. I even imagined I'd make it out of this biz alive to retire down in Saint Luthor's. But I never expected to be banned from Henchmen's.

Of all my assets this one was the most valuable. To prove it one final time Lee gave me an address I couldn't have found on my own. The last place the boys lived. Some run down holed-up house. Who knows, maybe it'd have a clue as to Scourge's whereabouts.

So no matter what happened, at least I could get Widow the truth about her brother. I could do that. And close my one and only solo black cape case.

#

The lobby was nice, as holed-up houses went. The red carpet didn't have a single bald spot, the walls were intact, and the chandelier, though made of glass, wasn't missing any tears.

I walked up the wide stairs to the sixth floor. Thermite and Firewall's door was at the end of the hall. When I got there I studied the lock.

It stared back at me with contempt.

Pulling out Rico and Lois I kicked open the door and charged in. To complete darkness. And no movement. The only sound was dripping water. I flicked the switch and lit the place up.

The single room was deserted. To my left was a small kitchenette with a tiny fridge, a hot plate, and a metal sink with a faucet that was spitting every ten seconds. To the right was a television next to a table with two chairs, and on the far wall, near the bathroom, was a king size bed.

Closing the door behind me I set about searching the place.

I started with the bathroom. All I found were a couple towels and some shaving gear. Then I moved to the bed. There was nothing underneath it but carpet, and the clothes on top had bare pockets. So I checked the table where I discovered a trove of old takeout menus and empty bottles of beer.

The place was looking like a dry mine. But then, in the kitchen sink, I found some gold in the form of a small pile of half burnt pictures. I sorted through the singed shots. There was a generic one of the Coconut. One of the back of the museum. The vent on the roof.

Jackpot. This was where they planned the heist.

I kept going. The next shot was of Doodle and Tera outside Wetlands. My kid looked pretty, but she always did. Then I saw one of me. I was coming out of the hospital. But something about the picture was odd. I looked closer and saw what: my hand wasn't singed from the crematorium.

Son of a...

The shot was taken a day before I met Monday. The day before Scourge sent us to the ocean floor. They'd been trailing me since the beginning. My blood got hot enough to overcook pasta.

I kept rifling through the stack and came to a letter. It was mostly burnt, but I could make out some of the words.

> *-didn't come through so my*
> *financial problems have gotten worse.*
> *Please, don't contact me. I'll be away*
> *trying to earn enough to keep Robby in*
> *the hospital. And thank you for the*
> *offer of assistance. But I'm afraid that*
> *I need so much money that such a*
> *small amount won't help. However, if-*

Bundy, you bastard. The boys were trying to stay straight, and wouldn't come in on your job, so you used your knowledge of their guilt over Robby to push them into it with a forged letter and fake story from Shelly.

Did he get a copy of her handwriting when the three of them shared a cell? Who knows, but it served as further proof that Bundy and Scourge were working with the boys. What it didn't tell me was why they killed them.

If I was going to get that answer, and protect Doodle, I'd have to find Bundy, Scourge, or Swamp, and since only one of those guys had a steady address it was time to swing by Wetlands. See what Swamp would say now. See if Vec and Victor were the same person.

Only this time it'd be different. This time I wouldn't just pull my Kapowitzer, I'd use it. That should get me the answers I needed. About Doodle. And the dead boys.

I dropped the letter and pictures back in the sink, walked to the door, and reached for the knob.

From the other side somebody said, "Hey, the lock's busted."

I ran across the room and dove under the bed. As quietly as I could I pulled Rico and Lois. Whoever was out there, Swamp or Scourge, they were getting a surprise.

The door opened.

One man walked in wearing black boots. He stopped at the center of the room, then paused before saying, "It's clear."

Someone else came in and said, "Damn. Where is that bitch?" And that someone was Swamp.

"Who knows? You want to check with the street sweets again?" That had to be Vec.

"Come on, Vector. If they didn't see her two hours ago, they wouldn't have seen her since. That Tera's a shifty little rabbit. I bet they got their warren stashed someplace deep. We're never going to find her."

So I was right. And Toby got it wrong. Vec wasn't Victor. He was Vector. And Vector said, "Can't we just contact the buyer?"

"I don't know, genius. Can we?" Swamp said.

"I guess not."

"No. And now that we've crossed Scourge, I doubt he'll tell us." Swamp kicked the table over sending the contents against the wall. "If only that fatso Teenie had come through with our explosives we wouldn't have had to hire those bitches. Why didn't you get those pics back?"

"Because Curse stopped me. Why didn't you kill him outside the club?"

"I thought about it, but who knew he'd be such a pain? The real question is why'd I trust Tera and her spawn?"

Vector plunked down on the bed right above me. "Maybe because you were banging them both?"

Swamp marched over to us. "What did you say?"

"You heard me."

"I must not've, because it sounded like disrespect."

Vector got back up. And squared himself with Swamp. "So?

What're you going do about it, waterman?"

The pair stood toe-to-toe for a few seconds. While I silently prayed one would kill the other and halve my workload. But instead Swamp said, "Nothing now. But we'll revisit this later. In the meantime let's just find the girls."

Vector took a couple of deep breaths. "Maybe they left town."

"No way. Tera wants cash, and this is the place she'll get it. They're going to meet the buyer, we just got to figure out who that is."

"Or where the drop's going down. But that could be anywhere."

"I know."

"And even if we find out where the drop is, what if Scourge's there, too?"

"What?" Swamp said. "You scared of Gunmetal?"

"Only an idiot wouldn't be."

"Well, I don't give a damn about her. We got to find Scourge and ask him hard. Or anybody else who may know where she is." Swamp paced the room a few times. Then he stopped. "Ha, I just had an idea. Who else is in contact with that little cooz?"

Vector stayed silent.

"Her old man. We go find Dane and follow him. I bet he'll lead us right to her."

"Nice. You know where he lives?"

Swamp said, "No clue. But I'm sure we can find somebody who does."

Good luck with that. Only three dames know, and two are in hiding while one just left town.

"Ok, let's go."

"No. First let's toss the room. Who knows what Scourge and his muscle left in this crap hole?"

And then a dark chocolate hand reached under the bed, and flipped it off of me.

Chapter 41

Swamp yelled, "Holy crap."

Vector dove to his friend.

As I fired my Kapowitzer. It exploded loud. The kick knocked me into the corner, and when I blinked my sight back both men were on their knees, a few feet away. Completely untouched.

I looked at the hole in the ceiling that Lois' narrow shot left. Damn. How did I miss from so close? No idea, but this wasn't the time to complain about poor marksmanship. I rolled to my knees, aimed Rico at Swamp, and fired. His head exploded in a green slosh sending jade goo everywhere while the body beneath it flopped to the floor.

I turned to give Vector some. But Rico grew heavy in my hand. It felt like he weighed tons. I pulled up, but his muzzle fell to the carpet. I dropped Lois, grabbed the Thumper's grip with both hands, and heaved. But it didn't move.

I was afraid of this.

"Nice try," Vector said. "Boss?"

I looked at Swamp's headless corpse. The green liquid on the floor was flowing back to his neck stump. And as sure as teachers love tenure, his head reformed and turned to flesh. Then Swamp, once more whole, got to his feet. "I'm alright."

With Rico's nose planted firmly on the carpet I said, "I knew it, you got TK."

Vector laughed. "Yeah. My telekinesis is pure badass." He held out a hand and his power pushed me into the floor. My ears, my brow, the brim of my hat, it all slid downwards.

Swamp wiggled his jaw. "So, big guy, where's your daughter?"

"How should I know?" I said.

"Wrong answer. Vector, pull back."

His pressure let up, but not enough to escape, and Swamp took a step towards me, then wrapped his hand around my mouth. It turned to liquid. The bitter juice flowed down my nose and throat. I tried to cough it out but neither lung was up to the task. Instead pain stabbed my eyes and temples. I shook my head. But the liquid mask stuck firm. My world got dark. Again.

But Swamp removed his hand.

I gulped air.

And Vector pushed me back down.

"That bitch ex of yours," Swamp said, "had Sketch sign my name on the caterer sheet at the gala, so when they investigated the attack it led back to me. I've lost my club. I've lost my life. I'm a wanted felon. And now she's trying to snake my payday, too? I need that cash. So tell me where she is."

"Even if I knew I wouldn't say."

Vector's pressure eased a touch and Swamp clamped down on my mouth again. I pulled away some. It didn't help. His thick, briny fingers formed a watery mask over my face. It ran into my eyes, and brought the now too familiar pain from asphyxiation with it. After what felt like an hour he let up and his pal crushed me some more.

Swamp said, "I don't know what it is about this family, they all seem to enjoy choking on me."

Vector laughed.

"Last chance, Curse. Where're the women?"

I coughed, and said, "Screw you."

"Since you don't know anything there's really no reason to keep you alive then," Swamp said. "I'll send your slut kid to you soon."

The force Vector was exerting let up, and Swamp clamped down on my face for what I suspected was the final time. The two men stared at me. So intent on watching my eyes go dull they were unaware I was lifting my pistol up. I only got it an inch, but it was something. Then a cold heat ran through the back of my head. I ignored it. And kept lifting. I was. Almost there.

Vector's eyebrows jumped. "Gun."

I blasted off two explosive tips. They blew a hole in the floor a few feet from me.

Vector and Swamp leapt back. And the pressure on me eased up. Just enough for me to lift Rico a few inches higher. It would suffice.

I started blazing away at the carpet like a kid at a carnival booth. My bullets blasted hole after hole in the floor, and the two boys sock hopped from one foot to the other dodging the blasts. Then, with a loud crash, the wood collapsed beneath them both, and the darkness below swallowed them as they fell straight down one floor.

I grabbed Lois, got to my feet, ran around the newly made chasm, and burst into the hallway. It was all clear. But below me a door opened.

"Where is he?" Vector yelled.

Swamp said, "Find him. He couldn't have gotten past us."

I turned from the stairs. At the other end of the hall was a window. Slipping my iron under my jacket I charged towards it, and crashed through the glass. The night air was cold. And I fell through it fast. Landing rough, I tumbled to the asphalt. And when I got to my feet I was near a black Jalopy.

Diving into my sled I floored it out of there, leaving Vector and Swamp to cast their aspersions at my tail through a cloud of exhaust.

I should've felt good. But with North Point a wash, and now Wetlands too, the hard truth was I had nowhere left to go.

Chapter 42

I took the stairs up to my apartment with the boxes from my office, and when I opened my door I flicked on the lights. But it stayed dark.

The busted bulb.

The only thing I could see was the swath of light on the floor from the hall lamp outside. I looked down for Doodle's telegram. It hadn't arrived. Yet.

So I dropped my office gear and walked towards the lamp in the corner.

I got two steps when the door slammed shut. And someone struck from behind, driving me to one knee and clamping their sharp fangs tight around the back of my neck.

Gunmetal.

I swung left and right, but she was dug in.

Then the lamp clicked on.

"Don't move." Scourge was sitting on my chair, wearing a black three-piece suit. His pair of size nine two tones were resting on the coffee table between us. Covering his dark, greasy hair was a black derby, and beneath its brim, but above a cheek full of scars, sat a left eye that was an inch larger than the right. In his hand was Doodle's red rose. "Hey Dane. Long time. No see."

"Scourge," I said. "You son of a mother fu-"

"Easy there. Keep it civil or she'll sort your hash." He motioned to my left. "Of course you remember Gunmetal."

I glanced back. Gunmetal's green eyes stared at me like emerald fire. One of them winked.

Looking at Scourge I said, "What do you want?"

His smile was an ugly, twisted thing. It fit his face perfect. "You seem unhappy."

"I'm always happy," I said, "with a mouth like Gunmetal's wrapped around me, but it's a little weird with you making eye contact."

Gunmetal sent a red jolt through me. Every muscle in my body locked up. For a few very slow seconds I couldn't move, couldn't breathe. When she finally eased up I went limp in her arms.

"Hey Dane." Scourge dropped his feet to my floor and leaned forward. "You still with us?"

I coughed up some smoke. "Sure am."

"Good. Now tell me." He held out a red envelope with my name across it in a familiar feminine scrawl. "Why's this so important?"

"No clue. I've never seen it."

"Then why were you looking for it?"

"I wasn't," I said. "What you saw-" Without telegraphing I thrust my head back into Gunmetal's chin. She popped off my back like a New Year's cork and hit the wall. I jumped to my feet, pulled Rico, and shot her twice in the chest with explosive tips. Then I turned to Scourge and lunged at him head first over my coffee table, reaching out for the red envelope.

He leapt aside, yanking it out of reach. "Ole."

I landed flat. But bounced to my feet like the king of bad checks, and spun to Scourge with my piece leveled. "Give me that letter."

He waved the red envelope in front of him like a cape. "Come on big boy, toro, toro."

No more yapping. I cocked Rico. And a red bolt hit my chest. I flopped backwards, dropping the iron.

Gunmetal leaned over me, and pointed to her stomach. There were no insides hanging out. Just two large, toasty holes in her shirt with kevlar underneath. "Nice shot, but I'm wearing a vest."

Scourge laughed.

Gunmetal held both her hands over me. And out flowed dozens of electric red charges. They dug in like spears, pinning me to the ground. My skin turned to fire. A lump of agony grew in my chest, and I couldn't stop it. Couldn't reach it. Seconds ticked and I felt a madness flowing in. But then finally, mercifully, it came to an end.

Gunmetal reached down, grabbed a fistful of locks, and pulled me to my knees. Then she slid behind me and clamped her fangs down like before. Only this time she twisted around in a more defensive position.

"Make sure you hold him tight this time." Scourge righted my chair, and took a seat on it. "I don't want to kill you, Dane. Not yet at least, so don't do that again. Now, we both know you want this, and we both know who it's from. What we don't know is what it says. So let's find out." Scourge slid a straight razor from his sleeve, and slit the envelope open.

He leaned back, crossed his legs, and removed the letter. As he consumed Doodle's words his head turned side-to-side the way a hungry man cleans corn off a cob, and when he finished he looked over the top of the paper and smiled at me. "You call her Doodle. What's that, a childhood name? It's cute."

Gunmetal pulled her mouth off me. "What's it say?"

"It tells us when and where to find Sketch."

She laughed. "That's good news."

I pulled against Gunmetal but she tightened her grip. I said, "You got what you came for, so scram already."

"This?" Scourge held up the envelope. "Oh, this is candy I'll grant you, but I crave something sweeter."

"I can pour some sugar on my loafers and kick your teeth in," I said.

Scourge grabbed my face and leaned closer. "Don't get cute ape, you don't got the gear for it. I'm talking about the diamond. They'll see me coming a mile away but you, you can get it for me a lot easier."

"You're kidding?" My brow slid down like an avalanche. "After your pass with Thermite and Firewall, then last night's stunt, the security in Wentorf Hall's going to be tighter than a fat man's pants. I'll never be able to steal that thing."

Scourge looked at Gunmetal before returning his attention to me. "Stupid comments waste time you don't have. This says you got until sun up. That's less than five hours away, and by then I expect the Coconut to be delivered to this address." He removed a small piece of paper about the size of a business card, and placed it on my table.

I looked at it, then at Scourge. "Not a chance."

"Are you sure? Don't you want to know what'll happen if you decline."

A low level jolt from Gunmetal's hands sent my neck hairs to a more attentive state. "Go on, ask him," she said.

"Fine," I said. "What happens when I decline?"

"I'm glad you asked," Scourge said. "Because it's the same thing that happened to your secretary."

"What?"

"You must be wondering how we found your pad. Mrs. West told us." Scourge pulled a bag from the floor. He put it in his lap, and pulled out a silver wig.

No. No no no. Wigs don't have skin still attached. And they don't bleed. "You scalped her, you son of a bitch!" I ripped free from Gunmetal. And lunged at Scourge. But a bolt hit me and I dropped to my back.

Scourge looked down at me. "Yeah. Mrs. West put up one hell of a fight. And she didn't say much. Initially. But an hour under my knife and the old girl wouldn't stop talking." He held up the hair, then put it back in his bag. "As souvenirs go it sure beats a mug, but I'd still prefer something with a bit more sparkle. So, if you fail to deliver my diamond, or jerk me around in any way, then it'll be us, not you, who Doodle finds waiting. And if that happens…" He leaned down lower, and whispered in my ear, "I'll peel her like a banana, and leave your little girl as wet and red as a butcher's block." He straightened up, and nodded to his crony.

Then Gunmetal hit me with enough juice to power the city for most of December. It was worse than before. I writhed on the floor, trying to get away. But didn't get far. And when she finally finished I was face down, barely awake.

Scourge dropped Doodle's rose on the rug an inch from my face. Then he stepped on it, and ground the bloom into the carpet. "Tick tock goes the clock, Curse. Hurry up. Your daughter needs you."

They left me smoldering on the floor, and slammed the door shut behind them.

Taking a deep breath I summoned all my strength, and tried to get up.

But I failed.

It was a habit I was getting tired of.

Chapter 43

By the time I found my feet Scourge and Gunmetal were long gone. So I grabbed the boxes from my office and plopped them on the table next to my computer. In order to save my daughter from Scourge I had to get him the Coconut. But it was locked up, and though I'm a whiz bang burglar, five hours wouldn't be enough time to successfully plan the job, let alone execute it. And despite his sadistic streak, Scourge knew that. So the request made no sense. In fact, nothing about this case did.

It was time to force it to.

By going back to the beginning, and focusing on what I knew.

Bundy Strong put the boys up to the job by convincing them that Margaret Shelly needed a large amount of money for her son. He had Scourge plan the gig, and Swamp equip them, and then he sent the pair into Wentorf Hall to snatch the Coconut, but inside those walls the two boys died. Those deaths were covered up by Scourge who's protected by Gunmetal, and both have been working hard to keep me off this case.

Now for what I didn't know.

Is there a moneywoman behind all of this, or was Bundy lying to me? He's definitely capable of putting this into motion himself. After all, he knows the players. And since Swamp, Vector, Scourge, and Gunmetal were at throats looking for Doodle and her mom, instead of him, maybe he was hiding out somewhere, pulling the strings. But if so, what're they all after? The payout from the attack on Greenie? How much could that be?

No. That's too much distraction. Let's solve the original question: who killed the boys?

I had no clue.

But they were light enough to walk over the pressure sensors, small enough to get through the lasers, and strong enough to lift the Kessel Glass.

There was only one person that stuck out. Vector. Initially I thought he had strength, but now I knew that show of power the other night was the result of telekinesis. That was helpful to float over the tiles and lift the glass, but it wouldn't do squat for lasers.

Still though, it was time to dig deeper.

I fired up my home computer, typed his name into Sandtrout, and pressed enter.

Staring at the screen I shook my heavy head.

I had to be pretty desperate. If I never heard of this black cape, it was doubtful any law enforcement or press outlets had. And even if there was something out there, it might take hours for Sandtrout to come back with it.

In the meantime, I'd turn my attention to the box from my office. I reached in for the pictures from the crime scene. And next to them was the gift that Mrs. West left me. I opened it up to find a bottle of scotch. I popped the cap and lifted it up. "Here's to you, Wags. Sorry about… everything."

I shot it straight from the bottle. The booze tasted like the crisp, late autumn air. I took another gulp. And from inside the scotch came a clink.

What the hell?

I held the bottle up to the light. Floating inside was some sort of tube. That was weird enough, but what really had my noodle bent was that the vial was wider than the neck. So how did Mrs. West get it in there without breaking the glass? Or the seal?

Whatever the answer, I wouldn't be so crafty.

I smacked the bottle against the table's edge. Its neck cracked off, spilling glass and liquor onto my floor. Reaching in I retrieved a plastic bag. It held a vial full of red liquid.

And a note.

> *Dear Dane,*
> *I know we've never been too sweet on each other, but Carl saw good in you and so do I. We helped so many people over the years, and now it's your turn. I know you'll make him proud. For the record, I already am. Oh, also enclosed is a small gift from Ms. Marcus.*
> *With very warm regards,*
> *Mrs. Laura West*

Ms. Marcus? I looked at the vial. This was the anti-venom from Redback I asked Widow for. Finally, some good news. The next time I met Gunmetal I'd be prepared. Now I just had to figure out a way to inject it. And also become impervious to electricity. Then all my problems would be solved.

From my computer came a ping. Sandtrout was done. But that was too quick for an in-depth search. When I turned to the screen I saw why.

I hadn't switched over from the normal search engine setting I'd used for Margaret Shelly, so all I got was a list of words that went with Vector, and its definition. But not the black cape it applied to.

I read it for hoo-hahs. After all, a black cape's name often implies a lot about-

What the?

I didn't get three lines in before every last clue, each bit of evidence, finally made sense.

A botched robbery that went according to plan.

The double murder for cover.

That sloppy assassination which was dead on target.

Even the joke outside of Wetlands about being attractive.

And finally, four deadly black capes on a quest to kill my kid.

My guts tightened. *Doodle. What have you done?*

I had to save her. But I couldn't do it alone. I'd need help.

From the one man in town who trusted me least.

Chapter 44

I grabbed the phone and dialed my office. It rang. And rang again. In fact that bell tolled eight times before Monday picked up. "Hello?"

"You're supposed to say 'Dane Curse Detective Agency.'"

As silences go this one had teeth, and it chewed on the air between us for quite a while before Monday said, "Where are you, you son of a bitch?"

"That all depends. How many people are in there with you?"

"Zero." He growled more than spoke. "It's just me."

"Really? Still fixing to lay iron on a black cape sans backup?"

"No. But after getting dumped in the bay, that disastrous car chase, and failing to apprehend a cop killer assassin, not even the dispatcher trusts me, so I'm here solo. And when you come in I'm going to slap some Trumite cuffs on you solo. And if need be I'll drag you to Impenetron solo. I hear they've got a hole I can throw you down that's so deep you'll die of old age before you hit bottom."

"I bet starvation would get me first."

There was more silence. "You're not going to be so jokey when I lay my mitts on you. The first thing I'll do is-"

"I hate to stop you, but instead of making what's sure to go into the Threat Hall of Fame, why don't we go nab the guys who killed those two kids, and retrieve the Coconut so I can solve my case and you can be a SPEC," I said, "just like we agreed?"

"Retrieve the Coconut?" Monday said. "The Coconut's safe in the museum."

"Actually," I said, "it's not."

#

I explained everything to Monday as fast as I could. It actually sounded more unbelievable out loud than it did in my head. And after I strained his credulity beyond any reasonable man's belief, I threw in a request for two items that could only be found in Gold Coast Police Headquarters.

All in all, I had to say, he took it pretty well.

"Really, your daughter?" he said. "Alright, I can't believe it, but I'm in. Meet me on the museum steps in thirty minutes."

"Make it ten." I hung up the phone, ran down to my car, and

raced there as fast as I could.

Monday, true to his word, was waiting out front where we first met.

"Hey," I said. "Did you get what I asked for?"

"It wasn't easy." He pat his chest. "But yeah."

"Great. And the curator's here?"

"Ms. Johan's waiting inside, but I wouldn't expect to see her happy."

"She's about to get a lot less."

We walked up the steps, through the gold gates, beneath Poseidon's gaze, and into Wentorf Hall where a very tall, very serious looking woman was waiting. She was fortyish, with blond hair and gray eyes, and had one arm in a cast, bandages on her chin, cheek, and legs, and a brace around her neck. Ms. Johan said, "Why am I here?"

"For the Coconut." I walked up to the diamond's display. "Is it for sale?"

She turned to Monday. "Officer, if this is some sort of ruse, I'm not laughing."

"He's a detective," I said, "and it's not a joke. In fact, after you hear what I've got to say you'll be crying so hard that by the time the waterworks shut off you'll be desiccated enough to pass for one of your mummies. Hell, you've already got the bandages."

Even when wounded she looked haughty as hell giving me the up and down. "And why, exactly, is that?"

"Because," I said, "that's a fake. The Vandenberg Coconut's been stolen."

"You must be mad," she said.

I motioned to the rock. "Then shuck that shell, and show me just how nuts it is."

"This is a waste of time." Johan turned to go.

"No, it's not. And if you walk out that door now you'll find out I'm right during your biweekly audit of the displays with law enforcement on one side and insurance vultures on the other. Imagine the headlines." I spread an imaginary banner above my head. "Dr. Johan's Shredded Coconut Security Surprise. Catchy ring to it. Who do you think'll play you in the TV movie? With your bone structure I'd say-"

"That's enough," Johan said. The anger was still there. Only now there was some curious fear as well. "You have exactly one minute to convince me before I make an official complaint to the police department."

"Monday," I said, "start the clock. Ok, so a few nights ago a team of three black capes came in to steal the Vandenberg Coconut, a-"

"There were only two," Johan said.

"No. You only found two. There was also a guy named Vector who can manipulate gravitational fields. And together the trio snuck up the outer wall, through the vent, and down to the floor quick as can be thanks to how light Vector made them. From there Firewall opens the door-"

"I know all this," Johan said, "but the inner alarms couldn't be shut off because he'd need to touch the controls directly."

"Which is exactly what happened," I said. "Vector escorted him through the room by making them both light enough to walk over the pressure sensitive tiles and-"

"But the lasers, they would've intersected the beams and set off the alarm."

"They had a gravitational field around them so..." I looked at the cop. "Monday?"

He was nodding with both eyes on his watch. "Light bends."

"Exactly. By encapsulating them both with the field, Vector was able to bend the beams around their bodies without cutting them and setting off the alarm." Like he did earlier with my Kapowitzer's narrow blast.

Johan's face was losing blood.

I felt bad. But continued anyway. "And then all that stood in their way was the Kessel Glass, which Firewall unlocked and Vector made light enough to lift. Then they plucked the diamond like a mote from your eye and replaced it with a fake. Probably some high tensile glass, but whatever, with the booty snatched, and the decoy in place, Vector pinned both boys to the deactivated ground sensors and sprayed them with the nitro-tri-phosphorus he'd brought. Then he dropped the canister along with some filament to complete the scene, confident that if anyone did notice the deception they certainly wouldn't care."

Johan looked at the case.

"But they still had one issue," I said. "You."

And she snapped back to me.

"Didn't you think it was strange that you were the only one hurt at the gala?"

"I was standing near Mayor-"

"That explosion wasn't aimed at Greenie. They needed you out of the picture so no one would be able to check on the diamond's authenticity for weeks. Maybe months. And by then the ice would be in someone else's freezer, far from here." I glanced at Monday. "Time?"

"Fifty-eight, fifty-nine." The cop looked up from his watch. "And sixty."

Johan may've been wrapped in gauze and plaster casts, but the worry lines cut deep in her brow looked far more painful. They twisted on her face, shifting back and forth like fault lines, before she finally said, "Ok."

"Ok what?" I said.

"I'll open it. But we'll have to wait hours before it's high enough to check the diamond. Maybe if we call in Al Mighty or Retroflex-"

"Retroflex is out of town," Monday said, "and Al Mighty's laid up with pneumonia thanks to a lungful of water."

Ha. "Don't worry," I said. "Just get that glass up an inch and I'll handle the rest."

"You can do that?" Johan said.

"Come on. Chop chop."

Johan pulled the purple curtain next to the display aside, opened the panel there, and punched the digits on the pad like she was making a collect call to Moscow. Behind the wall there was some clicking. Then some groaning. And the Kessel Glass rose one inch.

I walked to its center, spat on my hands, and slid all ten fingers into the gap. I turned to Johan and said, "You know, this would be so much more fun if that rock was authentic."

"We won't know that for certain until you do your duty," she said.

"I hear and obey, memsahib." I took a deep breath. And lifted. The massive piece of Kessel Glass slid up one whole foot.

Johan stepped to my side. "Isn't that heavy?"

"What? Yeah, but the longer I hold it the lighter it gets."

"Really?"

"Grab the rock already," I said.

Johan slipped her hands inside and pulled out the diamond. "Good lord, he's right."

I dropped the pane and looked at her.

She was staring at the shining orb, her face as grotesque as any gargoyle's.

"How can you tell?" Monday said.

"The weight. The weight alone. It's too light. This is a fake diamond. What'll I do?"

"The only thing you can." I extended a hand. "Pass it to me."

Her look was a frantic one. "Why would I do that?"

"Because I'll take that dud and trade it for the real one."

"How?"

"Don't worry about it."

Her eyes got real slim. And she chewed her lower lip. I'd seen the look before. On a lot of people. But it's always scariest on a dame.

"Monday," I said. "Could you give us a moment? The curator and I need to discuss something."

He looked to Johan.

She didn't say a word.

"Ok. I'll be by the cars." He turned and disappeared through the door.

"Now," I said, "let's get down to brass tacks."

"Yes, lets." Johan pulled out a small device from her pocket, and pressed the button on its side.

All three exits slammed shut with doors made from unbreakable Trumite. And through the thick metal I could hear locks clicking.

The potentate's jewel box was now shut tight.

"What do you think you're doing?" I said.

"I'm capturing the man who stole the Vandenberg Coconut."

Chapter 45

Johan was grinning. Why, I had no clue. She clearly thought she knew something I didn't, but truthfully, I could read her thoughts like they were tattooed on her forehead in a triple digit font. "You don't really think this'll work, do you?"

"Pinning the whole farce on you? Most definitely."

I strolled to the middle of the room and looked around. "Really? You think the white capes will pick me up and all you got to do is slide that back into place so during your next audit, when it's revealed as a fraud, you can blame the whole thing on me?"

"Of course, by then-"

"Stop. Just stop. You know, you're as bad as any black cape I've met. You're all thick. You're all sad. And you're all deeply infected."

"With what, exactly?"

"With dark hope. I can see it in your eyes like I've seen it in a thousand others. You got the bloody bad optimism of amateur crooks who think they won't get caught because they're child-of-destiny special. But here's the thing, no one's that special. And when that rock's made for the scam-zanite it is, you'll be blamed. Those bandages will net you no sympathy, and you can alibi yourself to I-didn't-do-it-istan, but they'll peg you for a thief or a fool, and they'll be right on one of those counts. But by then it'll be too late, because nobody will believe the truth: that this wasn't an inside job."

There are cats with a mouthful of mouse that don't look so satisfied as Johan did. "After that attack the mayor feels very inclined to help me, and when I tell him my side, the one your kindly Officer Monday will happily corroborate, I'll be blame free, but you'll be-"

"Wait, that's your hole card? Detective Monday? Lying?" I threw back my head and laughed so loud I'm surprised none of the displays cracked. "The guy whose life I saved twice? The guy who tried to prosecute a cop over Mr. Boogety's murder? You're expecting him. To bend. For you? I'm liking my chances more every second."

Johan stayed silent, and her expression doesn't have a

description.

"Look, I'll give you one last chance. Hand over the fake and I'll return your diamond. I can. I promise. But I have to move now."

She gazed down at the crystal ball she held. "No. I like my plan better."

"Fine." I took two big steps and towered over her. Then I pulled Lois. My Kapowitzer jumped to life with a bright green glow. "See this, you Sasquatch? This here's the most powerful handgun ever made, and it can sear a hole through Trumite. Not a big one, mind you, and it has to be a thin sheet, but a hole nonetheless. So imagine what it can do to you. Go on. Imagine."

Johan stared at my pistol with real big eyes.

"Good," I said. "Now forget about that because I'm not going to shoot you. I'm going to beat you against that door until you're dead or it opens because you're the only two things standing between me and my daughter. Now I want you to pay attention like you never have before and listen to every word I'm about to say. I'm taking that fake and leaving this place. You can't stop me. The SPECs can't stop me. Even Team Supreme can't stop me. Now give it here. I got things to do."

#

I walked down the museum steps to find Monday leaning against my car.

I held up the fake rock. "Better than that sly fake around Anubis, huh?"

"It's impressive for certain. What about the other things, you want them now?"

I opened my door and tossed the Vandenberg Faux-conut into the passenger seat. "Yeah. Please."

Monday pulled off his jacket, tie, and shirt until he was just wearing a black vest.

"That the same one you had on the night I shot you with the stunner?"

"Affirmative." He ripped the shoulder velcro off, and handed it over. "Now remember, it can absorb a lot of juice, but only from a direct hit."

I disrobed until I was completely naked above the belt, tossed my threads on the hood of my car, and slipped the vest on. "Got it."

As I re-buttoned the white shirt beneath my gray jacket Monday said, "I'm not kidding. If that broad gives you a jolt in the arm or the leg it won't protect you."

I put my black overcoat on, then tightened my tie. "But if her electricity hits dead center?"

"Then you'll be fine."

"Huzzah," I said. "And that other thing?"

Monday pulled his pistol, popped open the cylinder, and removed a Trumite dart.

"Thanks." I took it and poured the tranquilizer onto the sidewalk. Then I reached into my jacket, removed Widow's vial of anti-venom, and poured half of it into the dart. Capping both tight, I placed them in my shirt pocket.

"So where to now?" Monday said.

"Uptown. York Avenue."

"How many black capes are waiting for you?"

"Two."

"Two, huh? That doesn't sound like a day at the fair," Monday said.

I opened my door. "Like a cop once told me, life's not a fair." I hopped in. And rolled down the window. "Where's your sled?"

"A few cars back. I'll give you some room, but don't get too far out ahead."

"No problem. Just don't follow me down York. If you get made I don't think we'll see the real Coconut ever again."

"You know, York's a dead end."

"So are most of the streets I've travelled. Just hang back at the opening. If I fall, and Scourge gets out, I'm going to need someone to save-"

"The diamond."

"No," I said. "Something far more precious." I put my keys into the ignition.

"Hey," Monday said. "I never thanked you for saving my life."

"Yeah you did, right before the ambulance arrived."

"No, back at North Point. I know you blocked that rubble, and I... I appreciate the effort."

I looked up at Monday. He was a good man. An honest cop. I said, "Shut up already. Let's go."

He walked back to his car and I pulled into traffic.

Next stop, Scourge.

Chapter 46

Thirty minutes later I turned down York. There were no streetlights to illuminate my path, but I could still make out the run down row homes that stood shoulder-to-shoulder on both sides of the street. I crept along at five miles an hour, looking left and right for an ambush. I didn't know when Scourge would make his move, but on this road there wasn't a bad place for it. The only witnesses would be the army of unseen rats and roaches, and a single rusted out car on the sidewalk.

But I got to the end in one piece, and turned around, parking with my nose facing out in case I needed to make a quick getaway. At the other end of the block Monday drove by without a glance. He'd go another few yards and wait. For me, or Scourge. But not both. Because tonight one of us was going to die.

And it was going to be him.

After all, my plan wasn't half bad. I'd walk in there with the Faux-conut, hand it over, and when Scourge reaches for it I'd grab him like a human shield, then put a hole through Gunmetal's skull. But if she blasted me, all the better. I'd pretend to be wounded, and when she drops her guard, do the deed then. Even if she got a bite in, so be it, Widow's anti-venom would handle it courtesy of Monday's Trumite dart.

And then, it'd be just me and Scourge. I'd promise not to turn his head into a warm slurry if he slides me Doodle's address. And once he did, I'd break that promise, thump the whole story out of him, go get my daughter, return the Coconut to Monday, and tell Widow what really happened the night her brother died.

Like I said, a good plan.

I got out of the car with the fake diamond and did the self pat down. Both guns were ready. I had the dart and half full vial in my shirt pocket. I even had a lock pick. Not that I'd need it. The front door was wide open. I took the eight steps up the stoop and walked in.

And found myself in a long hallway. At the other end was a door. Nothing stood between me and it besides some creaky floor boards and two burning light bulbs with wattage in the single digits.

When I got to the end I kicked open the door and stepped into a dark room with no furniture and an old carpet. Scourge was on the far side, still in black with his scars and weird eye below a dark derby, while leaning in the corner was Gunmetal, wearing all black as well. She said, "Didn't think you'd show."

"Yes you did," I said, and took a step towards Scourge.

He said. "That's far enough."

"What?" I held out the fake diamond. "Don't you want your candy?"

He had the kind of smile that would shame a wolf. "Frankly, I didn't think you'd get it. Tera must've put up one hell of a fight. How'd you find her?"

"I'm a detective," I said. "And when I want something I usually get it."

"That's the one thing we have in common," Scourge said. "Now roll it over."

Roll? That was no good. I wanted to get close to Scourge. Get my paws on him before Gunmetal could blast away. "Here, just take it." I took a step forward.

"No." Scourge looked to my left and right. "Don't move. Stay right where you are."

I glanced both ways. And smelled a bushwhack. "No thanks." I took a step onto the carpet. And my foot squished. The rug was soaked.

"Got you," Gunmetal said. A red jolt of electricity jumped from her hand onto the wet rug. It cut a jagged red line to my foot, and shot up my leg. I locked tight. And dropped the diamond. It landed on my shoe, and skittered away.

When the juice stopped flowing I fell to my knees.

Gunmetal ran over, grabbed my left arm and twisted it. I fell forward, and caught myself with the other hand. She bit down on my wrist. Her fangs cut through my clothes, but stopped just short of breaking skin.

Scourge walked to the diamond. He picked it up and said, "I can't believe this is real."

"It is," I said. "Now-"

"Your declarations rank pretty low on things I'll buy without a warranty, so you'll forgive me if I double-check." Scourge removed a small magnifying lens from his coat, plunked it over his eye, and looked at the diamond. "Good lord."

With my arm still in her mouth Gunmetal said. "What is it?"

"It's the fake we put in the display. You really thought we wouldn't check? I guess we'll do this the hard way, and pull it from your baby girl's skinless hands. I wonder what part of her I'll keep." Scourge pocketed his eyepiece and nodded.

Gunmetal bit into my left arm. Her venom flowed into me like lava.

"Arg!" I pulled away. But she came with. So I plowed an uppercut with my right fist into her ribs. Gunmetal flew off me and into the wall. I rolled to the side, pulled out Rico with my uninjured hand, and aimed at her.

Only now she'd been replaced with a fuzzy pair of twins. Damn venom, it already had me seeing double. But I knuckled through it, and shot at the one on the right. And missed.

"Dane Curse," she said. "I've got the perfect spot on my belt for your notch." She had her hands up and flung a red jolt my way.

But I ducked. And the bolt struck the wall behind me. Burning splinters and the hot smell of rotting wood filled the air. Through both I aimed, and fired again. This slug hit her chest. Gunmetal grunted, and tumbled back.

I got to my feet. Scourge was clutching the diamond in the corner. I'd handle him soon. But first I aimed at his bodyguard's face.

From her back, Gunmetal threw another bolt my way.

It struck my right shoulder. I stayed on my feet but Rico dropped to the floor. So it was time to unleash Lois. I went to grab her. But the burning in my left arm had given way to numbness. My hand was now too cold to feel. Too cold to move.

Gunmetal got to her feet. "There's a lot of fight in him."

"I told you," Scourge said.

I looked down at Rico. If I lunged for him Gunmetal would attack, and that was too risky. Who knows what part of me she'd hit? No. I needed her closer.

"You want me to finish him off, or let the venom work its wonder?" Gunmetal said.

"Why don't you cook him some? Dane always said he was a rare sort, but when I pay for a job I expect it to be well done."

"No," I said. "Please. Stay away."

Gunmetal walked over. "Time to send you to your secretary." She grabbed my shirt with both hands. And poured her power through it. She really gave me all she had, too. Her fists glowed so bright that even though I clamped both eyes shut I could still see her crimson shine.

I dropped to my knees next to Rico. And shook some. But it didn't hurt. Not one bit. Monday's vest took the entire brunt and kept me a balmy ninety-eight point six. Until finally she let up, and the room went dark.

"And that's that," Scourge said.

"No," Gunmetal said. "Something's wrong. He should be burnt umber by now." She grabbed my shirt and ripped it open. "What the?"

My eyes popped open. "Nice shot, but I'm wearing a vest." I grabbed my Thumper from the floor. He was so heavy that I couldn't lift him high, but I got his muzzle against Gunmetal's knee. And fired. The bullet ripped through her cartilage. Then her bone. And spread both out on the rug like a spilled bowl of borscht.

"Arg!" Gunmetal grabbed her leg and flopped to the ground.

I turned to Scourge. "Now for you."

But that damn venom. I moved too slow. And Scourge put a fist across my chops.

I didn't roll with it.

"God damn it." Scourge dropped the diamond and jumped back, cradling his hand. "I think you broke it."

I stumbled to my feet. And turned his way. "I'm going to break more than that."

"What?" Scourge danced back. "You're not making any sense."

And he was right. Both my lips were numb. And my left arm still wasn't responding. It was like I had a stroke. If I didn't get that anti-venom in me immediately I'd be dead. So I dropped Rico, reached into my jacket, and wrapped my hand around the dart. I got it, along with Widow's vial.

"He's going for the Kapowitzer." Scourge threw his shoulder into me. And bounced off without making a mark.

But somehow Gunmetal leapt onto my back. She clawed my face. And pulled me down to the carpet. Quick as a cat that tiny dame had me straddled, and pinned the hand that held my dart and the antidote. There was a madness in her eyes. "No more guns." She drove her fist down on the back of my hand.

And something snapped. But it wasn't bone. I yelled, "No." Holding the dart and vial tight, I pulled my right hand out and backhanded Gunmetal across the face with it. She flew off, and rolled into the corner.

I sat up. And looked into my palm. The vial of anti-venom was shattered and empty. But Monday's dart was still full. Thank God for- *No*. I was wrong. The dart itself may've been fine, but its needle, it had broken off.

Now there was no way to inject the antidote.

Now I was a dead man.

Killed by Scourge and Gunmetal Gray.

But nuts to that. I may be worm food, but if I killed those two humps, Doodle'd be safe. So that's what I'd do.

Tossing the syringe aside I scooped up Rico.

"I'll be in the car." Scourge had the Faux-conut in hand as he ran for the door.

I fired at him. Again and again. But he made it out unscathed.

"Son of a bitch." Struggling to my feet I staggered after him. "Wait."

"Bastard," Gunmetal said. "I'm going to kill you."

I spun her way. The tiny dame was limping towards me, her hands outstretched. I could only lift Rico waist high. So I blasted her other leg. More meat and blood sprayed the wet rug, and Gunmetal toppled.

I meant to run through the door. But instead I slumped against the wall. My head felt like it was packed with wet cotton.

"Still coming, Curse."

I looked down. Gunmetal was clawing her way to me like a crippled lioness.

Lifting Rico I aimed at her face. Just as my left eye went blind. It didn't matter. My right was still good enough. I used it to line up my shot. And blasted away. But the lead sailed wide, and hit the rug.

So I fired another.

It landed wrong too.

Gunmetal reached out and grabbed my ankle. She yanked hard and I crumbled to the ground. Pulling herself on top of me she said, "Son of a bitch, you're about to die."

"Ladies first." I lifted up my piece.

Gunmetal swatted it aside. And pinned my hands to the ground. Her mouth swung open. Wide. And she bit my shoulder, sending another few CC's of venom oozing into me.

It was like magma flowing under mantle. And I writhed as she held my meat in her jaws. But then it all stopped throbbing. I went still. My muscles were limp. Their fight, gone.

Gunmetal eased her mouth open, and straightened up. Then she grabbed my lapels and pulled me up so I was an inch from her face.

I said, "What… you doing?"

She looked at me like a hawk stares at lunch. "I like to watch the light die."

And the angry dame was close enough to do it. But instead of shrinking I said, "Me… too." Using all my strength, I somehow wrapped my left arm around her lower back, and hugged her tight. Then I slipped my right hand under her armpit, snaked it back over her shoulder, and grabbed her face.

That bird of prey look was gone. "What the?"

I pulled down against her chin, trying to fold her straight back over my left arm like a towel. She twisted. And clawed. But still I poured on the pressure.

"What're you doing?" Gunmetal said though her fangs and my fingers.

"Letting you… watch the… light die." I pulled her chin harder, trying to break her in half. And although the vertebrae were clinging to each other with bony tenacity, her spine was separating. Just a bit.

Gunmetal panicked, and grabbing my chest she blasted away with every bit of power she had. Her hands glowed bright red. They lit up the room like the heart of a star.

But I didn't feel a thing.

Finally she stopped. And the room went dark. But I could see she was sweating. Panting, too. The famous assassin was all out of strength.

But I had one meager helping left. And I used it to squeeze. And squeeze. And then, with a sickening thrunch, Gunmetal's spine snapped in two as she folded backwards over my arm.

I dropped the broken broad on the floor. And slumped over next to her.

She was staring at me. And damn it if she didn't blink. "Good move, Curse. Didn't think you had it in you."

"Most people don't," I said.

She took two sharp breaths. "Which one of us… Do you think'll die first?"

I tried to say, "You." But my mouth didn't work. So I lay still. Thinking of Doodle. She was in so much danger. But I was a dead man. There was still some antidote in Monday's dart, but even if I could reach it there was no way to inject it. The venom inside me couldn't be stopped. Not anymore.

As my world went dark the last thing I saw was Gunmetal. Her spine may've been busted, but her spirit was unbroken, and through the black veil that settled over my eyes I saw her shining smile.

Chapter 47

Wait. That's it.

I may be near dead, with no fight left, but my baby needed me. So I dug down to the last store of strength that only a father keeps for his daughter, and took the king of all breaths. Then I rolled to my side, and threw a numb leg over Gunmetal. Pushing myself up I straddled the tiny woman. And the room pitched back and forth. I forced it to stand still, then searched for Rico. He was a few feet away. Reaching over I grabbed him. He felt like an anvil. But I put my rapidly weakening back into it and dragged him to me.

Gunmetal gazed up. "What the hell?"

"Stop talking," I said, and pushed my muzzle into her mouth. "This has to be perfect."

"What're you doing?" she said around the cold metal.

"This." I angled my rod so it pressed against the roof of her mouth, and pulled the trigger. My pistol blasted loud. Skull bits and meat exploded from the front of Gunmetal's face. Wet blood poured from the gaping hole. But there was no scream. Just red bubbles churning.

And in the middle of that crimson cauldron, hanging by a thin, meaty thread, was a Trumite fang.

I tossed Rico aside, pinched the tooth, and plucked it like a rose. Shredded, bloody gum still clung to it like pulp on an orange slice. I cleaned it off the best I could, then crawled over to my dart. As I grabbed it my sight kicked off entirely. I was blind. My pulse picked up its pace.

And I willed it down. The faster my heart beat, the quicker the poison would finish its job. And that job stood mostly done. So I steadied myself. And on feel alone I dragged the dart's opening around the dull end of the fang. Finally, after a lengthy search, it clicked into the tube Gunmetal's venom traveled through. The fit wasn't perfect. So I wrapped my hand around both and squeezed them together, hoping to make a seal.

Then I held it out. And as fast as I could, jammed the fang into my chest and pressed the plunger. Cold antidote flowed into me. My muscles drank it like a burnt sponge getting its first taste of water.

And slowly, the room came into view. Feeling returned to my limbs. I grabbed Rico and jumped to my feet.

From the carpet, Gunmetal vomited the words, "Curse… Kill me."

Half her face was missing, like it'd been chewed off by an industrial accident. But despite the soupy mess I could still see the human pain in her eyes. The fear. The need for mercy. "No," I said. "Wouldn't want you to miss out on that dying light." Then I charged down the hall and out of the building.

Scourge was next to the rusted car on the curb with one leg inside it. He flinched at my presence. "You? How?"

"Stand still, I'll show you." I lifted Rico. Too slow.

Scourge jumped into the clunker. And it roared to life like a volcano. The rear tires squealed, and it shot forward.

I slid my still heavier than normal pistol into its holster, ran to my sled, and hopping in I followed as fast as I could.

Scourge was almost at the end of the road. Only now his car's rusty hue was matte black. And the exterior shifted around until it looked exactly like my Jalopy. Even our license plates were identical.

He took a quick right onto the street. I turned after him. Monday was waiting, and as I zipped by I hit my horn. The cop got on my tail and together we chased Scourge through traffic.

But the slippery fiend was driving maniacal. He hit a car to the left. It spun out, and stopped in my path. I veered to the side, clearing it easy. And so did Monday.

Then my quarry swerved right. And clipped an oncoming motorcycle's rear tire. The rider went down. But his bike flipped up. It rolled nose over tail, right at me.

Jerking the wheel left I barely slipped past it.

But Monday took it head on, pinning the cycle beneath his frame. Metal shrieked and sparks flew as my backup ground to a halt.

Leaving just me and Scourge.

Up ahead the traffic thinned, so Scourge poured on the throttle. He was flying now, putting some distance between us.

But then he took the next on-ramp.

I looped up behind him. And smiled. We were getting onto the I-93.

Finally. This road was going to help.

A row of bright yellow barrels blocked the path. Scourge crashed through them without slowing down. I followed him past the wreckage and onto the deserted patch of highway itself. Scourge started to pull away. I let him. And came to a stop, waiting for what I knew was coming. The bridge up ahead had a missing segment. He wouldn't be able to go any farther.

And right on time like Tokyo trains, Scourge's brake lights turned angry and I heard skidding. He turned around. And revved his engine. Then his Jalopy came barreling back at me around eighty miles per hour, dragging a cloud of dust like an angry avalanche. That was no small threat. The car he was in would probably rip through mine easy. The smart move would be to pull over, let him pass, and follow until I could overpower him somehow.

But instead of the smart move I hit the gas. My car's tires spun and caught and I blasted off the line.

Scourge kept coming. Right at me. And he was getting closer. Fast. Maybe a hundred yards separated us. Meanwhile the needle on my speedometer reached the top of the sky, then started to set. I downshifted, and it dipped below the horizon. Out front, Scourge's Jalopy was coming in hard. It was like playing chicken with a mirror. We were just seconds away from impact.

So I unclicked my belt, jammed an open hand through the roof, and peeled it back like a tin of sardines. Then I put both heels onto my seat.

And, with Scourge mere meters away, I jumped.

Up and out of my car I sailed through the night air. And as I went I extended my heels, aiming them at Scourge's head. Beneath me metal shrieked, tires exploded, and glass shattered as our Jalopies kissed like two drunk Frenchmen. Right as I hit his windshield with both feet.

I burst into Scourge's car in a hail of shattered glass. It swerved and screeched and came to a stop. It was dark. I looked around but couldn't see a thing.

Then the light clicked on.

I was upside down. In the backseat. I searched for Scourge's severed head, figuring I'd kicked it off like a soccer ball. But I was all alone. I pulled myself up, and looked into the front of the car. And I couldn't believe it. That wretched skunk was still in one piece, crawling out the door.

"Come here, you." I lunged over the seat for his ankle. And got his pant cuff.

He turned around. There was fear on his face.

"It's time to get wet and red. Just like a butcher's block." I pulled him to me.

"Not likely." Scourge slid the straight razor from his sleeve. And sliced at my left eye. I shut it tight. But his keen edge slipped between my lids. And slit open the soft tissue beneath. Pain shot through to the back of my skull.

"You bastard!" With my free hand I clamped down on the injured orb. But the other still held his cuff. With it I pulled him closer. "I'll kill you."

Scourge took a second swipe with the razor. This time he hit his pant leg, right below my grip. It cut the fabric free, and I tumbled back as Scourge slithered out of the car and ran.

Keeping pressure on my injured peeper, I jumped out and went after him.

We were on an elevated portion of the highway. There were no other cars for miles. And the buildings around us were short, and dark. Beyond them was the ocean. Its wind gusted fierce. And Scourge was limping through it.

"Oh no you don't." I pulled out Rico and fired into the sky.

But Scourge continued on his way. He was just a few feet from the edge of the highway. The wall there was only three feet high, but on the other side was a two-story drop.

That fall might kill him. And I wasn't letting him die like that. So I used my right eye to aim carefully. And when I got my sights lined up nice I fired. The slug knocked his derby off, and it hit the street rolling.

"Ok. Ok." Scourge froze. He was right at the edge. But he turned around. And raised both hands high. In one he held Doodle's red envelope. "Don't shoot."

"Good boy," I said. "Now slide me that address."

He dangled the envelope over the edge. "No."

"You're not giving orders."

"Well I'm not taking them, either."

"Yes you are. Orders, or this heat." I motioned to Rico. "You're taking one."

"Nope." He smiled, and shook the red letter. "Because if I drop this you'll never see your daughter again."

"Maybe," I said. "Maybe not. But if I put a pill in your liver, she'll be safe either way. And you know what? I can live with that." I aimed my rod at his stomach. Truthfully, I had no idea if it was the part that housed the liver. But even if I perforated his bladder I'd still count it as a win.

"You might be able to live with that," Scourge said, "but Doodle sure won't."

My finger had the nasty fun urge that can only be calmed by pulling a trigger. But there was something unnaturally earnest in Scourge's tone. So I stayed my hand. "What do you mean?"

The wind around us picked up. Scourge had to yell. "You know what's going down tonight? Your scumbag ex and her spawn are auctioning off the Coconut to the highest bidder."

I raised my head from Rico's sights. "Tera wouldn't. She's not that dumb."

Scourge laughed. An ugly, rasping thing. "Stupid enough? No. But greedy enough? Definitely." He looked at me. "Oh Dane, you think your daughter, who's never left her mother's side, broke away to send a telegram to only you? That pair's reached out to every black cape in town who can rub two millions together to auction off the diamond." He laughed again. "I mean, come on. A telegram? In this day? Sketch doesn't want you to save her, she needs you to stand in the way of those who don't win the diamond while her and Mommy escape with the green. How did you not see it? I knew your skin was thick, just not that thick. Your kid's been using you. From the beginning." Then Scourge got more sly. An impressive feat. "You think one of them tipped off Swamp? Something like this usually doesn't stay quiet for long." He lifted the address higher. The wind had it flapping like his gums. "In one hour every black cape's going to show up for a diamond, or your baby's blood. Shoot me, and you'll never know where."

"No." A bidding war. Tera was going for a bidding war. That daffy dame-

"I'm bored," Scourge said, and gave my letter to the breeze. The red paper flew from his hand and danced right at me, twisting and turning in the wind. I reached out for it.

But with only one eye open the telegram sailed clean through my fingers. I turned and chased it. But the paper flew skyward, like a butterfly. I watched it sail up and away, taking with it any hope of saving my daughter. Higher and higher it went.

Then the wind died. And my letter drifted down like a leaf, landing right in front of me. I stomped on the paper, trapping it to the ground. And spun towards Scourge, ready to add three pounds of warm metal to his torso.

But the shifty rodent was gone.

I placed Rico back in his perch, then snatched up the address. As I walked back to my car I blinked a bit, trying to calm the throbbing in my left eye. It didn't work, but amazingly I could still see fine from it. Scourge's blade must've only hit the whites. It was good news, especially since I could read the letter clearly.

188th Street. An old abandoned girly club called Crush.

I knew it well. But I had to be there by four am. That meant there was only a little over an hour left before the meet. Still, that gave me some time. But then I saw my ride.

The front end was crushed. And the axle had snapped. That thing was going nowhere.

But sitting nearby was Scourge's ride. And his Jalopy was perfect, save for the Dane size hole in its windshield. I ran to it and looked in. The keys were still there. I turned them and the car came to life, purring like a happy tabby. Perfect. I loved the idea of a sled that could change its face. I threw one foot inside. But next to my other, with a loud clang, landed a metal canister the size of a football.

I said, "Son of a-" as the metal tube exploded in a cloud of blue smoke. I covered my eyes and stumbled away from the car, hacking. Another canister landed nearby. It erupted too, adding more viper vapor to the already thick air. I dropped to a knee. I could barely breathe. Then two vans pulled up the on-ramp. They came to a halt, and belched out a dozen black clad lawmen. Across their chests were the four letters I was learning to hate.

"SPECs, fan out and watch your fire. The gas should daze him, but let's not make any mistakes."

A rifle butt struck my temple. I fell to my back. Somebody kicked my flank. I rolled to my stomach and tried to get up, but a dozen hands pinned me down.

Even with their combined strength they shouldn't be able to hold me.

Turns out it was going to take more time to heal from that venom than I thought.

My hands got yanked behind me. And even over their yells I could hear the sickening click-click-click of Trumite handcuffs.

Then there was stillness. And the smoke was abating.

But my head still swam in a hazy pool of nauseous blue. I rolled onto my back and looked up. Standing there was an old friend. He spoke into his radio. "This is SPEC Commander Waters, bring up the dragon wagon, we got him."

Chapter 48

"And the Coconut, too." Waters was talking proud. Monday said these guys weren't cops, but they sure sounded like them when they made a collar. "We'll be bringing him to Impenetron in the wagon. What's that, please repeat? Affirmative, the diamond goes home first. Waters out." He turned to me and smiled. "Tried to steal the Coconut, huh? You've gotten the farthest of anyone. Fortunately the museum pegged you the second you got outside, and now you're heading to the clink. Hope you like bars as much as you hate sunshine. Box him, boys."

Two SPECs reached under my shoulders, hoisted me up, and hauled me to the dragon wagon. Its insides were completely smooth, with two benches against the walls, and all of it was made of thin Trumite sheets. They shoved me in and slammed the doors. I lay there with my hands behind my back. It was dark. Silent.

But then the wagon came to life. And even in my drowsy state I have to say it lived up to its name. If real dragons were as loud as this one I haven't been giving Saint George enough credit.

It pulled out and I slid to the rear. We were now heading to the museum. And after that it would be a straight shot to Impenetron.

That didn't leave a lot of options for escape.

But Doodle was up north with her mom, getting ready to open a can of black cape worms that would kill them both unless I freed myself from this rolling cage. And I never let having no options stop me before.

My first step was getting the cuffs off.

Then I'd break those doors down. Somehow.

Sitting up I leaned against the back wall. Sliding the cuffs below my knees I pulled both heels in. Then I slipped my hands beneath them, and out in front of me.

I pat my jacket. Both pistols were still there. I guess when you bag black capes guns aren't something you naturally look for. That was their first mistake.

Leaving me my lock pick was their second.

I pulled it out and heard Carl Cutter's voice in my head. "Learn to use this. Muscle isn't an all-purpose tool."

Thanks for the advice, pops.

Taking a deep breath I steadied myself. The blue smoke was still floating behind my eyes, dulling all five senses. Fortunately I was just working with cuffs. Door locks are a hell of a lot harder, but still, I pushed the hazy numbness down, thankful that invulnerables can withstand an unhealthy amount of sedatives, and focused. Using my left hand I steadied the lock, and slid the safeguard that covered the keyhole aside. Then, with my right, I guided the pick's thin metal point inside.

Slowly I twisted the lock clockwise, like I was winding a watch. I got from noon all the way to midnight. But nothing happened. So I rotated it in the opposite direction.

The mechanism spun. And it gave a click. The cuff stayed locked, but it was almost there. Then the wagon came to sharp stop. I slid down the floor and rolled, dropping my pick. Outside the front doors opened. Then shut. And we started moving again.

That had to have been the museum. Next stop, ten years of my life.

Pawing the floor I found the pick. Then I clicked the cuff's guard out of the way again, and pushed the thin metal inside. Rotating counterclockwise I got the mechanism all the way around, and the cuff opened wide.

Halfway there.

I pulled my left hand free and gave it a shake. Then I passed my pick to it and started on my right. I moved the guard and spun the same way. After one pass it stayed locked. That's the problem with my left paw, it's about as useful as a palsy hand. I jammed the pick in as deep as it would go. And spun again. This time the mechanism gave a satisfying click, and the cuffs dropped to the floor.

I pocketed my lock pick, pulled out Lois, and depressed her trigger halfway. She doubled in size and width, and bathed the room with a green glow, which I used like a lantern to study the doors.

Both were as smooth as a conman's tongue. There were no handles or locks. Not even hinges. And the gaps between the wall and door were too thin for a needle.

That left me one choice. The one I warned Johan about. The one Carl cautioned against. Muscle.

I clicked off Lois' safety and her grip spit the twin bracers that ran up my arm like latticework, strapping her to me. I stepped back and aimed at the spot that should be between the two handles on the other side. My Kapowitzer was the most powerful handgun on the market. And the Trumite was probably so thin I might burn a hole through it.

But would that hole be big enough? And what was on the other side? Could be nothing.

Could be a car with a family of four.

So I stepped closer. And pressed the barrel to the door, clicked on narrow shot, and angled it upwards, high enough so the blast would sear through the metal, but wouldn't hit anything save the man in the moon. Then, with my cannon prepped, I braced myself.

And pulled the trigger.

The Kapowitzer blasted hot light. I flew back, bounced off the far wall, and fell to the ground.

With a ringing head I got to my knees. And shook the buzzing in my ears away. Slowly my sight returned. Lois was glowing red. But she wasn't the only light source in the wagon. Now there was a hole in the door about the size of a baseball.

I jumped up, and charged, throwing my weight into the exit. The impact knocked me back and I fell as the gate stayed shut.

The locks were still in place. *Damn it.*

I crawled back, and peered out the hole. There was traffic. But it was all civilian. And I could also see the door handle a few inches to the right. I pulled out the lock pick. Lois illuminated it with her red glow.

And I heard Carl say, "Learn to use this. Muscle isn't-"

Shut up, old man. I get it.

I holstered Lois, then took the pick in my left hand and fished it through the hole. Finding the key slot on the other side of the door, I slipped the thin metal inside. Now all I had to do was unlock it. Backwards. And blind. With my left hand. While moving.

Yay.

I began to fish the metal around. The tumblers were there. And they wanted to line up. They wanted to release so badly. All they needed was a push. So I moved the pick up. And down. I jimmied it side-to-side. I twisted it left. Then right. And the door swung wide open.

Holy shit...

Behind the wagon a whole lot of traffic and tall buildings were flying by. We were downtown. Inside the city. And traveling maybe forty miles an hour. Five or six cars were following close. And not one of those drivers failed to notice me. With my right hand I yanked Rico out, and pointed him their way. With the other hand I lifted a single finger to my lips, and shook my head.

The cars all slowed down, and pulled to the side.

With my wake now clear I stepped out.

And hit the street rolling like a tumbleweed. Coming to rest I jumped up. A vehicle zipped by on my right. Two more passed on the left. It was like being in a stampede.

A car came charging towards me. It hit the brakes. All four tires locked as their rubber painted the road. And it came to a stop a few inches from my knees.

The driver rolled down his window and said, "Hurry up, get in."

"Monday?"

The blond Viking was behind the wheel. "Let's go, we don't got all day."

I ran around to the passenger side and hopped in. "188th street, driver. And step lively."

"Done and done." Monday hit the gas, and took the next turn.

I looked at the cop. "Not that I'm ungrateful, but how and why?"

"After I got that cycle out from under my car I arrived on scene, but they already had you cuffed and stuffed. Outside the wagon Waters was talking to central and Johan's claiming you're behind Firewall and Thermite's death. She says you scuffled with the boys and ended up killing them during your first try, but then learned from the mistake and succeeded tonight."

"How's she saying I got the rock?"

"Don't know. Mind control? Doppelgänger? This town's not normal, so I'm sure she'll cook something up just north of unbelievable."

"Fat chance."

"You think? They got eyewitnesses who saw you break into the Amphibia Theatre a few nights back. They got Johan saying you were in Wentorf tonight, too. And since you lifted that Kessel Glass display they got your prints underneath it as-"

"And my DNA," I said, "because I spit in my hand. But you were there, you know the truth."

"So? I got a feeling if I speak up they'll try to pin it on me since on your first day I followed you out for a tete-a-tete. And maybe they'll say I helped you escape after your dance with the SPECs, too."

"Damn." All of a sudden Johan's thinking didn't seem so bad. Maybe she was child-of-destiny special.

"Cheer up. If we retrieve the real Coconut we should come out of this fine. Now where in the Outskirts are we headed exactly?"

"A closed down club called Crush."

Monday pulled onto the expressway. He grabbed his radio. "I'm going to have to call it in."

"Please do," I said. "I need as much backup as possible. And considering the likely black cape turnout I don't care if your boys are wearing blue suits or white capes."

"Really?"

"Yeah. It's going to be a convention."

"What if I can only get patrolmen, will you be able to handle it solo?"

I thought about who might be there. With Gunmetal rotting away on some dingy floor all I had to contend with was Scourge. Maybe Swamp and Vector. Possibly Bundy Strong. Along with a large helping of the wealthiest, most antisocial black capes inside these city limits. That stacked the odds against me coming out in one piece. But when it's your kid, coming out in one piece odds don't mean much. I said, "Sure thing."

Don't worry, baby. I'm on my way.

Chapter 49

Crush, the old dance club, was one story with walls mostly made of boarded up or blackened windows. The buildings around it had been demolished, or simply crumbled of their own accord, so it sat on the block like a stumpy monolith, completely alone save for a few fancy automobiles parked out front.

But when we got three blocks from it, a cop jumped out from the corner and waved us over. Monday pulled down a side street and stopped behind a building. The young kid ran to the driver's side and leaned down. "Hey detective," he said. "We got the perimeter set up as ordered."

"Good," Monday said. "How many you got?"

"About eight."

"Cars?"

"No, men."

Monday sighed. "So you're not surrounding the building?"

"Oh, we are. It's just not with as thick a blue line as you'd like. But we got a team on every corner, four blocks from the club in all directions."

Monday nodded. "And the SPECs, they onsite?

"Not yet. But we saw Manfred Mayhem arrive about ten minutes back and called it in, so they should be here soon. Hopefully along with a white cape or two, though this won't be a priority since there's no action yet, or civilians around."

I leaned over. "What're your men armed with?"

He looked past Monday. "Just service pieces, shotguns, and viper vapor."

"Gas?" I said. "You guys are going non-lethal?"

"With a guy like Mayhem it's bullets that're non-lethal. At least the vapor's got a chance of knocking him flat."

"Thanks," Monday said. "Get back in position."

The officer tipped his cap and returned to the corner.

"Park this thing over there," I said, "in front of Toots' Sweets."

Monday pulled up to the candy shop, and we got out.

"What're we doing here?" he asked.

"There's a back door into Crush, and I'm about to use it."

"You sure?"

"My kid's in there with Manfred Mayhem and who knows what other villains, and soon the SPECs and white capes will arrive, so yeah. I'm going in, grabbing her, and coming back out as fast as I can."

"Do you want me with you? Maybe get the force to run interference?"

I thought about charging into a stolen diamond auction with Monday on my elbow and the GCCPD at my back. They wouldn't do much to stop whoever was in there. Blood would definitely flow, most of it blue. And of course it would cement my status as a turn cape. "No," I said, "let me get the lay first. If I need help, I'll fire off a shot."

"Fine. One gunshot and we're lobbing enough knockout gas through the windows to bring down a stampede."

"It's a plan." I ripped off the door to the candy shop and ran through to its back room. There was an old, dilapidated refrigerator in the corner. Shoving it aside revealed a rectangular hole, and steps that led down into darkness. I took them, and the yellow orbs of Tunnel Town lit up at my feet, illuminating the way. When I got to the bottom I ran through the red rock corridor, and in less than a minute I was taking the stairs up to Crush. There was a large, metal door. I pushed against it, but the thing was stuck. I threw my shoulder into it and nothing. Then I gave it a kick.

The boom echoed down the tunnel, but the door didn't give. Gunmetal's venom, it was still working a number on me. So I reached for Rico, but stopped. Not because of Monday's warning about the gas. No, I was more leery of charging into a room full of black capes buying illicit materials with my Thumper out. They'd be jumpier than frogs in a coffee pond, and my daughter wasn't bulletproof.

So I took a deep breath and concentrated. Then I cocked back, and punched the door as hard as I could. It blasted off the hinges and slid to the far wall.

I charged through the opening. And into Crush's kitchen. Not breaking stride I moved into the main room. The stale smell of must filled the cavernous room along with scattered, broken furniture. Beyond all the flotsam, in the far left corner, was a raised, circular stage.

Gathered around it, on the club's floor, was a collection of black capes. There were fewer than I expected, but what they lacked in numbers was more than made up for in power.

Nearest to me was my gal pal, Dastard Lee. She had Psy-ball, her onyx barman, with her, and they were flanked by those twin giantesses from Henchmen's: the black beauty queen Kalamity, and Slamazon, the pasty dish of dog's dinner. Both had mini-chain guns strapped to them.

To the right was a nasty piece of work known as Manfred Mayhem. He was my size, made of German muscle, and wore black slacks and a black t-shirt. But his eyes were bright white and burned with nuclear fire. Behind him stood two men in suits I'd never seen, each holding a large, wooden chest.

On my left, standing alone, was Perry Mortem. He wore an old-fashioned top hat and a green Victorian suit with tails, and he was leaking dark magic into the air like a squid does ink.

Finally, on the other side of the room, closest to the stage, was my old friend and missing fake cape, Bundy Strong, holding a large suitcase.

I looked around again. No Scourge. No Swamp. No Vector.

That was a relief.

But the consolation was short lived. Because at the end of the stage the moldy curtains parted and out walked Tera with my little girl on her elbow. And in my cute kid's hand, as big as a bowling ball and sparkling like the promise of prom night, was the one and only Vandenberg Coconut.

Chapter 50

"I'm glad you could be here," Tera said in her Tagalog tinged accent. "For the bidding war of the century."

"I'm not bidding on anything," Bundy said and looked my way, "until the curse among us is lifted."

"Get bent," I said.

Perry Mortem spoke in a way that was half dandy, half mortician. "I concur with our strong friend."

"Ja." Manfred Mayhem had more kraut in his words than they do in Dusseldorf. "No turn capes here."

Bundy I couldn't have been less scared of, but the other two men were hitters of the heaviest means. Despite that, the one thing I've learned about black capes is they always mistake kindness for weakness, so I pointed a finger at them and said, "Button your lips before I fatten them. Lee, where we at?"

"Bidding war," she said, "and it's about to get hot."

I passed my gaze over the gathered villainy. "So I see. How'd you all hear about this?"

Lee said, "I got a telegram, along with every other gold laden diamond devotee around. How'd you get in here?"

"Tunnel Town," I said. "And thanks so much for passing the info about this on to me."

"I tried, but your office line-"

"Enough chatter," Tera said, "get him out of here."

Slamazon pointed her chain gun at me. "Glad to."

I swatted her heater aside. "Stifle it, plugly."

"Slam. Be easy," Lee said. "This ain't the place to go all slap happy."

"Listen to your boss," I said. "And-"

"Why are you here, anyway?" Bundy said.

"To protect my kid. From the cops outside waiting to raid this place."

The collected capes didn't show fear. But there was concern. Or confusion.

Mayhem glanced around. "There are cops outside?"

"Don't listen to him," Tera said, "this is just another one of his ploys."

Lee looked at me. "Is it?"

"Sorry Lee, it's no ploy. Have Psy-ball take a peek out front."

Lee gave a nod and the kid ran to the window. The panes of glass were blacked out, but he peered against the wall and looked to the left and right. Then he turned back around. "Dane's right. There's a bunch of cops out there. No lights, no barricades, but cars and mortars. About four blocks back."

The room started to mull about.

Lee was loud. Her lips curled nasty. "You brought the cops with you?"

"Damn snitch," Mayhem said.

Perry Mortem covered his mouth with a black kerchief. "Such a scabby fink, bringing the constables."

I raised my hands. "Lee, Jerry, Fancy Pants, you got it all wrong. They-"

Mayhem loosed a white blast from his right eye. It struck my shoulder. I flew backwards, hit the ground, and skidded to a stop. "Always the hard way," I said, and jumped to my feet. I reached for Rico. But the spot where Mayhem hit me throbbed. I looked at my shoulder. The clothes there were burnt away. The skin was blackened and bubbly. I grit my teeth, pushed the pain aside, and went for my piece.

But before I could snatch it Perry Mortem said, "No, I think not." He stepped out from the shadows behind me, and wrapped his hands around my face, covering both eyes.

And my world turned black. I couldn't see a thing. I spun around and swung my left hand through him. It was like running into a cold patch in a warm pool. My whole arm went numb. I grabbed it and shuffled back. "You got it wrong," I said, still blind. "I'm here to help."

"Help this." It was Slamazon. And her strike came in hard across my chin. My formerly split lip tore open. Blood filled my mouth, and I stumbled away.

"And this." Kalamity joined her friend. And drove what felt like a kick into my gut. The air blasted from my lungs as I collapsed to the floor. But they didn't let me rest long. One of those broads snatched me up and held me tight while the other one tucked in for a workout. First she jabbed my nose, breaking it again. Then drove a hook into my temple. And kicked my junk for good measure.

I went limp in the arms of whoever had me. My face was wet. The body beneath it swam in nausea.

"Kill him already." I couldn't see Bundy, but the glee in his voice was evident.

"As you request." It was Perry Mortem. He pulled me free from the mystery dame's clutches, then wrapped both hands around my neck. The skin there went icy numb. I tried to swallow some air. But nothing happened. Pressure built behind both eyes. It was like my head was a water balloon, and Perry was squeezing more liquid up into it. Bursting was imminent.

But then, "Let him be, Perry. Or we'll see what's what."

There was a long pause. Finally Mortem said, "Very well, Lee. Since we are the oldest of friends." The building pressure eased. Then the hands released my throat. And my skull returned to its resting state of painfulness as I flopped to the ground.

The bitty patter of tiny feet came scurrying my way. And the familiar voice of Dastard Lee said, "What's up, kid? Why'd you drag the fuzz this way?"

"I didn't. They were waiting when I arrived. And while there aren't too many here right now, more are coming, so I'd suggest anyone who doesn't want to see the inside of Impenetron should rabbit back down the hole to Tunnel Town."

"Like fun," Bundy said. "How about we kill-"

"Wait," Lee said. "There are only a handful of bulls out there?"

A few seconds passed before Psy-ball said, "Yeah Lee, I count eleven all day."

"Eleven?" Lee said. "That's nothing. Give him back his orbs."

"Very well," Perry Mortem said. And with that the black veil over my eyes lifted. The dark dandy was staring down at me with that half mad look he made famous. "There. He can see all this splendidness again. So, shall we commence the bidding?" He slid a hand inside his coat and removed a green duffel, one that was far too big to have been in there. He slipped open the top revealing a whole lot of bound dollar bills. "I've brought my fee."

"Yeah, let's." Bundy clicked open his case and held it up. The thing was lousy with crisp hundreds. "I came to play, too."

"Show them, schnell." Mayhem motioned to his twin monkeys. Each opened their chest and filled the room with gold bullion shine.

"Excellent," Tera said. My ex was grinning like a Midwest divorcee on his first trip to a Thai whorehouse. "Now get Dane out of here, and we'll begin."

Every eye turned on me.

Lee pulled me to my feet. "Sorry, but like your old flame says, it's time to go. Kalamity, Slamazon."

The two broads started my way.

But Psy-ball jumped in their path. "What the hell?"

"Stay frigid, kid." Lee pulled him back. "The muscle's doing its thing."

"No, forget about Dane." Psy-ball pointed at Bundy. "We got a problem."

"What is it?" Lee said.

"Those bills are marked," the onyx kid with the big, white eyes said. "With the kind of ultraviolet ink that only cops use."

Chapter 51

Lee spun to Psy-ball. "What did you say?"

"Those hundreds are marked. He's undercover," Psy-ball said.

Bundy slammed his case shut. "No they're not."

"Yeah they are. And I can still see them." Psy-ball turned to Lee. "All of them, too. That briefcase is glowing like a Vegas hotel fire."

Kalamity stepped forward. "Why would they be marked?"

It was a good question. Why would a fence like Bundy have so many marked bills? Then it hit me, and I looked the scoundrel's way and said, "I know."

Bundy stared into my eyes. "Shut up."

"You had those bills marked so the cops could nab Dread Division."

He stepped back, hugging the case. "You can't prove that, maybe I stole them."

I pulled out the note I tried giving Psy-ball earlier, and read the date in the corner. "Nope. There hasn't been a bank job that big in half a decade, and these bills were printed this year. Even so, the cops don't mark every bill. No. You worked with the law. Had them set up that cash. Then somehow you got Subatomic to use you as a fence, and you gave him a bunch of dirty dollars."

Kalamity shook her head. "Why would Bundy set up your old team?"

"Because," I said, "he needed us out of the way so he could steal the Coconut."

"What?" Mayhem said, "Bundy planned the theft?"

"No. Scourge did. But Bundy put the team together. It's his specialty. But to plan the job, execute it, and cover it all, he needed Scourge, who wouldn't step foot back in town so long as Dread Division was breathing free air.

"So Bundy called in the big guns: the state. And offered them the team who stormed Top Tower. All of them. Every last one. See, there are a lot of members of Dread Division, and each one got a cut, even the ones that didn't do the gig, which he knew through Scourge, even though they didn't have the full roster. So you had the cops mark every. Single. Bill. Only by the time you got to work, I'd moved into the snooping sector." I squeezed the air from my fists. "Must've burnt those biscuits to know one got away. I can't believe you skimmed that much from the state. If you'd just been less greedy you wouldn't be holding a case full of evidence that you're a liar."

The room mulled some. But I heard no dissent.

Until Slamazon said, "Wait. Hold on. Maybe Bundy's got an excuse."

The entire room turned his way.

Bundy said, "I don't... He's not... I don't know anything about this."

"Really, nothing?" I held up my rotten bill. "This one's got a print on it. You want to prove you never touched this dough? Come on over and let bright eyes here study your nimble pickers."

It was brisk inside the dump. But Bundy looked uncomfortably warm.

"Come on Bundy, prove it," Slamazon said.

"Show us," Mayhem added.

Bundy looked around. "Listen, maybe I got some ultraviolet ink on my fingers but that... that could happen to anybody. Maybe I..." He trailed off.

And I didn't blame him. Who knows where that sentence would've ended up? Not the people in the room. They were all silent, down to the last man. Even Tera shut up.

Finally Kalamity said, "You son of a bitch turn cape no good reg. You did it. You really did it. You're the one who ratted out Dread Division."

"I'm not a reg," Bundy said, "and so what if I did? I wasn't alone. We-"

"You filthy louse," Lee said. "You know what we did to guys like you in the old days?" She lunged my way, grabbed Rico from his holster, and aimed him at Bundy. "This."

"No." I reached out for my piece.

But it was too late. Lee blasted away. And the bullet, a high-velocity, struck Bundy's cheek and spread his thoughts in a red cloud behind him. Then, with his head pumpkin hollow, Bundy dropped his case and fell to the ground.

"Give me that," I said and yanked back my iron. "Do you know what you just did? Now we all-"

"Sorry about banning you. I should've... I just shouldn't have,"

Lee said.

"Yeah," Kalamity said. "Damn. Sorry. I thought-"

"Let's save the apologies for later. The cops are about to start lobbing gas our way. Assuming the SPECs aren't already here and ready to-"

"So? Who are the SPECs?" Tera yelled. "Listen up, we got the Coconut here. Bidding starts at five million."

"There's no time," I said. "A regiment of very-"

The Kraut said, "Five million."

Tera's eyes were shining. "That's five million to Manfred Mayhem. Do I hear six?"

I looked at Doodle. And caught her gaze. I motioned to the exit. She looked at her mom. Then she nodded, and came towards me. But she only got two steps before Tera pulled her back.

"Six million," Lee called out.

Perry Mortem waved his kerchief. "Seven lucky."

I yelled, "Hey, cut it out. We got to get moving, otherwise-"

A metal shell burst through a window on the far wall, and landed on the floor.

Lee said, "What the hell is that?"

Out both ends of the canister came a stream of thick, cobalt viper vapor. Above it two more windows exploded as another pair of bombs came bursting in, spitting out the same viscous haze.

As the smoke filled the room I covered my mouth and said, "Lee, the stuff they're using is grade-A knockout gas. We got to split."

"We can still handle this," Mayhem said.

"Absolutely." Perry rolled up his sleeves. "Just give me the tiniest of moments."

I said, "And what about the team of white capes that're surely on their way here?"

The room got quiet.

"Yeah, you think they're not coming? The museum knows the Coconut's been stolen, and the first call their security system makes is to Team Supreme." I wasn't sure that was exactly true. After all, I had no clue what Johan had done or who she'd informed. But still I said, "Ok. Ignore me. Just don't kick yourselves too hard during your own ten year tour of Impenetron after Pinnacle and Glory Anna catch you in a room with the same notes they pinned on Dread Division."

All eyes turned to the case lying next to Bundy's corpse.

"Damn. Dane's right," Lee said. "Mayhem, Mortem, on me."

The three formed a triumvirate right there.

"No." Tera's eyes were wild. "We do this now."

The gas had filled the far side of the room like a ten-foot snowdrift, and it started rolling our way.

"Really, Tera?" Lee said. "Not every cape handles night-night juice as well as invulnerables, and I'm one of them."

"Me too," Mayhem said. "So what's the call, Lee?"

"Ok. All we got to do to avoid the hoosegow is leave down Tunnel Town together. I know we don't trust each other completely, but I think instead of going for throats over the diamond now, and dying in prison, we can agree to put off the bloodletting until tomorrow."

"What certainty can be offered that none will attempt to filch the gem before the allotted time?" Perry Mortem said.

"Because if any of us moves on Tera, the other two will clip them clean and clear. Right?" Lee looked at both men.

"Right," Mayhem said.

Perry Mortem smiled. "I believe that reasoning to be sound."

"Alright, let's motor. Together." Lee and the two mighty black capes charged my way. "Dane, where's that door to Tunnel Town?"

I threw a thumb over my shoulder. "Back through the kitchen."

"No!" Tera was raging.

"Let's skedaddle," Lee said. Then she, Perry, and Mayhem vanished through the door together as the wave of noxious gas rolled ever closer.

It was only twenty feet away when Mayhem's lackeys charged past me, followed closely by Slamazon and Psy-ball. Kalamity was the last one out, but she paused and said, "Sorry about everything, Curse. I was wrong as hell. You're a standup guy."

"You can buy me an Octane later," I said. "For now, split."

She knocked my shoulder. And ran out the door.

That only left Tera and Doodle.

"Come on, sweetheart. We got to go," I said.

"Ok." Doodle took another step towards me.

But Tera yanked her back again. "Dane, I always knew you'd ruin everything." The old broad's eyes were wild. Her face twisted like a tiki. "But you'll never do it again." She took a deep breath. I'd never seen her inhale that much before, and whatever was about to come out of her mouth was probably going to do a lot more damage now that I was already weak from the venom.

So I ducked down. And covered my ears. Prepared for the worst. But it never came.

I glanced up.

Tera was standing still. Her look of anger turned to confusion.

I didn't blame her. The blue gas that was rolling in thick like a sandstorm had stopped. And it was floating up into the rafters along with the three canisters it came from.

I lowered my hands. "What the hell?" It was like a bright thundercloud localized above us.

But then something cut through the azure fog. Someone, actually. Three of them. They sailed down and landed on the floor gentle. And I knew the storm hadn't blown over.

It had just started.

Chapter 52

The three men stood in the middle of the room. Swamp was closest, looking furious. Vector was right behind him, with enough confidence on his face to go around. But the one that gave me the chills was Scourge. He was staring right at my kid and her mom when he said, "Remember, we split the rock three ways, but the dames... They're all mine."

"Agreed," Swamp said. And he and Scourge charged for the girls.

I ran at them with Rico in hand, ready to intercept. But coming towards me fast was Vector. I raised my piece and-

"Where do you think you're going?" Vector extended his hand.

And my body got heavy. Rico dipped as I dragged both feet across the floor like I was knee deep in oatmeal, and came to a stop.

"Dane!" Doodle lunged towards me.

But Tera grabbed her arm. "Forget your father, stand by me."

My daughter looked my way. "No," she said. "He needs me." And she tore completely free from her mother's grasp.

"What?" Tera said. "You stop right-" She spun from our daughter, turning to the pair of men running towards her, and screamed. The force wave blasted a hole in the floor. Scourge leapt over it, and kept moving left towards Doodle, as Swamp veered to the right in pursuit of Tera.

Doodle made it two steps in my direction before she saw Scourge was coming and stopped.

"Forget Dane," the fiend said. "You're mine."

My daughter, still on the stage near her mother, snapped towards him and pulled her pistol out.

"Doodle," I said, "look-"

"Hey," Vector said, "we've got unfinished business." He swiped a hand to the side and his power jerked me backwards through the air.

I landed flat on my chest. Blood from my head wounds poured down my face. While ahead of me, Doodle, still clutching the diamond, fired at Scourge. He rolled behind a column to the left. She couldn't see, but he pulled out a gun of his own.

"Are you listening to me?" Vector said. He circled behind me.

I was still stuck to the ground like it was glue. No good. My baby needed me. So with my Thumper still in hand, I pressed against the floor. And managed to get a few inches up. Then I glanced back. Vector was right behind me now. Perfect. I slid Rico under my left arm, aimed comically high through the back of my coat, and fired.

The bullet shot upwards. But because of the heavy gravity the slug changed trajectory, rocketed down, and hit Vector's flank. He yelled, "You bastard," and clutched his hip where a red spot was spreading beneath his fingers.

Finally. I'd managed to put a pill in him. But he'd need more. I flipped over, aimed at his chest and fired again.

Behind him a window shattered.

But then another gunshot came from the stage. And Doodle screamed.

I looked over. Scourge was pointing his smoking piece up at my kid. She was bleeding from her thigh. Yet Doodle stood straight, and keeping the diamond close with one hand, fired down at him.

The slippery fiend ducked back behind his column. And chunks of plaster fell to the ground as my daughter blasted away.

Next to her, on the right, was Tera. She screamed and sent another sonic wave down at Swamp. It hit square, bursting him apart like a popped water balloon. But he reformed in seconds as a green, liquid waterman. Tera shrieked at him again. This time he flattened out like a puddle, slithered to the side, and popped back up, whole and unharmed.

Vector stepped to my flank, and looked down on me. "Still not getting it, are you?"

"I'm a slow learner." I was flat on my back, with Rico pressing down on my chest. I aimed him up at Vector's face as best I could. And fired another round.

It blew a hole in the ceiling.

"You must be. If I can move beams of light around my body, and compress gas, shifting the trajectory of bullets is easy." Vector pushed both hands out and his power hit me like a waterfall, pressing down so hard the wooden planks beneath me groaned.

I turned my head so I could see my kid. She was on one knee now. Still shooting at Scourge. But then her clip ran dry.

Scourge poked his head out. But stopped when he saw me. He

licked a lip, then pointed his piece my way. I could tell he was aiming for an eye. And with me stuck still, and his quality vision, he'd probably hit square, and blind me for life.

Doodle yelled, "No." She manifested twin blades from her forearm. And tossed one at Scourge.

It hit his wrist as he fired at me, and the bullet sailed wide, striking my shoulder. Blood poured down his arm as the gun fell from his hand. "You bitch!"

"Oh yeah," Doodle said. And then she tossed the second knife.

This metal shiv hit Scourge's leg. He screamed again, and fell.

Doodle looked at me and winked.

But she didn't notice that Scourge had landed right next to his pistol. He scooped it up, and from his back he shot again. This bullet hit my kid's hip.

She spun, and dropped the Coconut.

Tera screamed, "No."

I thought she must've seen Doodle.

But I was wrong.

Tera was staring at the Coconut as it rolled off the stage and fell onto the floor. She shoved our wounded daughter aside and dove after it.

Both Swamp and Scourge moved towards the diamond. Vector took a few steps that way, too. And his power eased some.

I rolled to my stomach. More blood ran into both eyes.

"What're you doing?" Vector said.

"Shooting your boss." I pushed Rico out, lifted him up, and tried to aim at Swamp. But the blood in my orbs was blurring my vision as the cut Scourge put in my left eye throbbed. Meanwhile the shoulder Mayhem blasted ached. And the gun, it was still so heavy. But I strained. And a number of muscles ripped in my arms.

Vector laughed. "You still think that'll work? Bullets slide right through him. Man. Sketch was right, you are an idiot. Here. Go nuts. You'll probably hit Tera." He was confident. Cocky. He let up a little more so I could aim at his boss.

Ignoring the pain, I got Swamp in my sights.

"Is this what fatherhood is?" Vector said. "Being so stupid that you'll give your life, and everything you've got, to help a dumb kid that resents you?"

"Yes. That's exactly what it is." I pulled my trigger five times.

Each bullet hit Swamp's back dead center. Green liquid sprayed from his chest. But he didn't even slow down as he moved towards the Coconut.

"See?" Vector said. "You didn't do squat."

"I wasn't aiming at him."

"Huh?"

"Those were target seekers." As I said it the bullets turned in the air, and came back hard like a squad of angry hornets, seeking the tracer I'd put in Vector's torso moments ago. And because he didn't know they were coming, and was far enough away from the gravity field that had me trapped, those bullets hit true. They ripped through his body like hungry rats. Vector doubled over and grabbed the green guts and red blood that poured out of him like meat from a grinder. He opened his mouth, and blood leaked out along with a meek, "How?"

"Don't worry about it." I jumped to my feet, put Rico to his forehead, and pulled the trigger. The explosive tip spread his brains onto the floor, and Vector fell to the ground, not quite as attractive as he once was.

Then, without his power to hold them up, the canisters belching out viper vapor dropped like stones, while the massive cloud of blue smoke above us descended in slow motion.

I ignored the encroaching danger, wiped the blood from my eyes, and turned towards Doodle.

Scourge, with his gun out, was walking her way. His look was sickening. Between me and Doodle, Swamp danced with Tera. She somehow had the diamond in her hand. But Swamp was holding onto her head and had it encased in his watery grip. She still had some fight in her though. And my ex let loose a scream that would've vaporized a normal man. But Swamp was liquid. The sound waves passed through him harmlessly.

Tera thrashed some as her air supply diminished. Then, in a desperate last ditch effort, she pulled a pistol with her right hand, put it up to Swamp's flank, and emptied her clip with abandon. The slugs all passed through their target. Three of them slapped the far wall. The fourth hit Scourge. He fell to the ground and stopped moving.

But Tera's fifth bullet hit Doodle. And it sent a bloody spray from her shoulder.

Then my world went red. All I saw was her. All I heard was static. I screamed, "Doodle," and charged.

And my daughter looked at me. Not her mom. Me.

And how I don't know, but with one hole in her leg, another in her hip, and now a third in her arm, that wonderful woman stood tall. She didn't tumble or anything. But she did take a step. She was coming my way. But another few feet and she'd fall off the stage. Which was a five-foot drop.

In her dazed condition maybe she didn't notice it. But if she dropped from that height, her bones would break easy. Maybe one in her neck. Either way, it wouldn't help the three holes in her body.

I had to catch her.

But between us stood Swamp. The diamond lay on the ground at his feet. And Tera hung dead in his hand. He dropped my ex next to the rock, and turned to me.

I didn't slow down. I had to plow through him and catch my baby.

But then, just like that night outside Wetlands, he became a wave, and crashed over me.

Suddenly everything went cold and quiet.

I was inside of Swamp. And when he spoke his voice had an echo. "I told you I was going to get her."

I thrashed, writhed, and twisted inside him, trying to push myself out. But I couldn't see a surface. There was nothing to swim towards.

"And I told you why. You raised a bitch, a dirty little slut. Should I tell you what she did to get the secret of that rock from me? You want to know what she's capable of before you die?"

I focused. And beyond the thick, green water I could see Doodle. Barely. She was blurry. And wounded. But if I could get to her I could save her life by stopping the bleeding like I did with Monday, back on the-

"Answer me," Swamp said. "Or are you afraid of the truth? Afraid of knowing what she is?"

No more talk. No more time.

I reached into my jacket and pulled out Lois. She jumped to life and clung to my arm. I put her on scatter shot, aimed towards the front of the club, and pulled the trigger.

And she roared. Bright light flooded from her. And the kick sent

me flying out of Swamp. I hit the ground and slid away. Blinking twice I got my sight back. The front of the building was now gone. So was much of the roof. It had cleared some of the blue vapor away, but the canisters were still belching out more.

In the middle of it all, Swamp, once again made of flesh and blood, was somehow still standing. His eyes were wide open. But they were dull. Slowly, he spun around. And the back half of the body, the skin, the organs, and the bone, were completely gone. Lois' energy blast had vaporized half his liquid form, so when he solidified he was only partially there.

He collapsed. But before he hit the ground I was up and running for Doodle. She was already falling off the stage. And coming down hard. Her head was sailing towards the floor. Sprinting two steps I dove, sliding on my knees.

And snatching her from the air, I caught Doodle soft in both arms.

I did it. I saved my little girl. I helped her when she needed me most.

I looked down. And couldn't believe it.

From chin to belt, my kid was a wet, red mess.

I looked at her shoulder. It was untouched. A few inches away though, on her neck, was a tiny hole. And it was spurting. Too strong for a vein. But too weak for an artery.

"Doodle. Talk to me. Say something."

My daughter looked up at me.

"Baby. Don't worry," I said. "There's an ambulance outside. I got the cops. They'll save you. They'll-"

Then something brushed my cheek. It was gentle. And soft. It was a butterfly. A lone butterfly. With bright blue and pink wings, and long, curling antennae. I looked at Doodle's arm. The beautiful clutch of fluttering insects that she'd tattooed there were leaving her. One-by-one they peeled off her skin and jumped into the sky in search of their sisters, and as they did they brushed my cheeks.

When they were all gone there was movement beneath her shirt. And a pair of doves crawled out of her sleeve, and flew up into the rafters.

Then, from Doodle's back, a pair of white angel wings unfurled, their tips landing on the ground. She pointed upwards. "Pretty," she said. "So pretty."

Above us, like a kaleidoscope, the butterflies and the doves shined and shimmered as they flew in a large circle.

I gazed at her work. And was moved. Then I looked at her. And was awed.

My daughter. The artist.

Her chest was rising. But those breaths were shallow. And with a hand that shook when it moved, she reached up and touched my face. "Hey Dad," she said. "I knew you'd come."

And then she smiled.

The dewy kind.

Right before she died in my arms.

And I sat there. It was quiet. The blue mist was thinner. Most of it had moved to the hole in the front of the club. But there was still enough floating around me to make it all seem unreal.

I was snapped from my trance by something striking my shoulder.

It was a dead dove.

The second one landed to my left. And then, like autumn leaves, the butterflies floated down. The angel wings fell to the ground in a pile of feathers. All the knives and weapons, the flowers and fairies, peeled off and fell from Doodle's body, and for the first time in forever she didn't have a mark. Not a smudge. She was pure and perfect, and about as heavy as a baby bird.

I put her down as gentle as I could, then lifted my two shaking hands and wiped my face. There was no blood though. The tears I just realized I was weeping had washed it all away.

Then, from a few yards out, came an, "Uhg."

I quelled my crying and looked over.

Something in a black suit, with an oversized left eye and some tangled scars beneath it, was crawling away.

I got to my feet. A few steps away sat the Coconut. With steady hands I scooped it up, and brought it over to Scourge.

"You forgot your diamond," I said.

Scourge flipped to his back. "Dane. Dane, listen."

I got over top of him and sat on his chest.

He said, "Listen. Listen to me, I don't... I didn't... I never wanted to hurt her. I just wanted the stone, see?"

"You want the Coconut?" I grabbed his jaw and held it shut as I raised the diamond high. "Then have it."

Scourge looked at the shining orb with naked terror. Its bright reflection lit up his eyes.

And I brought it crashing down onto his forehead. The skin there split as the skull beneath it cracked. Scourge's eyes went funny. I lifted the Coconut up again. And hammered it into him once more. This time his skull collapsed while his throat made wet sounds like a garbage disposal.

But I could still recognize him.

So I beat his face with that rock again. And again. And again. I beat his head until nothing remained that would make you think he was ever human. And when I finished, everything above his neck, his skull, eyes, teeth, and brain, were pounded into the planks below. And that wood was wet and red. Like a butcher's block.

"Drop it, police!" someone yelled.

I turned. Standing alone on this side of the wall of smoke, with his service revolver drawn, was Monday. "Dane, are you… is that you?" He holstered his sidearm and ran over.

I rose to my feet, walked over to Doodle, and scooped her up in my arms.

He looked at what I had. "Is that…"

"Yeah," I said. "The most precious thing in Gold Coast City. And a God damn diamond."

Monday spun around and yelled, "Do not enter. The building isn't safe. Gas is too thick, hold your fire I'm coming out."

From beyond the haze someone said, "Hold your fire and positions, officer coming out."

Monday covered the distance between us. "Is she dead?"

I had his answer in my eyes.

"I'm so sorry. But you have to… you have to go. I'll take her from here."

I didn't move. I just stood there.

"Dane, the SPECs are here. All of them. And a few white capes, too." He reached out. "Give her to me. I'll get her home. I promise."

As gentle as I could I handed my daughter to him. Then I took the Vandenberg Coconut, far and away the world's largest and most valuable diamond, and placed it on her lap.

Monday swallowed. "I'll ride with her myself." He turned away.

But I grabbed his shoulder. "Tell them to go slow," I said. "She always loved to drive."

Chapter 53

The sun was shining bright and strong the day I buried Doodle. But a soft ocean breeze kept it cool. You could smell cut grass, and the birds were singing in almost every tree.

It was that kind of a day.

I had her laid to rest in Ayers Cemetery. Not on the hill, but next to family, beside my brother, Raymond. And she had a stone right from the start. It was big and white, and inscribed on its face was no black cape handle, but her real name.

Jamie Beatrice Curse.

According to her birth certificate that wasn't her official title, but it was my call, so I made it.

There were no mourners. No priest. It was just me. And the whole service... You know, I don't have the words.

After, I stopped at Henchmen's. Lee was alone, behind the bar. She said, "You look like you need a drink."

I tossed my hat on the bar and plunked down on a stool. "Octane. Three fingers."

"Think I'll join you." She grabbed two glasses and the half full black bottle, and poured one for us both. Then she reached below the bar and pulled a copy of The Chronicle from a few days back. "Here. Thought you might not've picked up a copy with everything that happened and all." She shook her head. "You see that headline? Hero Cop Saves Coconut. Can you believe it? He got all the credit."

I looked at the front page. It was a shot of Monday, coming through Crush's demolished wall, with thick streams of smoke rising all around him, and my daughter and the Coconut in his arms.

It was a nice picture. He looked heroic.

"Says he'll get a medal, and a promotion to the SPECs," Lee said. "Apparently he's the first cop to do that."

"He deserves it. He's a good man."

"Well, we all know who the real hero is. Dane Curse. Killer of Scourge and Gunmetal Gray. The man who beat Al Mighty in a straight up scrap. The PI who never turned rat and always closes the case. I'll tell you kid, your business is going to be booming." Lee lifted her glass up. "To the Dane Curse Detective Agency."

I lifted mine. "To Doodle."

"And to Doodle." Lee took a sip of her Octane and pulled a face. I just looked at my shot. "I got one question, Lee."

"Is it why we drink this stuff, because I don't have the answer."

"No," I said. "It's how?"

She looked at me with those grandma eyes. "How what?"

"How are you going to sit there, smiling at me for the next few years, knowing you set my kid up to catch a slug in her neck without ever feeling nothing?"

"What do you mean?"

"Don't. There were photos of me at that holed-up house. From my first day on the case. And the only people who knew I was working it that soon were Widow," I said, "and you."

Lee's face slid an inch. She put her drink down. And dropped both hands to her sides.

I whipped out Lois. And pointed her at Lee, real threatening like. "You don't want to try anything, moms. I'm not in one of those live and let moods."

She looked down my pistol's gullet. "So it's like that?"

"Oh yeah." With my glare I bore two holes through her face. "It's exactly like that."

She sighed. "Kid. That rock. It's like I said before, sparkle struck. You know I've always wanted it. Finally the urge got the best of me."

"So when Bundy got out of prison you had him put together a team."

"All he needed to get it going was more dough. And my inside intel on Wentorf Hall. All of it of course, not just the parts I told you."

"Yeah, but he also needed Dread Division out of the way," I said. "So Scourge would return, and put your intel to work."

She couldn't look me in the eye. "Yeah."

"Was it your idea to set them up?"

"No, I wouldn't-"

"Don't." I clicked on Lois. She glowed an angry green, and wrapped herself around my arm like a cobra. "You're about to be singing with angels or screaming with demons, and neither one likes lies."

"It wasn't my idea. I swear. But he said we needed Scourge so I went along with it. It was easy enough. One night Subatomic comes in and I sat him down, told him he couldn't trust his usual fence. Then I vouched for Bundy who paid out the dough the cops provided."

"And that's why you shot him. So he wouldn't implicate you."

"Yeah." She stared at her feet, probably trying to imagine what hell was like.

"And what about Doodle?"

"Damn your ex. We had the diamond free and clear. Vector was supposed to make the handoff to Scourge and Bundy outside Wetlands so they could stash it up at North Point. Only I'm guessing Tera figured out what we had, then she and your kid stole it before blowing the place up, and setting this whole thing off." Lee looked up at me. There were tears. "But I promise you, I never wanted any of this to happen. I tried to warn you off, and-"

"You were like a mother to me. You know that? I loved you."

She stood dumb. And nodded slow. "So what now? You going to kill me?"

I thought of everyone I'd lost the last few days. I thought of those I'd lose soon. And still I wanted to. So bad. But even though I can lift seven tons on any day that ends with y, there are some things you just can't carry. So I holstered my iron. "No."

She sighed and relaxed. "So what now?"

I stood up and drank my shot. "Now you sell this bar."

"What?" Her eyes nearly leapt out of her skull. "Why would I-"

"You're going to sell this bar and leave town. Today."

"But where will I go?"

"Don't care. Go to Saint Luthor's. Go to Australia. It doesn't matter. But you don't get to stay planted in this burg. You're a turn cape, Lee. You set up Dread Division, killed Widow's brother, and ripped my daughter from my arms when I almost had them around her again. So yeah, you got to go. And wherever you choose you won't be coming back."

"What if I do? Come back I mean."

I seized her Octane, drank it, and slammed it on the bar. The glass shattered and Lee flinched.

"If you set foot back in this town I'll find you and kill you. And if you doubt it, just ask Scourge. Ask Swamp. Ask the feared and fearsome Gunmetal Gray." I grabbed my hat and walked towards the exit.

"Dane," Lee called out. "They're all dead."

The red curtains in front of me slid open. I stopped. Put on my hat. And said, "You're God damn right."

#

When I arrived at my office building I plodded up the steps, prepared for the worst. I got the impression that before we made peace Monday had my place hollowed out and stacked neat in the evidence locker at precinct one-seven-who-cares. And I didn't want to see it that way. I'd never wanted to see what Carl built that way.

So when I got to the fourth floor I trudged down the hall in no big hurry. But when I stepped through the hologram, my office lights were on. Inside were the unfamiliar clicks of fast work on a keyboard. I pushed the door open and stepped inside. "Oh my God," I said. "It's you."

Widow was at the reception desk. Gone were her black threads, replaced with a yellow suit. And all four hands were on two keyboards, doing the busy fidget. "It is. And I have to say that detective work is right up your alley if you can figure that out with a single glance."

I closed the door and hung up my coat and hat. "I solved your case by the way. Sorry I haven't gotten back with the details sooner. It's just that I had a lot of-"

"It's ok. I know. Everybody knows," she said. "And thanks. I appreciate it."

"Yeah." I thought about the last few days. And what it cost me. But I shook those thoughts from my head and looked down at her. "So what're you doing here?"

"When I stopped by to drop off the vial of anti-venom I ran into Mrs. West. And we talked."

"So?"

Widow stopped typing and looked up at me. "She made this post sound not half bad. Especially compared to what I've been dealing with. So when she offered it, I accepted."

"What about the Spinnerettes?"

"I know." Widow leaned back and tapped her chin. "What about them?"

For the first time in days I laughed. "Ok. But you're overqualified."

Widow shrugged all four of her shoulders. "I need a job, and you got a vacancy. Now are we going to do this or are you going to give me trouble?"

I opened my mouth to say something, but I had no idea what, so I closed it and nodded. "Fine by me. But I'm betting you'll be bored in-"

The phone rang. Widow held up a finger and snatched the receiver. "Hello, you've reached the Dane Curse Detective Agency. Yes, that's correct, he's the one. May I ask who's calling? And what's this in reference to? Thanks so much, hold one moment please." She turned to me. "It's a woman, says she's Landslide's girlfriend and wants you to find his killer. Says she needs help. What should I tell her?"

I looked at the door. The glass read the same way she answered the phone, Dane Curse Detective Agency. Carl's name was gone. Now it was my turn to show this town who I was, and what was important to me.

I turned to Widow. "Tell her if she needs help to come right in. Tell her that's exactly what we do."

- The End -

Dear Reader,

Thanks so much for taking this trip with me and the denizens of Gold Coast City, I hope you enjoyed the ride. Before you leave though, I'm afraid I have to ask for a favor. Indie authors like me rely heavily on reviews from readers like you. If they're positive it helps drive sales, if they're critical it offers an opportunity to improve the next book, but mostly this feedback lets others know if the story's right for them. So please, however you felt about your time with Dane, I would appreciate it if you'd share your opinion on Amazon.com, and thanks again. We hope to see you back in Gold Coast City soon.

Other Black Cape Case Files
Dane Curse
Old Iron
Grace Killer
Gangland

Made in the USA
Monee, IL
26 September 2021